Praise for The

'Scenes from *The Good Son* are going round in my head months later. Paul McVeigh's is an original voice of which I, for one, can't wait to hear more.'
—PATRICK GALE author of *A Place Called Winter*

'A writer to be championed . . . utterly engaging . . . vivid, fresh and brought fully to life . . . written with a sharp eye and a big heart, *The Good Son* will establish Paul McVeigh as an important new Irish voice'.
—LUCY CALDWELL author of *All the Beggars Riding*

'Charming, scary, witty and touching, this is a wonderfully written coming of age story.'
—CLAIRE FULLER author of *Our Endless Numbered Days*

'Paul McVeigh brilliantly achieves a very difficult thing: he turns a coming-of-age tale into high art. Mickey Donnelly navigates The Troubles like Huck Finn navigates the Mississippi River letting us see the human condition through penetratingly fresh eyes. *The Good Son* is a work of genius from a splendid writer.'
—ROBERT OLEN BUTLER, Pulitzer Prize-winning author of *A Good Scent from a Strange Mountain*

'I was knocked out by this stunningly intelligent, compassionate, and mordantly funny debut novel. *The Good Son* is a brilliant portrait of both political and familial unrest, and Paul McVeigh is a wildly important new talent.'
—LAURA VAN DEN BERG, author of *The Isle of Youth* and *Find Me*

'Someone's going to make an exceptional movie out of this amazing, cinematic, perfectly structured and realised book.'
—CATE KENNEDY author of *The World Beneath*

'From the very first page I knew I was in the hands of an accomplished storyteller, McVeigh's vibrant and irreverent prose carrying along a novel that is both hopeful and big hearted at its core. It deserves to be widely acclaimed and widely read.'
—CLAIRE KING, author of *The Night Rainbow*

'Paul McVeigh has created a strong, unique, and funny protagonist, able to reveal the everyday intricacies and the broader politics of the Troubles in a fresh, engaging way. I fell in love with Mickey Donnelly.'
—SARAH BUTLER, author of *Ten Things I've Learned About Love* and *Before the Fire*

'Brilliantly sparky and original. Fairly ripples with wicked humour, warmth and coming-of-age wonder.'
—SARAH HILARY, author of *Someone Else's Skin* and *No Other Darkness*

'A real page-turner. Mickey Donnelly is a brilliant creation – a captivating, complex boy on the cusp of young adulthood. A poignant, devastating, funny, unforgettable read.'
—VANESSA GEBBIE, author of *The Coward's Tale*

'Beautifully written, heartbreaking story of a young Belfast boy during the Troubles. There's something very brave about the writing and wild about the character.'
—LIZ NUGENT author of *Unravelling Oliver*

'Paul McVeigh is a story-teller of the highest order. *The Good Son* is a joy to read, truly a page turner, and at the same time, its structure is masterful, and its nuanced use of language, dialogue and narrative create a remarkable journey of discovery. The last book I felt this strongly about, in terms of its completeness, its build, its pacing and punch, its lyrical perfection, its use of a young protagonist to reveal exceedingly adult issues, and its voice was *All the Light We Cannot See* by Anthony Doerr.'
—NANCY FREUND author of *Rapeseed*

'There's no nostalgia in the depiction of simmering brutality and intense claustrophobia in a place where everyone – a full-colour close-up of life in a no-go area.'
—*The Guardian*

'. . . transportingly vivid. The effect is often very funny and then touching; the injustice of a life spent half in fear, the pleasure of a life half lived in laughter.'
—*The Big Issue*

'One of my favourite books coming out in April, this completely charming, pitch perfect story stole my heart. Has to be one of the best voices of 2015.'
—*A Case for Books*

'Heart-rending. It has everything. It's so real, one the best protagonists I've read in a long, long time . . . The last time a character had stayed with me like that was Holden Caulfield in *Catcher in the Rye*. Takes you from sadness to humour to horror to a whole range of other emotions quite often even in the space of one page which is not an easy thing to do.'
—BBC Radio Ulster, Book of the Month

# THE GOOD SON

*Paul McVeigh*

CROMER

PUBLISHED BY SALT
12 Norwich Road, Cromer, Norfolk NR27 0AX United Kingdom

© Paul McVeigh, 2015

The right of Paul McVeigh to be identified as the author of this
work has been asserted by him in accordance with Section 77 of the
Copyright, Designs and Patents Act 1988.

Printed in Great Britain by Clays Ltd, St Ives plc
Reprinted with corrections 2015

Typeset in Sabon 10/13

ISBN 978 1 78463 023 2 paperback

3 5 7 9 8 6 4 2

*To my Ma*

# THE GOOD SON

# I

I was born the day the Troubles started.

'Wasn't I, Ma?' says me.

'It was you that started them, son,' says she, and we all laugh, except Our Paddy. I put that down to his pimples and general ugliness. It must be hard to be happy with a face like that. I almost feel sorry for him. I spy a dirty, big love bite on his neck and store this ammunition to defend myself against future attacks.

Steamy, flowery-smellin' disinfectant fills my nose and joins the sweet tastin' Frosties in my mouth as Ma passes with the tin bucket and yard brush. Ma only cleans the yard when somethin's up. That would be Da, as usual.

'Do you want a hand, Mammy?' says me.

'No, son,' says she, disappearing out the back. She didn't even look at me. I'm worried about her after last night.

'*D'ya wanna hand*?' Our Paddy says in a girl's voice. 'You wee lick.'

'I'll tell m'Mammy on you,' I say.

'*I'm tellin' Mammy on you . . .*' Paddy mimics me.

I look at Wee Maggie and give her the *We hate him, don't we?* look. She gives me the *Yes we do, he's a big, fat pig!* look back. I was taught how to give looks by a monk on Cave Hill. I trained like a Jedi Knight but my lightsaber was my face. I became *Look Skywalker*. My mission: To defend all weaklin's and youngest ones in families against the evil that is older brothers. Wee Maggie is now my disciple.

To test her telepathy training, I send – *Don't worry about him cuz he's gonna be knocked down by a car then a lorry will run over his head makin' his eyes pop out*. Wee Maggie smiles. She got it. I think we're actually twins born years apart in some CIA super-genetic-test-tube experiment.

Paddy gets up, leavin' his dirty bowl on the table like he's King Farouk.

'Don't leave that for Mammy,' I say.

'Mammy's boy,' says he.

'Shut up you,' I say. 'At least I don't have a dirty, big love bite.'

Wee Maggie laugh-chokes and Frosties shoot from her mouth onto Paddy's jumper, just like that wee girl in *The Exorcist* I saw at the Pope John Paul II Youth Club.

'That's your fault, you wee gay boy!' Paddy slaps me across the head.

I try to kick him but my shin hits the table leg.

Paddy laughs, wipin' his jumper. 'And you're supposed to be the smart one? Grammar School? Away on.'

'I'm smarter than you, dumbo,' I say. 'By the way, does your girlfriend like suckin' the pimples on your neck?'

Paddy dives at me and trails me off the chair by the jumper.

'Mammy!' I shout out the back yard.

'What?' Ma screams. The house trembles like when bombs go off. Paddy lets go. Not even Muhammad Ali would mess with our Ma.

'Nothin',' I shout back. Paddy grabs his blazer from the back of the chair and heads off. I raise my eyebrows and smile at Wee Maggie. 'Victory is mine!' I laugh like the Count from *Sesame Street*.

There's mess on Ma's good table. I run to the sink, wet the

cloth and rush back before Ma comes in and kills somebody. Somebody = me. Even though I'm the good son in the family, I get the blame if Wee Maggie does anything wrong cuz she's the youngest and I look after her. Wee Maggie could set me on fire and Ma would kick *my* head in for lettin' Maggie near matches.

Wipin' the table, I see my reflection in the smoked-glass. I look like a Black Baby we do collections for at school. I usually give them creamed rice. We get free tins from the community centre cuz we're poor and cuz somewhere there's a place called Food Mountain made from tins of creamed rice and corned beef. I think it's in Switzerland.

One day I'll be President of Ireland. I'll be so kind and good. I'll bring all Black Babies to Belfast where there's free food for poor people and they can live in new houses like they're buildin' at the bottom of our street.

I've only ever seen black people on TV. Apart from the ones starving in Africa, there's ones America stole to make slaves, which isn't very nice, but at least they gave them some clothes. You wouldn't be allowed to walk around America with no clothes on. Or Belfast. Maybe if they lived with the Protestants. I've only seen Protestants on the TV too.

'Mickey, stop spacing out,' Wee Maggie tugs me. 'You're going to be late for school.'

I throw the cleaning cloth in the sink and run through the living room and up the stairs. I tip toe into my room cuz I don't want to wake Da. Ma took him back in when he hammered the door in the middle of the night. He brought men with him. I listened from the top of the stairs. I told Paddy I heard Da cryin' and they were talkin' about money. The men said they'd come back today.

Paddy thought Da wasn't comin' back this time. But Da

always comes back. I don't know why Paddy even bothers trying to think.

I grab my schoolbag and run down the stairs and into the kitchen.

'Ma, I'm away on,' I shout to the yard.

'Did you get washed?' Ma shouts back.

'Aye,' I look at Wee Maggie through the doorway, pretend to pick my nose and wipe it on my jumper. She laughs into her hand. She thinks I'm like one of them from the TV. Like *Laurel and Hardy* or *Abbot and Costello*. We play them sometimes. She says it's not fair that we don't play any girl funny ones but I say it's not my fault that girls aren't funny. Cuz if they were, wouldn't they be on the TV?

I get on my horse and ride him, dodgin' the chair and table, swerve round the half-open door into the livin' room, side-ward round Da's chair and past the sofa.

'Cham-p-ion The Won-der Horse!' I sing, salutin' the TV. I gallop out the front door, Wee Maggie running after me.

'Don't be doing that in the street, Mickey,' Wee Maggie says, like she's the one who looks after me.

'I'm not stupid,' I say. 'Go on you.' I push her back into the livin' room.

The waste ground in front of the house becomes an open prairie and the aul half-knocked-down houses to the right now an abandoned Gold Rush mining town in the Wild West.

I ride Champion off into the sunset.

∾

'Mr Donnelly, what time do you call this?' says Mr McManus. I'm in the doorway lookin' at my feet. 'Sorry, Sir.' He's a funny frigger Mr McManus, cuz he's sayin' that, but I know he doesn't care, due to my telepathic abilities. A power like mine comes in very handy so you know when someone's really bein' real. He's just pretendin' to be annoyed, so I'm pretendin' to be sorry.

'Go and sit down, Donnelly,' Mr McManus says, goin' back to readin'.

'So what's happenin', Fartin'?' I say, slidin' into my seat.

'Shite,' says he.

'Well, now we're all here,' Mr McManus gives me the side eye, 'I thought we could have a little competition. Some creative writing, one page in length, on any subject and there will be a small prize for the winner. If you're not taking part, you can read quietly at your desk.'

The room groans. Since we finished our 11+, ages ago, it's been singin' and stories and everybody hates it. Not me. I love singin' and stories. I'm gonna write somethin' but I'll have to hide it from the Hard Men who would love to kill me cuz I'm smart and not hard. Thank the Lord, His Holy Mother and the Little Baby Jesus, I've got my mate Fartin' Martin. Fartin' is cool *and* hard but not one of them. Without him I'd've been murdered about seventeen times.

## MY DOG KILLER

*My dog Killer, he is great.*
*My dog Killer, is my mate.*
*I take him walks about the street,*
*And he stays right beside my feet.*
*Because he does what he is told,*
*And he's never, ever, bold.*
*He knows what to do because he's dead cool,*
*Though he's never even been to school!*
*He's my dog and he's the best,*
*I bet he could even do a test.*

*Late at night he likes to bark,*
*Because he's scared in the dark.*
*He sits in my Da's chair,*
*And he covers it with hair.*
*Then my Mammy goes mad,*
*And tells him he is bad.*

It's not one of my best but it's only for fun. Are you allowed to tell lies in a poem? They'll all be dead jealous if they think I have a dog.

'Have those of you who're entering the competition finished?' asks Sir.

'Yes, Sir.' Everyone tuts and stares at me and the two brainers who answered. I always get too excited about things. Why can't I just keep my big mouth shut until I get to St. Malachy's and away from this school?

'Who would like to read first?' asks Mr McManus.

'I will, Sir,' The Blob says.

Everybody looks at each other tuttin'. That'll distract them from me. You can depend on The Blob. He's always first. First with his hand up, first to offer things and first to get his head kicked in. But I won him in the exams cuz I didn't get some wrong on purpose like I do in class.

The Blob clears his throat then reads with his put-on voice of a somebody not from here. Mountains and the sea and somethin' about *beauty*. I mean, who talks about those things in Ardoyne? You'd think he'd know by now what to hide from the Hard Men.

The Hard Men *starrin' Wee Twin McAuley, Big Twin McAuley – co-starrin' Ma's-a-Whore and Monkey McErlane. It's a filim about stupid people – how they do bad at school and beat the shite out of everybody that's got a brain cell. Comin' to a cinema near you.*

Wee Twin is starin' at me while chewin' a straw from our bottles of milk. He must've nicked it cuz we haven't had our milk yet. That's the kind of bad thing he does. He's shootin' pure hatred at me from his good eye. The other is pointin' towards our display of Carrickfergus Castle. The bendy eye followed a bullet that grazed his face and decided not to come back. So would I, if I was his eye. Havin' to see that face in the mirror.

'Thank you, Mr Campbell, that was a great effort, well done,' says Sir. 'Now, who's next? Mr Close?' he says.

Status Report: *Sean Close – AKA Helmet Head – under observation – moved into my street last month – posh – therefore probably a Protestant double-agent as who's ever heard of a posh Catholic – has no mates – thinks he's great. Conclusion – I hate him.*

Helmet gets left alone cuz somebody tried to beat him up on his first day and he kicked their head in with Karate. Definitely suspicious. A Protestant child spy trained in Kung Fu? I wouldn't put it past them.

'This is a story called "Monty the Fly",' says Helmet. I snigger the loudest. ' "Monty was from Surrey and flew Spitfires for a living. He was a short-sighted fly, so he had to wear very large spectacles." '

He's talkin' but I can't hear. I already know how brilliant it's gonna be. Some things you just know right from the word *go*. If it had been homework, I'd've said his posh Da must have helped him. It's not enough he's moved into a new house near me and into my class, but he's movin' in on my action too. It's me that comes up with brilliant stories in here.

I could never think of somethin' like that though. Never. Maybe if I didn't come from Ardoyne, but from a place where you're allowed to learn things. But I'm goin' after the summer. St. Malachy's Grammar School, here I come! I'll learn to write brilliant stories like his.

He's gonna win me today. I can't let him. Never let them win.

I put my jotter down the back of my trousers. 'Toilet, Sir?' I stand up.

'You shouldn't interrupt someone, Mr Donnelly, it's very rude,' says Sir.

'I'm desperate,' I squeeze my dick like pee is about to explode out. Like when you should've gone ages ago and now it's killin' you. Like that. *Oh, I'm in agony. Oh God, I'm goin' to die.* Hold on, I'm only actin'. I actually believed myself there, I'm that good. I should be an actor.

Sir waves me out like a bored king. In the corridor the class doors are open and the teachers look out as I rush past. At Mrs O'Halloran's I slow down and look in. We have a secret, me and Mrs O'Halloran. She looks up and smiles.

'Well, if it isn't Michael Donnelly. Come in a moment,' she coos like a dove.

I'm in love with Mrs O'Halloran. I was the only one she got to take her notes to Mr McDermot. She used to call me her *Wee Currant Bun.* Her *Wee Pet.* She said I was different. Not like the other boys. I bought her a necklace on my last day in her class. It cost one whole 50p. It had a little golden heart and on the back it said *I Love You.*

'Now class, I want you all to have a look at Mr Michael Donnelly,' she says, her arm on my shoulder makin' my skin fizz. 'He is one of, in fact, he *is* the finest pupil ever to come out of Holy Cross Boys.' I'm completely scundered. I take a massive redner, my face burnin' like a slapped arse.

'St. Malachy's Grammar School. It doesn't surprise me at all. You see, class, this is what you can achieve at this school with hard work and determination,' she beams at me. It's supposed to be a secret, but I guess it doesn't matter if these wee

8

ones know. She's right too. I am determined. I've got a plan. Get away from this school. Get smart. Get to America. Get Rich. Bring Wee Maggie and Mammy over to live with me in my penthouse.

'Thank you, Mrs O'Halloran,' says me, in my good-boy voice, to prove to her class she's right.

'You'll be sorely missed around here,' she says, smiling. She whispers: 'Make sure to come see me before you leave today, won't you?'

'Yes, Mrs O'Halloran,' says me, now completely on fire like a human petrol bomb. I kick the leg of her desk, smile and speed-walk out. I do want to grow up and make all my dreams come true, but mostly I just want to be back in P3 with Mrs O'Halloran.

In the toilet, I take out my jotter. I rip out my poem and tear it up, throw it down the toilet and flush it away forever.

Everyone looks at me when I walk into class so I put my head down and go to my seat. I hide under my desk, pretendin' to tie my lace.

'Ah, Mr Donnelly. We've been waitin' for you,' says Mr McManus.

'What, Sir?' I say, like I'm completely thick and really stupid and cool.

'You said you had something for the competition?' says he.

'No I didn't.' That came out cheeky.

'Stand up, Mr Donnelly,' he says. I've crossed the McManus Line. Whisperin' and *oohh*s around the room. 'Are you now saying that you don't have something to read out?'

'Aye, he does, Sir. I saw him writin' it,' Fartin' says, and hides his head in his arm on the desk, laughin'.

'Well?' says Sir.

'No, look.' I hold up blank pages. 'See.'

'You are being very irritating today, Mr Donnelly. First

you're late and now this. What do you think will happen if you behave like this in St. . . . in secondary school? Why don't you stand there for a while and perhaps you'll remember what you did with your writing.' Mr McManus goes for a fag at the door.

Why does he even care? I love Mr McManus, but sometimes he gets on like someone shoved a duster up his arse.

'You're for it, now,' Fartin' laughs.

'What did you do that for?'

'Cuz I saw you write one. I thought you were only messin'. You don't have one?' he says, in complete eyebrow-raised disbelief.

I don't want to fall out with Fartin' cuz he's my best friend in school. My only friend. We don't knock about after school cuz he lives at the other end of Ardoyne near the Prods and I'm not allowed up there cuz of the riots. We won't see each other much after school finishes next week. And after the holidays I'm goin' to St. Malachy's and he's goin' to St. Gabriel's with everyone else. I wonder where Helmet Head is goin'? He thinks he's great with his blonde hair and blue eyes and *Oh, look at me with my brilliant stories and clean uniform.*

Mr McManus comes back in, followed by Mr Brown, the Head.

'Donnelly, come here,' says Mr Brown, and I do cuz he's one scary specimen. I'm never in trouble in school. I'm a good boy. Can't be about the writin'. Must be about St. Malachy's. Mr Brown said it was best not to tell the other boys and finished the sentence with the look *If you want to get out of here alive.* Mr Brown is whisperin' to Mr McManus, lookin' very serious. Mr Brown puts his hand on my back and pushes me into the corridor.

I stand by the windows lookin' out at the tarmac playground covered in glass and splats of colour from the paint bombs the Hard Men throw over the walls at night. Reflected in the window I see Mr McManus, hand over his mouth, starin' at his feet. Mr Brown has one hand in his pocket and the other is rubbin' his baldy head. Somethin's wrong. It's like one of those scenes in a filim where someone's bein' told bad news while the music plays and we know what they're sayin' even if we can't hear the words. Usually the hero is being told he's terminally ill or his parents have died in a car crash. We don't have a car, so . . .

'Follow me,' says Mr Brown. I do, but look round at Mr McManus who's still at the doorway smilin' at me like . . . I've got leukaemia! I did have a nose bleed last Christmas. I feel a bit dizzy.

At the end of the corridor, Mr Brown's office door is open. He walks in. I wait.

*I'm in my hospital bed, the whole family kneelin' by me cryin', I raise myself to say, 'I forgive you all. Even you Paddy.' I smile, touching his head, then die.*

'Come in, Michael,' says Mr Brown, which is the first time in seven years he's called me by my first name.

Holy Shite! Ma and Da are here. In their Sunday clothes. This is gettin' too TV.

'Sit down, son,' says Da, all nice. Hopefully Mr Brown can't smell last night's drink under Da's Polo minty breath. I sit in the empty chair.

'Michael, I know we've spoken about the offer from St. Malachy's, and I want to assure you that we're extremely proud of you here at Holy Cross,' says Mr Brown, fidgetin' with his papers. 'You're a big boy now, Michael, and there are certain things you have to understand.' He folds his fingers like a cat's cradle and taps the knotted bunch on his desk. He takes a deep breath. 'Michael . . . your mum and dad have asked me to talk to you, to help you understand that . . .'

Ma coughs, shifts in her chair and looks at the floor.

'. . . unfortunately . . . Michael, you're not able to go to St. Malachy's.'

Mr Brown's mouth moves but there's no sound. *Concentrate Mickey – don't space out!* I hear somethin' about 'five years . . . trips . . . uniforms and books . . . two buses there and two buses back.'

'But I love buses,' I say, lookin' at Ma to back me up, but she's starin' at Mr Brown who gets up from his seat and plays with the blinds, all the while talkin'. My breathin' is loud in my ears. I keep missin' what he's sayin', like when Our Paddy turns the sound up and down on the telly to annoy me.

'Your mummy and daddy can't afford it, Michael. They feel terrible,' Mr Brown says.

Ma's face is purple. She's not goin' to say anythin'. And whatever is jammin', the sound in my head is messin' with my powers. Is it the aliens? Or the Russians? Protestants!

'Now you'll be able to go to St. Gabriel's, just like Paddy,' Da smiles, puttin' his disgustin' orangey-brown, fag-burnt fingers on my shoulder. He means wear Paddy's old uniforms like I've done my whole life. Paddy's old everythin'. Even his bloody trunks.

I look at Da and know with absolute certainty that this man is not my father. Just as I know, by the smallness of his eyes, this is all his fault. Everythin' bad that ever happens to our family is because of him.

'We'll see ourselves out, Sir,' says Da, holdin' out his hand, actin' like he doesn't want to cause any trouble when that's all he's ever done.

'You can take Michael home with you, help him through the . . . transition,' says Mr Brown.

'No, I'm sure he'd rather be here playin' with his friends. Wouldn't you, son?' says Da.

*Frien-dah*! One friend. That's how much he knows. And no . . . 'Actually, I would like to go home,' I say.

'No problem,' says Mr Brown, lookin' pale and walkin' fast out the door. 'I'll get your schoolbag.'

Silence. We stare out the window and watch the sun come out from behind a big Fuzzy Felt cloud. All three of us squint and turn our heads makin' sure we don't catch each other's eyes.

'I . . .' starts Da, 'Mickey . . .' he sighs into the sandpaper shuffle of his hand along his stubble. 'I've got a big surprise for you. It's comin' tonight.'

I look at the stupid grin on his face. I check Ma; she hasn't a clue. He's a big liar. Ma nods to me, then towards Da, her eyes openin' wide. This means *Please Mickey, play along with your Da. For me. You know what'll happen if you don't.*

OK, Ma. For you.

I know we have no money and I would never scunder her about it. 'A big surprise? Wow,' I say, like some kid on TV. I look out the window. Then it descends upon me like the Holy Spirit. 'It's a dog, isn't it? Oh, Daddy, I'm so happy, that makes up for everythin'.'

Ha. I won him. I smile at Ma like I've no idea what I've just done. She's said *no* to a dog since I was five. She's gonna break every bone in my body. At least then I won't have to go to St. Gabriel's.

## 2

'C'MON YOU, WEE boy. And don't lift that dog or I'll kill ye,' Ma says out the kitchen window. 'You too, wee doll,' she says to Maggie. She's still annoyed with me about Killer, but I haven't said a word about St. Malachy's so I'm safe as long as I keep my mouth shut.

'I'll be two shakes of a lamb's tail,' I say and wink.

'Don't wink on a Sunday,' says she, her head disappearing back through the window.

I laugh. That's a new one. We're in the yard leanin' into Killer's box Uncle John made out of wood from the burnt-out houses in Havana Street. If anyone asks, we're to say Da made it cuz Ma doesn't want people knowin' he's useless.

'How's my wee son? Eh?' I scratch Killer's black back. He collapses and rolls over. 'How's my wee man?' I tickle his brown belly. 'He's brill, isn't he, Maggie?'

'Yes, oh my God, I love him,' says she.

'He can be yours too. Nobody else's, but.' I frown and wag my finger.

I really want to pick him up but I'm in my new *do you for the whole summer holiday clothes* to be debuted at the

Chapel's Summer Fashion Mass – the first Sunday after school breaks up.

A tumbleweed of curly, ginger hair sticks out the back door. Our Measles. AKA Our Mary, the eldest. Her chubby cheeks are so covered in freckles there's only a few white dots around her nose. Like freckles in reverse.

'Yous two better get movin' if yous know what's good for yous,' says Measles before dashin' back in to get the dinner on while we go to Chapel. She has to do everything round the house like Ma cuz she's a girl. Boys don't have to do anything but I always help cuz it's just not fair.

'Right!' Ma growls.

I run in, Wee Maggie, my stickin' plaster, behind me. Ma's us trained like those kids in *The Sound of Music,* but she doesn't need a whistle with a voice like hers. And I don't mean she sounds like Julie Andrews.

Ma gives the finger-on-the-lips signal cuz Da's still in bed. Everythin' has to be kept quiet so he doesn't leave us. Or worse – drink. Ma grabs Wee Maggie's hand and marches out of the house and down the street. I catch up.

'I swear to Almighty God, if I'm late for Mass I will not be held responsible for my actions,' Ma says, her tiny feet goin' 100 miles an hour.

The further down we go, the older and dirtier our street gets. They're knockin' these aul houses down soon. At the bottom, you can see across to Flax Street where they're buildin' huge, corrugated iron barricades, beside No Man's Land. To keep us in and the Protestants out.

We turn up Brompton Park road and head up the hill. Nobody's talkin' cuz we're rushin'. I don't care. I'm happy as a pig in poo cuz I have Killer and I can't wait to get back from Chapel to play with him. And it's the Summer Holidays so there's cartoons on every mornin'. *Flash Gordon* and old black and white films too. And even though I'm not goin' to St. Malachy's, St. Gabriel's is not til nine whole weeks. Plenty of time for me to come up with a new escape plan.

Everyone in Chapel is goin' to love my new T-shirt. It's cracker. I chose it cuz it has the American flag on it. Our Paddy says it's crap but that's just cuz he thinks he's great since he turned Rude Boy for Easter. If you want to change who you are, you have to wait til you get your new clothes at Christmas, Easter or Summer. Everybody turned Mod last Christmas. I don't know how they all know when to turn what. They must tell each other on the street when they're playin'. I don't play with the other kids. I play with Wee Maggie.

Look at me in my brill, super-duper, cool, Americano, baseball boots too. We call them guddies, Americans call them sneakers. I'm learning the names from the telly so I don't look like a *dork* when I go. I can't wait to get to America. I'm going to work in a diner. I've got dreams.

A Saracen crawls down the road, snipers' heads out the top. It's like a tank but fatter with bits bolted on, like Frankenstein. It's a *Tankenstein*. Ha!

I skip like a boxer and do a little dance up on the side of the road.

'Mickey! If you ruin them guddies you'll spend the rest of the summer runnin' around in yer bare feet,' says Ma. 'Now stop actin' the eejit.'

'They're not guddies, Mammy, they're sneakers,' says me.

'I'll sneak you a dig in the head if you don't stop contradicting me, wee boy. And then you'll know your arse from Joe McKibbon,' says she.

I have absolutely no idea what that actually means, but it will translate into pain inflicted on me. But Ma knows that really I'm a good boy, it's just I get on her nerves sometimes. But I can't help it. I'm lovin' myself right now.

At the top of Brompton Park I look down Balholme Drive. 'Mammy, I'm waitin' here for Fartin'.'

'You are, my shite. It's too dangerous, sure the Shankill Road's just there,' says Ma. The Shankill Butchers live there. They don't sell meat, they chop up Catholics. I don't think they eat us but it wouldn't surprise me.

'I won't go behind the Chapel, I'm not simple,' I tut. 'Look, there he's comin' now,' I point. 'Please!'

'Can I wait with him, Mammy?' Wee Maggie whinges.

'See what you've started, wee boy?' says Ma. 'You'd better not be late for Chapel, you hear me?' She trails Wee Maggie off by the hand.

I hate those bloody Prods livin' across there cuz it means I'm not allowed up to play with Fartin'. We arranged to meet here on the last day at Holy Cross. I didn't tell Fartin' I wasn't going to St. Malachy's.

In the shop window, there's an IRA poster. A man's face. Eyes starin' at you, frownin'. A bodyless hand covers his mouth. *Loose Talk Costs Lives* it says. You have to be careful all the time. Keep your mouth shut. I move and it's like the eyes follow me, same as the 3D Jesus picture in Aunt Kathleen's.

'Wait til you hear this one,' Fartin' says, like we're already in the middle of a conversation. 'Ye walk up to somebody and say, *You're lookin' well*, and when they smile, you say, *Who shat on you?*' Fartin' pisses himself laughin'. I think that's horrible, bein' nasty to somebody. 'I heard that yesterday on the street,' says he. 'Everyone's out playin' all the time. It's cracker. Are they in your street?'

'Yeah,' I say. 'I'm not goin' to St. Malachy's.' I had no idea I was goin' to say that. Shit, that's how *loose talk* works. 'I'm goin' to St. Gabriel's.'

'You're goin' to St. Gabe's?' says he, his eyes poppin' out. 'How come?'

'I told them I didn't want to go,' says me. 'I said I wanted to be with my mate. *I'm goin' to St. Gabriel's with Far-tin' Mar-tin and you can shove your posh school up your bums.*' I stick my two fingers up. 'I thank you,' I give a little bow.

I can see Fartin's totally blown away. God, I'm good. It's called improvisation. Marlon Brando does it. I saw it in a documentary.

'Well, I've got news too. I'm not going to St. Gabriel's,' says he, and an alien raygun disintegrates me.

'Why? Where are you goin'?'

'Some school far away. You go if you're special.' He grabs his dick with happiness then puts me in a headlock and grabs my nose. I don't try to get away cuz you get a Chinese burn on the neck in the struggle.

He doesn't even know that special means stupid. Damn it! I thought he'd protect me like he used to at Holy Cross. I'm going to be all on my own in St. Gabriel's.

He lets me go and we walk to the road waitin' for the cars to stop.

'I've got somethin' you can do when you get to St. Gabe's,' says he. 'The older ones in the street've been tellin' everyone all the tricks so they'll be OK.'

We run though a gap in the traffic, across Crumlin Road, to the gates of Holy Cross Chapel.

'You need someone else to make it work,' says he. 'They go up to somebody and say *Go up to Donnelly and ask him how his granny's gettin' on with her knittin'*, right? So yer man goes up to you and says *Donnelly, how's yer granny gettin' on with her knittin'*? And you say, dead serious, you say, *My Granny hasn't got any arms,* and they shit themselves cuz they think you're goin' to kill them. Class, isn't it?' says he, wetting himself.

'That's cracker,' I say, forcin' a smile. I think it sounds like somethin' a really horrible person would do. St. Gabriel's sounds like it's goin' to be Holy Cross multiplied by a hundred million. I'm goin' to ask Our Paddy. I'll have to be nice to him. *Shiver me timbers.*

The Chapel is enormous. Huge, grey bricks, ladder up to two high spires. Men stand smokin' outside the doors holdin' their babies. They pretend the baby's cryin' so they can leave for a fag. Me and Fartin' bless ourselves with holy water from the font – you have to, to get in – push through the latecomers standin' just inside the door.

Mass is bunged and we walk down the aisle lookin' for Ma and Wee Maggie. I use it like a catwalk. I know everyone is starin' at me. I don't look but I can feel their jealousy mixed with total admiration for my style and general coolness.

I push Fartin' into Ma's pew and everyone shuffles along. Ma narrows her eyes til they say *You've embarrassed me in front of the whole friggin' Chapel.*

The new Priest is so quiet it's hard to hear what he's going on about. Our Paddy says he's gay, but how can that be? He probably thinks that cuz Priests wear robes that look like dresses. They make altar boys wear them too. You'd never catch me wearin' one of them. I'd rather eat my own eyeballs soaked in bleach. It'd be like walkin' round in a T-Shirt that said *KICK MY HEAD IN PLEASE.*

The rows in front sink to their knees and like dominoes we follow.

'That new Priest is so borin',' Fartin' whispers.

'Shush, yous two,' whispers Ma. 'Mickey Donnelly, I'm warnin' you.'

It's not friggin' fair. And it's not fair I'm not going to St. Malachy's and Fartin' won't be in St. Gabriel's. That's God's fault.

*Mickey, that's a black mark on your soul.*

I wonder what your soul looks like. I reckon it's a red

circle. No, a heart is red, so a soul is probably pink. Pink is for girls though. I picture my circle soul now and it's definitely pink. I just won't tell anybody my soul's a girl's one.

I forgot the black mark. I'll make it an X for wrong. But I don't want to go to Hell. Wait a minute. What did Old Father Michael used to say? 'Ask for forgiveness and your soul will be cleansed.' Hmmm . . . I see a pygmy God, inside my soul, with a wee mop.

*God forgive me.* God mops the black mark off.

Sex! *God forgive me.*

Fuck! *God forgive me.*

*Big diddies.* Two black marks appear. Must be one for each diddy.

*God forgive me. God forgive me.*

Poor God is rushin' around on fast forward.

'Mickey,' says Ma.

'What?'

'Will you get up for Communion,' Ma scowls. I was last in on the pew so everyone's standin', waitin' to pass. How long have I been spaced out for? 'I'm takin' you to see the Priest afterwards,' says she, loudly for those watchin'.

'*I'm* goin' to Communion, Mrs Donnelly,' Fartin' says, with the voice of an angel, his hands together in prayer and his head tilted to the side like the statue of the *Child de Prague*.

'Mickey,' Fartin' whispers behind me in the line.

I bring my prayer hands up to my face and whisper into them. 'What?'

'Your Ma's mental.'

'I know. But you'd better watch yourself. She'll end up whackin' *you*, if you don't stop,' says me.

'The Body of Christ,' the new Priest says.

'Amen,' I stick my tongue out and he puts the white, card-board circle on it that sticks to the roof of my mouth. The nuns came to school to give us a special lesson on unstickin' Communion without using your fingers – that's a sin and punishable by Hell.

There's Martine. *Hey – did you happen to see the most beautiful girl in the world?* That terrible song plays in my head. Two wee cherubs fly out of the stained glass windows above and trumpet down to hover over her.

Martine . . . She's got long, blonde hair and everybody knows, long, blonde hair is the most gorgeous thing any girl could have.

Martine . . . she has a garage. She's so lucky.

Martine . . . is like Farrah Fawcett-Majors without diddies. *God forgive me. Twice.* And she's even an actress like her too. Last summer she put plays on in her garage. Everybody went mad for them. I hope I get to act in a proper play in her garage one day.

She smiled at me. Nah, it couldn't have been. Could it? Not unless she went temporarily Stevie Wonder. Must have been at Fartin'.

I sit up and let Fartin' pass. I nip him on the inside of his leg. He yelps like Killer and falls onto the pew. Ma digs me, givin' me a dead leg. 'Wait til Mass has finished, wee boy,' Ma says. She'll crucify me on the altar. I never mess around like this in Chapel. It's just cuz Fartin's here. He makes me do things I wouldn't do in a million years. Ma will never let him sit with us in Chapel again.

'May the Peace of the Lord be with you always,' the new Priest whispers.

'And also with you,' we all answer.

'Go in Peace, to love and serve the Lord,' says he.

'Thanks be to God.' Yeah, thanks be to God that's over.

Everybody legs it out. It's like leavin' the cinema. Everybody's pushin' to get out first.

'Mickey,' Ma says in a deep voice that she uses when she wants to shout but she can't.

'You go on, I'll have to go with her,' I whisper to Fartin'.

'Oh Donnelly . . .' he sucks in through his teeth.

'I know,' I say, noddin' my head up like it's all one big laugh but really I should start sayin' my prayers, for real this time.

Fartin' heads on and I slow down. A hand grabs my arm tight. I let it pull me any way it wants. We bless ourselves and go outside. The light is blindin'. I'm pulled down the steps, across the path to the side door of the Chapel. The new Priest is there, shakin' hands, all smiles, talkin' to the Holy Joes. Mrs Montgomery even has a grotto in her front garden, re-staging Mary's appearance to Bernadette at Lourdes.

Ma can't really be takin' me to the Priest. I'm a good boy really. It's all Fartin's fault for makin' me act the maggot.

'Hello, Father,' Ma says, half bowin', like she's talkin' to the Queen. 'I was wonderin' if you could have a word with my wee boy. He was actin' up somethin' shockin' in Chapel.' She looks at me: *Didn't I tell you I was gonna do it?*

'Mrs Donnelly, isn't it?' says he.

'Yes, Father.' Ma's over the moon he remembered her. That's it now. He could tell Ma to stick needles in my eye til I sang *Hail Glorious Saint Patrick*, and she'd say, 'Needles in just one eye, Father?'

'Och, Mrs Donnelly, I'm sure he's not that bad,' he winks at me.

I have to nip my leg hard to stop myself from sayin' *Winkin' on a Sunday, why Father, I'm shocked*. I am seriously on my *funny half hour*, as Ma would say.

'When I was his age I wasn't exactly an angel either. At least he comes to Mass with you,' smiles he. 'Where's Mr Donnelly?'

Ma near has a stroke; face frozen on one side and a cripple's smile on the other.

'He's sick, Father. Was ragin' he couldn't make it,' says she.

'Och, well, I hope he gets better soon. I look forward to meeting him. But I can see your wean is worrying you though,' says he, soundin' all Scottish. He speaks so soft in Chapel you'd never notice. 'If it makes you feel better, I'll certainly have a chat with young . . . ?'

'Mickey . . .' I say.

'Michael,' says Ma, diggin' her nails into my arm.

'Michael,' he says, smilin' at me. 'Why don't you come up and see me soon and we'll have a wee chat, OK?'

'Thank you, Father,' says she. 'Say *thank you* to the Father.'

'Thank you, Father.'

'Go in Peace,' he smiles and pats me on the head.

'There, that'll get the messin' out of you,' says Ma when we get out of the gates.

It wasn't as bad as I thought it was gonna be. I think Ma came off worse.

'Mammy, can me and Wee Maggie run on down to the house?' I say.

'After the way you've messed about in Chapel? Anyway, we're too far away.'

'Aye Mammy, dead on. Sure am'n't I gonna have to go past here to get to St. Gabriel's?' says me.

Ma goes purple. I wasn't sayin' it in a bad way.

'Mammy, can we not go on down to the house?' Wee Maggie says. 'We could set the table for you an' all,' she says, sweet as strawberry jam.

'No,' Ma says, but her heart's not in it. 'Go on then, give my head peace.'

'Thanks, Mammy,' I say and take Wee Maggie's hand. We walk ahead, down Brompton Park.

'Will we do our walk?' says Wee Maggie. We can walk at exactly the same time. We've been brilliant at it since we won the three-legged race at the Summer Scheme last year. God, the Summer Scheme, I wonder when it starts. We'll have to go back this year and win again.

'Jesus Christ!' Our Paddy nearly has a canary. 'Don't burst into the house like that.' He thought he was gettin' shot by the Prods. I want to laugh but I need him on my side.

Wee Maggie grabs my hand and we go into the scullery. Our Measles' face is the colour of a raspberry Slush Puppy, leanin' over the steamin' pots of potatoes and cabbage. She looks like a mad scientist in her lab. If we *were* gunmen, she'd be shot without even noticing, but I tell you, with her last breath she'd have reached up to turn off Ma's potatoes.

'Alright, Measles.' I run over and grab her round the waist. Maggie copies me.

'Awoooaaah!' I laugh, as my ear gets pulled off my head. Measles has us both by an ear and we're on our tippy toes, like naughty school kids caught by the headmaster.

'Shut that dog up before Ma gets home,' she says, throwin' us to the back door and pretendin' to kick us up the bum. We laugh. We love Our Measles. I wish boys and girls were swapped so Paddy had to do all the work around the house and then we could play with Measles more.

'C'mon, wee son,' I call, openin' the yard door, 'It's me and Wee Maggie to see you.' Killer runs out of his box barkin' and jumpin' up on us and burlin' round with his pink tongue floppin' out the side of his mouth. 'Isn't he the best dog you ever did see?' I say, in an American voice.

'Can you wait five minutes?' says me to her. She frowns. 'You can play with Killer all by yourself.'

'OK, hurry up but,' says she.

I sneak into the livin' room and slide onto the sofa beside Paddy. He's watchin' TV. I hate football in real life, never mind the TV. 'What's the score?' I say.

'2–1 to Everton,' says he, then looks at me. 'What you lookin'?' he squints.

I have to hurry before Ma gets back. 'What's it like in St. Gabriel's?' I ask.

He laughs. 'So you want info. What's in it for me?'

'I'll polish your shoes.' He completely hates them not bein' shiny.

'You can clean my football boots.'

I can clean them when Ma's polishin' Da's boots and we can be together. 'OK. It's a deal.'

'On the first day they'll have your head down the toilet,' he says.

My stomach churns. 'Yeah, right,' I say. Ma walks through the door behind Paddy. He doesn't see.

'They'll do a big shit in it first. And then they'll shove your face right in it. And flush the chain,' he says. He mimes wipin' his face then puts his hands under his nose and smells somethin' disgustin'.

I'm goin' to be sick. Ma looks like Medusa. She grabs the wee shovel from the companion set on the hearth and whacks Paddy on the leg. He screams like a girl, jumps to his feet and squares up to Ma. She takes a step back, eyes wide. He's gettin' too big for his boots. In that freeze somethin' changes, Paddy's chest unpuffs and he gets smaller. Ma whacks his elbow with the shovel. Paddy dances like a demented leprechaun.

'What're you sayin' that for?' she shouts.

'They do, to ones like him,' he points at me. 'Sure he still plays with his wee sister.'

Ma whacks him on the knee and he hobbles out the door.

'He's a good boy,' Ma shouts after him and she slams the door. 'Don't listen to him.'

'OK,' I say. Nine weeks til shite on my face.

Bangin' on the ceilin'. Da's been woken up and wants somethin'. Ma forgot not to shout.

'Go on, play with your dog,' Ma says, frownin' up at the ceilin'. She goes to Da and I go out the back. Paddy could be lyin'. Fartin' could find out for me. How am I goin' to see him? We didn't arrange anythin'. I wish we had a phone. I could get 10p and go up to the payphone on the Cliftonville Road, but that's more dangerous than going to Fartin's house, there's so many Proddy areas around it. Who else can I ask?

Wee Maggie's lyin' on the ground with Killer jumpin' all over her. I pick him up. He licks me. It tickles and I laugh but I can't concentrate. I need to ask boys, but I don't play with any. I hate them and they hate me. Why can't I live in America where girls and boys go to the same school? Girls would protect me.

'I've got sweee-eeets,' Wee Maggie sings.

'Yum yums,' I say, in my funny voice. We laugh and she shoves somethin' pink, soft and sweet into my mouth. I bite half off and give it to Killer so he knows he's my dog. Killer! The boys would love Killer. I can use him as my secret weapon to get behind enemy lines. Genie-Ass! Ha! Mickey Donnelly will never be defeated. *No surrender!* Shit. That's the Protestant saying. Luckily only me and Maggie can read minds cuz that would get me knee-capped. In the future, everyone will be telepathic and the IRA posters will say *Loose Thoughts Cost Lives*. I'd better be careful cuz they may already be testing this kind of technology.

# 3

I'M NOT ALLOWED in the house cuz it'll annoy Da. Which is really, really not fair cuz there's so much brilliant TV on. Ma said she doesn't know why I'd want to be sittin' in on a day like this anyway. She said every child in the world would want to be out playin'. I wish she'd make up her mind cuz most of the time she tells me not to play with the ones in our street. Everythin' changes in the summer.

Da's off the drink and fags again which makes him sick. He's really gonna try this time, Ma said. This'll be about the ten hundredth time. But you never know. He did get me Killer. Ma took Wee Maggie to work with her sayin' I was too wee to mind her, but big and ugly enough to look after myself. But she won't let me take Killer out – yet. I nearly did, anyway. I don't know what difference it makes if I take him out when Ma's home or not. I don't understand her. Like Weetabix, brown sauce, how TV beams across the sky, the Bermuda Triangle and the bizarrest of all, the off-side rule in football.

I have very clear instructions. Don't go to the top of the street cuz there's always riots. Don't go to the bottom of the street cuz there's No Man's Land and there's always riots. Don't go near the Bray or the Bone hills cuz that leads to Proddy Oldpark where they throw stones across the road from their side. Don't go into the aul houses cuz a wee boy fell through the stairs in one and broke his two legs. I think his neck too.

Ma could be exaggerating. Oh, and don't go onto the Eggy field cuz there's glue-sniffers.

Ma should have just tied me to the gate or locked me in a cupboard.

I step on two chewin' gum splats on the tarmac and go up on the balls of my feet. I swishy-twist my ankles in and out, clickin' my heels like I'm wearin' ruby slippers. I put my right foot in front and swishy-twist it. Bring left foot front and swishy-twist it. Swishy-twist right foot, change, swishy-twist left foot. Frig me, this is great.

Faster, faster. *Look at me!* Nobody else can do this. Americans – they could. Cuz they've got baseball boots like mine. Class. Beezer. Magic.

Someone's watchin' me. Why would they not, when I look this cool? I don't even look up. That's how cool I am. I wish Martine could see me do this, but she's playin' in the girls' gang. I wish Wee Maggie could. I'll show her later.

'Take a redner, Donkelly.' Only one person in the world thinks it's funny to call me Donkelly. Ma's-a-Whore from my class. He hates me and I hate him.

'Wise up, Donkelly. Catch a grip, wee lad,' says he.

'Jealousy will get you nowhere.' Who wouldn't be? Of my brill baseball boots. And the way I can swish.

'Wha'? Of them? Wise the bap! Why would I want baseball boots for? Sure nobody plays baseball in Ireland,' says he.

I stop. 'Yeah, well, I'm goin' to America on my holidays and everybody plays it there.'

'Aye, right, America? I believe ye, thousands wouldn't,' he laughs.

'Anyway, you don't have to play baseball to wear them. They're sneakers and everybody wears them over there.' Ha!

Hold on a cotton-pickin' minute. I bet you he's goin' to St. Gabriel's. 'So, what are you doin' now?' I ask.

'That's for me to know and you to find out.' He smiles and walks on. He's won me now.

It's so hard to let him win, but if I let him win cuz I want somethin', then really it's me that's winnin'. I smile. I watch him spit over his shoulder like the men do. Yuk. He's got the Ardoyne Hard Man Dander too. I might need this for St. Gabriel's. I catch up, puff my chest, hands in pockets, chin stickin' out and point my knees out as I walk. *The Dander*. I must be doin' OK cuz he doesn't sleg me.

'I'm goin' to St. Gabriel's. Are you?' says me, like I'm proud of it.

'Aye,' says he. 'I thought you'd be goin' to St. Malachy's?'

I hit a redner. 'Me? No way. They're all snobs.' I hope I get to be a snob when I grow up.

Silence. I keep walkin'. We turn the corner and walk along the land at the side of the Eggy field, where the burnt-out egg factory is. I hope he isn't goin' up there.

There's a crowd of girls at a lamppost where the Eggy edge meets the road.

'Dir-ty bitch! Dir-ty Bitch!' they chant. 'Brit-lovin' bitch! Brit-lovin' bitch! Dir-ty whore! Dir-ty whore!'

'A whore is worse than a prostitute cuz she does it for free,' says he. It's a bit weird him sayin' that, since everybody says his Ma's one.

As the circle breaks, I can see there's an older girl tied to the lamppost. She's covered in black stuff, like tarmac, with feathers stuck on her. She's a traitor. I see Our Measles.

'Move yous on,' Our Measles tells us, 'And Mickey Donnelly, you know you're not allowed in them aul houses.'

'I know,' I shout and tut, to sound cheeky. I pull Ma's-a-Whore into the entry, the alley behind our street. 'C'mon, before Our Mary whacks us.' I'd never call her Measles in front of him.

'Fuck, her diddies are even bigger!'

He's lookin' back at some wee girls watchin' the big girls. He means Briege McAnally. I hate her. Everybody is scared of Briege McAnally cuz she's evil, her Da's in jail for being a big IRA man and she has big diddies at eleven. But that's not why I'm scared of her. I'm scared of Briege McAnally cuz of the way she drinks Coca-Cola.

She steals money from us in the street so she can buy big bottles of Coke like your Ma buys to put in her vodka. She drinks with her head back and tips those big bottles up, lettin' the Coke flood in. She glugs in her throat like a lizard or an alien and goes on til the bottle's half gone. I tried what she does but with a can, and I near choked to death. I actually think Coke is dangerous.

And that's not all about Briege McAnally.

When you're eatin' an apple and somebody says *give us yer dutes*, you only eat the middle of your apple and leave the top and bottom to give to them; that is the *dutes*. Briege calls *second dutes* which means, after someone eats the top and bottom, she eats the bits normal people throw away – the core – pips'n'all. It's cuz she gets no food in her house cuz her Ma spends it on drink.

'Vincy lumbered Briege,' says Ma's-a-Whore. What's *lumbered*?

We walk and he talks all about girls, but dirty things. I want to go home and watch *Laurel and Hardy*.

'Take two of these,' he says, when we reach a dead end, fannin' out lollipop sticks, like he's the Child Catcher from *Chitty Chitty Bang Bang*.

He sits down, right on the road that's blocked off cuz of the aul houses. Ma would break my face. I check no-one's watchin' then sit beside him. He digs a lollipop stick into the tarmacy line in the middle of the road. The tar moves a little, like really thick, black, chewin'-gummy glue. I copy every-thing he does.

The tar is like the black glue they used on the girl. I wonder what they're doin' to her now? How's she goin' to get tar out of her hair? She must have done it with a Brit. She'll get put out of the district now. When we're finished I'm goin' round to see if she's still there. If there's no-one around I'll rescue her. Even though she's a Brit-lover, I don't think it's right. I mean, you can't help who you fall in love with. Look at Romeo and Juliet. Beauty and the Beast. Peters and Lee. What I can't un-derstand about *them* two is, the blind one is the ugly one – surely it should be the other way round?

We have big X's by crossin' two sticks and wrappin' the tar round the middle and pressin' the join together. He's made two but I've only made one.

'Did ye see that filim on last night?' says he.

'Which one?' says me.

'The war one where they build the aeroplane. It's my fa-vourite filim by miles. What's yours?' says he.

Let's see . . . there's *Star Wars*, *Grease*, *The Sound Of Music*, the one about the wee boy who dies of leukaemia – I cried my eyes out – and *Herbie Goes to Monte Carlo*. Hmm . . . It's between *Grease* and *The Wizard Of Oz*.

'*The Wizard of Oz*,' I say.

'Wise up!' he pisses himself. 'That's for wee girls and wee kids.'

'Right,' I say like *you know nothin*'. How could he not know that it's one of the best filims ever? I saw it in a docu-mentary so it's true. I'm the only person I've ever heard of who watches documentaries. I will find my people one day. And they will live in the US of A.

A rifle pokes out from the gable wall behind Ma's-a-Whore. A Brit's head appears over the rifle, lookin' through the telescope bit. He raises his arm and an army patrol come out from behind in a line.

Ma's-a-Whore gets up and walks off. I follow him along the backs of the aul houses.

'What are you lookin' for?' I say, after he passes the third house.

'Stairs,' says he. 'Here we go.' We stumble through the back yard and into the house. He creeps up the stairs, dead quiet, like there's still people livin' here. I stay at the bottom.

'C'mon you,' says he. 'What's wrong? Ye big woman.'

I need to get info quick and then get away from him. I creep up, holdin' onto the wall, and run the last couple of steps because in filims that's when they always collapse. From the empty window frame in a bedroom we see the Brit patrol walk in two lines across the waste ground, some walkin' backwards.

'I can't wait to go to St. Gabriel's, can you?' I say.

'I know. Best school there is,' he says.

Maybe Our Paddy's just messin' with me. Maybe they will have drama and music and I will learn how to be a brilliant actor, and how to sing and dance and maybe end up like John Travolta.

'You can smoke in the handball courts and the teachers let you,' he says. 'And you can mitch school for days and no-one even notices. Our Ta says ye can have riots every day with the Proddy school down the road.'

Sweet Mother of Jesus! I don't think I'm goin' to ask any more questions about St. Gabriel's. I want to go home now.

He picks up a plastic bag. 'Glue,' he laughs. 'You can do that in the handball courts too, if you're *in*.' I turn my nose up and he chucks it. 'Right, see who can throw theirs the furthest,' says he, walkin' to the window.

He throws his **X** out and his whole body goes ou
it, nearly. He's not scared one wee bit. I wish I was like tha

'Look at that,' says he pointing.

Looks like helicopter blades. 'Brill,' I say.

'Beat that,' says he, rubbin' his hands together.

I throw mine and it goes straight down onto the old road.
He laughs, slappin' his legs.

'You throw like a girl,' says he. That's why I never did PE
in school.

The army patrol comes into sight. Ma's-a-Whore takes
out his other **X** from his pocket. He holds it to look like a gun
and points it at the Brits.

'Down!' A voice shouts and the soldiers hit the deck. We
jump either side of the window, backs to the wall.

'It's OK,' a soldier shouts. 'It's those kids.'

Shit. They must have thought it was a real gun. Ma's-a-
Whore laughs. 'Did you see that? Beezer!'

This is what boys think is fun.

We sneak looks out the window and wait til the patrol
has gone.

'Last one to get his is a fruit,' he says, pushin' me back
against the wall as he takes off downstairs like he's had three
cans of Coke. I chase after him. In the yard, he slips and falls
over. I catch up.

'You alright?' I ask.

'My leg.' He's holdin' it, rockin' from side to side on the
ground. 'I slipped on bloody shit!'

I laugh. In here you wouldn't know if it was dog shit or
people shit.

'Come on,' I take his arm to help him up. He yanks me
down, flat on my face and jumps on my back, pinnin' me to
the ground.

'Get off me!' I shout. 'Let me go,' I wriggle, but I feel his

me so I stop. He rubs himself against my

gettin' hard. I can't put my face down cuz

his, aren't ye?' he whispers in my ear.

e on this Our Paddy will kill you.'

grinds into me hard and then he's off me.

ross his foot over onto his knee and struggle to keep his balance on one leg. Actin' like nothin' happened. Like what he did to me is normal. Normal for a dirtbird, maybe. I get up and walk around him, out the doorway to the entry while he scrapes the shit from his shoe with a lollipop stick.

Somethin' hits my leg and he laughs. I turn to see a lollipop stick with shit on it at my feet.

'You're disgustin'!' I say, checkin' my leg for shite.

'*Yer disgustin*',' he says, in a girlie voice and hangs his hands like they were broken at the wrists. He comes at me walkin' like a mixture of a woman in high heels and a horse. 'Fruity boy!' he says, scruchin' up his face in pure hatred. 'Go on and run to yer Mammy.'

I run away, down the entry and into the waste ground, him shouting after me.

I don't know why fruity means gay. Every time I play with boys they always end up calling me that. And he's won me now cuz *fruity* is the worst thing you can say to a boy. Well, there is one thing worser.

I stop and look across the waste ground. There he is, laughin' on the other side.

'At least I *can* get my Mammy,' I shout, 'Cuz she's not a whore that hangs round the Albert Clock!' I run like shite back towards the Eggy.

'I'll kill you. I'm tellin' ye,' I hear him scream. 'Just you wait.'

I know I shouldn't have said that, but he started it. He said bad things to me. And you have to say the worst thing back. You have to win.

I run down past the Eggy, past the girls around the lamp-post, but I don't look over.

I know what it's going to be like in St. Gabriel's, just like Holy Cross but with bigger, more horrible boys and no Fartin' to protect me. Could I pretend to be like them? Be a brilliant actor til I get to America? I don't think I'm that good. I have to get out of here.

I want Killer. I run home fast I as I can. I don't care if Ma said I can't go in, I'm gonna bring Killer in to watch TV with the sound turned down so I don't wake Da.

I open the door and: 'Wee Maggie, you're back!' I jump on her on the sofa. 'I've missed you so much!' I give her a big, giant hug. I wish Mammy wouldn't take her everywhere. I can look after her.

'C'mon we see Killer,' I say, runnin' out to the kitchen and out the back. Killer does a yappy bark.

*What's kept ye?*

Killer can telepath!

*Where have you been? You know you're my best friend and I've been just sittin' here waitin' to play with you. You can play with me and Wee Maggie all the time. We love you. You don't have to play with those boys. And St. Gabriel's is twelve million weeks away. And I've sent a letter to your Fairy God-mother to get you to America.*

I grab Killer's ear and give it a pull. 'C'mon, son.' I run back in, through the house to the bottom of the stairs.

'I've got 10p,' Wee Maggie says behind me.

'Brill! Let's go to the shop, now,' I say, grabbin' her hand and near pullin' her arm out of her socket. 'Mammy!' I shout upstairs, 'Can me and Wee Maggie take Killer just to the shop?'

'No,' she loud-whispers down, shakin' her fist. I forgot about Da.

'Ach, Mammy! It's not fair.'

'Take him and get out,' she says, lookin' back to the bedroom. 'And come you two straight back.'

I look at Wee Maggie and we hold hands and jump up and down. 'C'mon, wee son.' I pat my thighs and he jumps up on me.

I check up and down the street, make sure Ma's-a-Whore isn't waitin'. Killer barks. He would protect me. My bodyguard.

I pull Wee Maggie like we're runnin' away from boarding school or an orphanage or an evil stepmother. Killer goes mental. He thinks this is the best game in the whole world. So do I. I know Wee Maggie does too cuz we're the same. We laugh our heads off through the back alley to the shop.

We get to the back door of Toner's house. A shop in a house. A house shop. It's my favourite one. Their wee kitchen door is sawed in half with the top half always open. It's kinda like the doors in a saloon, only sideways. When I grow up and get my own house from the Housin' Executive, I'm goin' to do that to all my doors.

'Right, whaddayes want?' says Mrs Toner's wee girl, comin' out of her livin' room. Well, there's nothin' *wee* about her. She's as tall as a Brit look-out post. They could build a wee hut on her head and put a camera in it.

'What do you want?' Wee Maggie asks me, lookin' at the sweets.

'I don't know, what do *you* want?' We giggle. Killer barks.

'No, what do *you* want?' she says.

'*No,* what do *you* want?' I laugh.

'How does your Ma stick yous?' says Lanky Annie. I look at Wee Maggie and we want to laugh. Lanky stuffs sweets into a small, brown paper bag. 'Now, get out yous two.' She throws the wee bag at us.

'Excuse me!' I say, givin' her a big dirty look and 10p. I turn to Maggie, 'I'm sure I won't be partaking of this establishment henceforth, don't you know.'

Maggie folds her arms and sticks her head in the air.

'C'mon, Killer.' We all run down the path and out the back gate, like we really have to get somewhere.

I stop dead.

'Wha'?' says she.

'Wha-t? T,' I make the sound. 'You don't want to be like these hallions.'

'Excuse me,' Maggie says like the Queen, 'What-t-t-t?'

'Good girl,' I say and nod. 'We need the power of the sweets.'

'Yeah. We do. The power of the sweets.'

We're up to the high doe. I bend down and we rub noses together.

'I know! Why don't we do it like lucky dip?' I say, my eyebrows feelin' higher than my actual head.

'Mickey, that's ano'er brilliant idear.'

I wonder where idears come from? I close my eyes.

*A sign on the door says Idears Dept. It opens. A man has a big bundle of presents wrapped in paper and ribbon like you see in filims. I say, 'I'm gonna give them all to Maggie.' He smiles and says, 'Just right, Sir, that's the name on all the tags.'*

We put the sweets in our mouths at exactly the same time. As I suck, I shake all down my body cuz the power of the sweets is runnin' through me. I take off. I run up through the new estate, out into Havana Gardens. At the bottom of the Bray I stop, so she can catch up. I'm not going *up* the Bray. I'm a good boy.

I stop and look down to the lamppost where the Brit-

Lovin' Bitch was. The Brits must've untied her. She can't stay in Ardoyne now. She'll have to go England or they'll kill her.

'What's the matter?' Wee Maggie's scourin' the entry for what I'm lookin' at.

'Nothin'. You're too young. I'll tell you when you're older.'

'I'm not too young.'

'You have to trust me.' I saw that on the TV.

There's a big screamin' noise. We look and the Girls' Gang are playin' skips in our street. They think they're great. Killer appears from the back entry and does a wee wee on the post. Shit, I forgot about him. I'd get murdered if I lost him. Cheers from the other end of the waste ground. It's the Boys' Gang. They think they're great too. Why can't they all be like me and Wee Maggie?

'Do you want to go and play skips, Mickey?' says she.

'No way. Who wants to play with them?' says me.

'Ach,' she says, frownin'.

'Don't you want to play with me, Maggie?' I take a Whopper from the sweet bag. Her eyes light up.

'Yes, Mickey,' she says.

'Stick out your tongue then,' I say. 'Close your eyes.' I put the bag in my pocket, put the Whopper in her mouth, and when she's done I tickle her til she screams and forgets all about the girls.

# 4

MARTINE'S AT THE door of her garage. *I love you. Will you be my girlfriend?* She looks me up and down and laughs. I look down. I'm in Our Paddy's old, faded, brown pants with the pattern I really hate. I've a hard-on stickin' out towards her.

'In the US, of course, this is called a boner,' Martine says to a class behind their desks. She prods my hard-on with a long stick. Big boys grab me and drag me into Holy Cross school toilets. I can hear flushin'. Martine pokes my back with her stick. It hurts.

'Stop it.' I open my eyes. I'm in my bedroom, under Paddy's bed, facin' the wall where I go when I can't sleep. I must have dropped off cuz I was dreamin'. But somethin' *is* pokin' me. I roll over, careful not to get my hair caught in the springs above. A soldier is kneelin' down on the floor lookin' under at me. It must be one of those weirdy dreams when you wake up and then you're not awake. I close my eyes tight. Somethin' pokes me in the chest. I open my eyes again. The soldier's pokin' me with his rifle.

'Come on,' the soldier says, 'Out of there, kid.'

'Where's m'Mammy?' my voice soundin' like I'm about two and a half.

'Wot are you hidin', kid?' He shines his torch at me, pokin' his rifle around.

'Nothin',' I say.

'Downstairs. Let's go,' he says, gettin' up.

The landin' light pings on. I see him properly now. Rifle, camouflage gear and blacked-out face.

'Get a fuckin' move on up there, will ya!' comes from outside the room somewhere behind me. Like when I saw *Star Wars* in Dolby Stereo. Killer's bark comes through the open window. If they touch him, I'll kill them. I wiggle out from under Paddy's bed. He's not in it.

'Where's Wee Maggie?' I say.

'Everyone's downstairs,' he says.

Ma wouldn't go down without me. Out on the landin' the big light is blindin'. 'Mammy,' I shout downstairs. 'Where's my Mammy?' I warn him.

'What are yous doin' to him, yous bastards?' Ma screams from downstairs.

'Mammy!' I scream, runnin' downstairs. Big thumpin' behind me. A soldier jumps out in front of me aimin' his rifle at my face. Me and the soldier eye each other for about an hour and a half, like in the Westerns before they draw.

'Mickey!' Ma shouts. I see her arms grabbin' at the Brit but she's pulled back.

He puts his rifle down. *Go in*, he nods to the livin' room.

Ma's bein' held by a soldier. He lets her go. I hug her waist.

'It's OK, son,' she bends down. 'Don't let them see you cryin',' she whispers in my ear and pushes me away.

'Mammy, what about Killer?' I say.

'He's alright,' she says.

Everybody's bunged up on the sofa. I can hear shoutin' outside and helicopters jutterin'. I remember that's why I couldn't sleep. I squash between Our Measles, with Wee Maggie on her knee, and Our Paddy who shrinks from me like I've got leprosy.

'Did ya check the attic?' a big, fat, ugly soldier comes out of our scullery. He must raid people's fridges as well as their houses.

'No,' says the soldier who brought me down.

'Then get up and check it,' Buster Blood Vessel shouts.

'Where's m'Daddy?' I ask.

'Yer Daddy's not in,' says Ma, with a look like murder. He must be out. But he's supposed to be off the drink.

Wee Maggie runs over to Ma, who's on Da's chair, and jumps on her knee. We wait, sayin' nothin'. That's what you do. Ignore them, to show they're not winnin' us. We look at each other. Measles hunches her knees and pulls her white nightdress over them. All you can see is her ginger frizzball head stickin' out of a stumpy lump, her face lost in white make-up she uses to cover her ten million freckles. She must have been at the disco tonight.

'S'pose there's no chance uva cuppa tea?' Buster laughs, thinkin' he's funny.

'Go fuck yerself,' says Ma.

'Good Caf'lic then, are ya luv?' says Buster.

'Lip up, fatty!' I say, like in Buster's song, and the house wets itself. Even the other soldiers. That's never happened to me before. I'm a hit.

Noise like a thousand thunders from outside. Women bangin' their metal bin lids on the ground to warn the IRA to run and hide. Killer barks like mad out the back.

'Shut that fuckin' dog up!' says Buster.

Killer yelps.

'Don't you lay a finger on that dog. Yous are evil!' Ma
shouts to them back.

*You tell them, Mammy.*

A soldier stands on the hearth.

'Mammy, he's standin' on your good tiles,' I say, goin' in
for the attack.

'That's cuz he's an ignorant bastard, love. Don't worry,
they'll be out of here in a minute. They know they're not gonna
find anythin'. They're just tormentin' innocent Catholics.'

We are innocent cuz Da isn't in the IRA. He's always been
a drunk. But then again, Ma says the IRA is full of drunken
bastards cuz from the chippy she works in she sees them fallin'
out of the Shamrock Club every night of the week.

'Found somefink!' That comes from the top of the stairs.
Some-fink. Fink? I thought they were supposed to talk properly in England.

'Bring it down,' Buster shouts, his piggy cheeks all pleased.

We all look at each other. Ma looks worried. Maybe Da is
in the IRA. Maybe his drinkin' is just a cover – a disguise to
throw them off the scent of his secret identity. I know Briege
McAnally's Da is. She never shuts up about it. If Da is, and
they put him in prison, I could get to go to America in one
of those *help the poor sufferin' children of Northern Ireland*
schemes. God, I hope Da is in the IRA. And goes to prison.

The soldier comes in with two balaclavas. They're ski mask
things the IRA use to hide their faces. The odd nutter wears
them in winter under the hood of their snorkel jacket. They've
found our gas mask too. We used to play with it sometimes
when Ma and Da were out. Measles or Paddy would put it on
and chase us round the house – that's when Paddy was almost
normal and I nearly liked him. I tried it on once but I couldn't
breathe. Saves you from gas but suffocates you instead. What
genius came up with that?

'Right, take him,' says Buster and two soldiers pull Paddy from the sofa, arms twisted behind his back.

'Leave him, yous bastards!' Ma jumps from the chair goin' for the Brits. Two move in surroundin' Paddy. 'Let him go!' she screams. Buster pushes Ma back on the chair and holds her there.

'Don't touch her,' Measles screams at Buster, untanglin' her legs from her nightdress. Wee Maggie starts squealin'.

'Right, all of ya, out!' shouts Buster. 'Now!'

'Come on, move it!' another shouts.

We're pushed, Ma screamin' the whole time. Two Brits drag Paddy to a Saracen. I give Wee Maggie a piggyback cuz she's got her nice slippers on and she's not allowed to get them dirty.

Everybody's out, right up the street. The bin lids and the whistles are behind us now in Etna Drive. Helicopters everywhere. The noise is powerful.

We're huddled together behind Mammy and she screams right in the Brits' dirty, blacked-up faces. The street is packed. Paddy's gone.

'What about Killer, Mammy?' I ask.

We get a glimpse of Our Paddy dragged through the crowd. Ma breaks through the Brits and runs to him.

'Leave him alone!' Ma grabs at Paddy.

'Don't, Mammy!' Paddy shouts, the soldiers draggin' him to the back of a Saracen.

'I'll kill yous,' cries Ma, a soldier holdin' her at arm's length.

'Get away, Ma,' Paddy shouts. What's he shoutin' at Mammy for? She's only lookin' after him. I hate him. He's just like Da.

'He's only a child,' Mammy's cryin'. 'That's all yous're good for, isn't it? Takin' childer.'

43

Ma bites the hand of the soldier holdin' her.

'Fuck ya!' he whacks her across the face.

'Mammy!' Our Paddy roars and jumps out of the back of the Saracen, hands tied behind his back. He's cryin'. Our Paddy never smiles, never mind cries. All the women run to us. There's goin' to be murder.

A soldier cracks Paddy on the back of the head with the butt of his rifle and Paddy flies forward but he doesn't fall – he runs.

'Paddy, don't!' Measles screams, runnin' to him. A Brit blocks her with his rifle. She claws at his face like a wild cat.

Wee Maggie's screamin' in my ear, deafenin' me.

'That's my wee brother.' Measles gets free and runs in front of the soldiers chasin' Paddy.

'Don't!' shouts Aul Sheila from next door, grabbin' Measles by the collar, her nightdress tearin'. 'You'll only make it worse for him.' Measles is kickin' and hittin' Aul Sheila, who doesn't let go.

Three soldiers have Paddy. One pulls him backwards and he falls onto the road and is dragged along the ground by his stupid, long hair while the other two kick him. Two Peelers join and batter him with their black sticks.

The women surround Ma like they're her bodyguards. But really they're protectin' the soldiers, cuz if Ma gets her hands on one she'll kill them stone dead.

I can't see Paddy. He must be back in the Saracen.

'Takin' him for a fuckin' stupid balaclava,' Mummy cries to Aul Sheila.

'Sure, they're bastards,' Aul Sheila shouts for them to hear. 'They're liftin' every man they can get their dirty hands on.'

'But he's only a child,' Mammy cries, holdin' her hands up to the sky as if there's someone up there. I look up. There's no God, only helicopters choppin' the air, deafenin' us.

The Saracen with Paddy moves off. More men are dragged into the street. Police, Jeeps and Saracens leave and arrive. Engines. Bin lids drummin'. Screams. Shouts.

'Mammy,' I say. I'm scared.

'Yous cowardly bastards,' a woman in the crowd shouts. Then 'S-S-R-U-C!' over and over again. Everyone joins in. Buster comes over to our crowd.

'British Bastard!' Ma pounces. The women have her by the arms, her strugglin' to get free. 'Let go of me. I'm tellin' yous. Bridie, fuckin' let go or I'll kill you,' Ma does this scream like a howl. I don't wanna hear her. I don't ever wanna hear Mammy sound like that. Buster better hope she doesn't break free.

Wee Maggie's screamin' again. I have to let her down. She wraps herself around me and pushes her face into my pyjamas. That's what I want to do to Mammy, but she's too scary.

The soldier stares at Ma – smiles at her, like *Fuck you, love.* You don't do that, Mrs – *My Ma* – Donnelly. Ma puts her head back, heckles and spits right in his face.

Everythin' stops for a second like we're frozen in time. The spell gets broken by the women pullin' Mammy away. 'S-S-R-U-C!' The women chant, like scary men at football matches.

'What does that mean?' I say.

'S.S. – like Hitler's men,' says Measles.

'Right, clear the street!' Buster shouts.

'English Bastard!' Measles shouts.

'Come on, you cunts,' Buster shouts through a megaphone. 'Clear the streets. Bomb scare.'

Soldiers push the crowd with their rifles.

'Where's my kids?' Ma looks round for us, but I'm right here in front of her.

'They're here, Mammy,' says Measles.

'Take them two over to the gable wall,' Ma orders.

Measles takes me and Wee Maggie by the hand. Ma stays with the women.

'What about Killer?' I say.

'We have to wait here,' says she.

'But we can't leave him here if there's gonna be a bomb,' I say.

'There is no bomb,' says she. 'For God's sake, Mickey, when are you goin' to wise up?'

'Come on, move!' A big soldier shoos us along from the gable. Ma sees the soldier at us and runs over.

'Move, what for?' Ma says, but she's not as scary. 'Just let us back in our houses.'

The soldier pushes Ma. Mary doesn't do anythin' this time.

'Aye, yer awful fuckin' brave, aren't you?' Ma gets goin'. 'Why don't you fuck off back to where you belong, you black bastard.'

God, he is black too. I thought it was just polish on his face like the rest doin' the *Black and White Minstrel Show* thing. His black is real. My first real-life black man.

I can't believe that black people are sidin' with the Brits in our war. I've always sided with them. I hate them now. Britlovers. They're not gettin' any more of our tinned rice. You can't trust anybody. Serve them better to go and help their own ones in Africa. After everythin' the English did to them in the filims, I can't believe it.

The Brits push us with their rifles and we're movin' like the sheep on that really crap TV programme.

'Up the street. Come on,' Ma says, walkin' ahead.

'No, Mammy, what about Killer?' I say.

'He'll have to stay there, son. We can't bring him to somebody else's house.'

'But Mammy!'

'Stop it, now. My nerves are wrecked,' Ma shouts.

'Shut up, Mickey,' says Measles. She's never horrible to me, so I stop. Wee Maggie squeezes my hand til it hurts. I wonder if they're still beatin' the crap out of Paddy.

All of us Havana Street ones walk together. All the kids are in their pyjamas or just pants and we get pushed in front as we get to Jamaica Street. The street is full of women. They shout across to each other.

'Bastards!' Mum spits at the ground. Aul Sheila has her arm wrapped round Ma's shoulder.

'Alright, Josie,' says Minnie the Tick Woman who lends everyone money and writes it in her book. You can't miss her cuz of her beehive.

'Aye, a shower of bastards,' Ma says.

'You alright, Sadie?'

'Aye, fuckin' desper't isn't it?'

Women callin' out from everywhere. I watch everythin'.

'Who'd they lift?'

'Any men they could get their hands on.'

'God spares us, they'll all be let out the 'marra.'

'Aye, but in what state?'

'Stop that in front of the kids.'

'My hands are shakin'. I'm not worth 2d.'

We get to the top of Jamaica Street. Measles is carryin' Wee Maggie.

'Did they find any guns?' Mrs McAnally asks. Her Briege is behind her.

'I wouldn't know about that, would I?' Ma won't even look in her direction, so I shoot Briege a dirty look.

'Maybe it's time you did,' she digs at Ma. 'There's some round here think they're too good for the rest of us. And some that don't play their part,' she says, walkin' off.

Playin' their part. Is she sayin' Mammy's not a good

actor? I bet you if my Mammy wanted to, she'd be as good as Bette Davis or any of them. Judy Garland, if she wanted. Just because Briege gets to be in plays in Martine's garage, they must think they're special.

'She's a cheeky fucker,' Ma says to Aul Sheila.

'Watch yerself, Josie,' Aul Sheila whispers, 'She's vicious.'

'I'm not afraid of her. She runs about like she's the wife of Michael Collins and all her husband did was steal a bag of sausages,' says Ma.

'Yer a liar,' Aul Sheila laughs. 'Who tol' you that?'

'I'm not sayin', but sure he's a fuckin' joke, near on a half-wit. The boys sent him to rob Denny's warehouse and when the Peelers caught him in there, sure all he had on him was a big bag of sausages he stole for her.' We all laugh. 'They only did him for the gun they found at the house, used on a Brit and his prints all over it. He'll never get out. She's taken care of though.'

Imagine leavin' your prints on a gun. I've known that since I was two. Did he never see any TV programme in his entire life? He *is* a bloody half-wit.

'Still, Josie, wasn't even him killed the Brit,' says Sheila.

'You're right. You're right. She just turns me, that woman,' says Ma.

'She's hard to like.'

Talkin's makin' Ma normal again.

'Right, Mary, you take the kids round to Mrs Branna-gan's,' Ma says.

'Where are you goin'?' asks Measles.

'I'm goin' to look for yer Da.'

'What am I supposed to say to Mrs Brannagan?' Measles looks pissed off.

'Just tell 'er that yer Mammy sent you round and tell 'er what's happened.'

'Can you not come round?' Measles says, takin' her life in her hands.

'Well, what the fuck d'you want me to do?' Ma screams. 'Tell me!'

Measles doesn't say anythin' and walks off, ragin'. We run after her and grab her hands. I look back at the women huddled under the lamppost, talkin'. We walk across the waste ground beside Aul Sammy's shop and the barricades on Alliance Ave. Measles tries to tuck her ripped sleeve into her bra. I'm tryin' not to step on any broken glass from all the riotin' here. We're lucky our Aunt Kathleen and Uncle John buy us slippers every Christmas or we'd be in our bare feet like the McDermot's over there.

At Etna Drive, the women are out smokin' and talkin', some still with their bin lids in their hands. They nod as we pass, and whisper with stony faces. In Stratford Gardens, Measles turns up a path and we follow to the front door. Curtains move, a face through the net curtains. The big door opens.

'Hello, Mrs Brannagan, Mammy sent us round cuz they've raided our street,' says Measles.

'I heard the bin lids. Get in, in the name of God, yous'll catch yer death.'

'Thanks, Mrs Brannagan,' says Wee Maggie, as cute as a button.

'Thanks, Mrs Brannagan,' says Measles, walkin' in.

'Thanks, Mrs Brannagan,' I say to the floor as I pass her into the livin' room.

'Any of yous hurt?' says she.

'No,' says Measles. Mrs Brannagan is Ardoyne's nurse for big cuts and stuff, so you don't have to walk through the Prods to get to the hospital. Unless you have money for a black taxi.

Wow. Her house is like museums I've seen on TV. Millions of ornaments. And pictures. Mary holdin' Baby Jesus. The

Pope. President Kennedy. Elvis Presley and the Sacred Heart with a red, flickerin' candle bulb.

'Yous kids shouldn't be up at this time of the night, yous may get straight to bed,' she says, clutchin' her dressin' gown to her neck. 'Mary can stay in beside me,' says Mrs Brannagan.

That's cuz there is no Mr Brannagan. Blown up by his own bomb. They gave him a big funeral with the Irish flag over the coffin. Fired shots in the air. Come to think of it, the IRA are quite nice cuz both Mr McAnally and Mr Brannagan completely made a mess of things and the IRA don't seem to mind.

'Right, Mary love, I'll be down in a minute and you can tell me what happened. Yous kids follow me.' She leads up the stairs. Me and Wee Maggie look at Measles, who nods for us to follow. Over her shoulder, President Kennedy is smilin' at me.

I don't want to go upstairs. I want to go back to ours. I hate this smelly house. Wee Maggie doesn't like it either.

'Yous can jump in here together.' She opens a bedroom door and turns on the light.

There's a single bed pushed against the wall under the window and an open wardrobe, empty but for a couple of wire hangers. Imagine havin' a spare room. And an empty wardrobe.

Mrs Brannagan pulls down the blankets. 'Jump yous two in. Yous don't mind sharin'?'

Don't mind! Don't friggin' mind? Me and Wee Maggie have dreamed of this all of our lives.

'No, Mrs Brannagan, sure we do it all the time,' I say. Wee Maggie's smilin' like it's Christmas.

'But keep your clothes on,' Mrs Brannagan gives us a funny look. She doesn't leave.

'Take off your slippers,' I tell Maggie, dead serious, to show Mrs Brannagan I can be sensible.

We both sit on the bed and kick our slippers off.

'Get in,' says Mrs Brannagan.

Maggie and I get into bed and Mrs Brannagan puts the blankets over us and tucks us in. Like parents do on the TV.

'Don't let the bedbugs bite,' she says, turnin' off the light. The door closes and we're in the dark.

'Oh my God,' Maggie giggles.

'I know!' says me. 'Dreams can come true Maggie, see?'

We laugh and talk and when I hear Mrs Brannagan and Mary come upstairs I tell Wee Maggie we have to go to sleep. But she can't.

'Will I do what I used to do when you were a baby-boo-boo?' I say.

'The magic sea shell?' she says and she puts her thumb in her mouth.

'Turn over,' I say, 'You know it doesn't appear if you try to look at it.'

Maggie turns to the wall and closes her eyes tight. I snuggle in close and cup my right hand around her ear. 'Can you feel it?' I whisper.

'Yes,' she whispers back.

I blow, and make gentle wind sounds into her ear through my thumb.

When she's asleep, I lie back and stare into the dark. I think about my wee Killer all alone in his box.

*Please God, take care of Killer tonight. I promise I'll be a good boy forever and ever.*

*Oh and maybe check our Paddy. But only if you have the time. Amen.*

# 5

BIG, SLOPPY-TONGUE LICK. Slobber gloops onto my leg.

'Killer, stop it!' I shout, lovin' it. I want them in the street to hear and come to our wee front garden to see him. Our garden is actually a bit of concrete under our front window cordoned off by a wee wall.

'Mickey, get in here,' Ma shouts from the livin' room.

'Come on, Killer.' I pat my knees and run inside.

'Keep him out, wee boy, he pisses everywhere,' shouts Ma. 'Make sure that gate's shut.'

Of course it's shut. She's said that a hundred times. Ma's on Da's chair, grippin' the arms. Paddy comes in from the back yard with a bulky grip bag. Weird. Not like he'd be cleanin' the yard or hanging up the washin'. He pushes past me and heads out the front door sayin' nothin'. He's never in the house anymore. Hardly said one word *since*.

'Where you goin'?' Ma shouts after Paddy, lookin' out the door.

'Out,' shouts he, already down the path.

'Out where?' she calls after. He doesn't even turn round. Who does he think he is? Just cuz he got beaten up he thinks he's special. And he thinks he can be horrible to my Mammy. She looks really annoyed. Cuz he was so ignorant. I know I've always won the best son competition, but now there's not even a contest.

Killer runs in past Ma.

'Put that dog out the back!' Ma really shouts.

'Sake,' I tut. That's Our Paddy's bloody fault Ma's annoyed. Who even cares about him, anyway? None of us even like him. I lift Killer, lock him in the yard and come back onto the sofa.

'Josie?' That comes from our path. It's Aunt Kathleen.

'Come in,' Ma calls.

'How's Paddy doin'?' Aunt Kathleen sits on the arm of the sofa.

Ma telepaths somethin' to her.

'D'ye wanna cuppa tea?' Aunt Kathleen squints.

'Aye,' says Ma.

'I'm goin' to your Aunt Kathleen's for a wee minute,' says Ma. Damn. I can't earywig. 'I'll take Wee Maggie with me. You look after the house.'

Wee Maggie went out to play with the girls like a wee traitor. Snipin' off. Just cuz I wanted to stay in and play with Killer. But I'm goin' to have Killer *and* the house all to myself. Ha!

Ma lifts her purse from the mantelpiece and puts it in her coat pocket. She squints round the room. 'Your Da'll be back soon. Ye'd better not leave this door wee boy, d'ye hear me?'

'Yes, Mammy,' I say, in my good-boy voice. 'Catch you guys later.' I smile, American-style. I watch them leave, disappearin' round the hoardin's they put up yesterday for more new houses.

Da won't be back before Ma. Now he's supposed to be off the drink, he's always at the bookies or playin' cards with his cronies. Nobody here. I can do whatever I want. A big glass of milk. I'll have to be quick in case somebody comes in, cuz Ma's not made of money. As I tip my head back, cold milk trickles on my cheeks and down onto my neck, but I can't stop drinkin' til it's done.

'Ahh . . . Man that's Bass!' I wipe the escaped milk off my face with my arm then lick it off. I wash and dry the glass, holdin' it with a cloth up to the light from the window to check there's no fingerprints, then put it back exactly where it was on the drainin' board, like a detective at a crime scene. Not like Briege McAnally's *Dopey Dick* Da. I'm tellin' you now, it's lucky I'm on the side of *good*, cuz if I was a *bad* . . .

Out in the yard, Killer jumps all over me goin' completely *Nuts, whole hazelnuts, Uh! Cadbury's take them and they cover them with choc-o-late.*

'C'mon, my wee son. C'mon, Killer,' I run through the livin' room, dodgin' him. He barks his wee yappy yelp. Da says when Killer grows up he'll be able to growl and bark like a proper dog. But I don't want him to. Why can't he just stay a puppy forever?

Killer attacks my ankle but I shake him off and run up-stairs, him floppin' up after me. He's not allowed up here, but so? Nobody will know. In Ma and Da's room, I kick off my baseball boots and get up on their bed.

'C'mon, son. Up here. Up, up.' I pat the bed.

He tries to jump but gets stuck, hangin' half way. I laugh. He doesn't give up cuz he loves me so much. I pull him up by the scruff like Da showed me. But gently, not cruel. Killer tries to run but his claws catch on the blanket. I bounce up and down, jump as high as I can and try to touch the ceilin'. Killer's laughin' away in dog language. I laugh in Dog-ish, too. He hasn't telepathed me again – yet. I pick him up and a bit of wee comes out of his Wee-Willy-Winkie and drips onto my T-Shirt.

'Yuk, you dirty pig,' I throw him down on the bed. I smell his pee on my T-shirt. Stinker. I bounce on top of Killer and scratch his belly and he stretches his legs and arms way out like he's yawnin'. His floppy tongue's out. He's lovin' it. I love Killer more than I love anyone else in this whole entire world.

He's my Number One. And I could tell him anythin' and he wouldn't tell. *And* Wee Maggie. She wouldn't. She's my joint Number One. I jump off the bed and Killer follows me, pantin' away. He's up to the high doe.

'Come on, son!' I lift him and bring him into Maggie and Measles' room.

I look around for somethin' to play with. On top of the chest of drawers is Our Maggie's Girl's World with her long, blonde hair, like Martine McNulty's, who's just as beautiful. I bet you Martine will be a model when she grows up.

Round the neck of Girl's World is a long string of pearls. You have to be careful they don't get tangled. I bought them for Ma. Paid one whole pound. Saved up for ages. I told her to leave them to Wee Maggie in her will. Maggie's asked a few times when Ma might die. Ma says: *It won't be long the way yous torture me.*

I tickle Killer's ears. He closes his eyes in happiness. I've discovered the secret thing he loves. I'll do it to him all the time now.

I hear singin'. Out the window, the girls are hangin' at the gable. Me and Maggie have been watchin' them for days and lettin' them see we have more fun than them. Some are singin' *Awalla Jim,* playin' Two Balls against the gable on the huge, white painted letters of *Tiocfaidh ár Lá.* It's Irish for *Our Day Will Come.* The day when we win the Brits.

Others line up for a chance to play Swings. Three ropes tied high around the lamppost. Briege McAnally is swingin' round last and gets to crash into and crush poor Siobhan and Cathy.

I'd love to swing one day. But never with Briege.

'She's the oldest of us all and she's the biggest, baddest, nastiest, evilest bitch in the whole-wide-world EVER! Her Ma is Mrs McAnally, a big bitch too. Their family are like the

Olsens from *Little House on the Prairie*, I showed you this mornin' on TV. Only Mr Olsen isn't in the IRA. That throat of hers is like a snake's, any-thing, any-size, can go down there. Once, Killer, ages ago, I was walkin' past Havana Street entry and I saw her with her head right back and her arms high in the air. She was danglin' somethin' over her mouth and it was wrigglin', tryin' to get away. When I looked back again it was gone. Disappeared. And I'm not coddin'. So when you get big and go out in the street, you stay far, far away for her.'

I hope he doesn't get nightmares. But you have to scare him to put him off.

Briege McAnally gets off her swing, walks over to the gable and leans against it. The girls stand round waitin' for Briege to decide what game they'll play.

Martine! Comin' out her back. She's been watchin'. Just like me. Are we the same? Are we meant to be? I drop Killer onto the bed and put Girl's World on the window sill so I can see Martine behind it, in the street. I pull back Girl's World's yellow hair and kiss her on her mouth while lookin' at Martine behind. I try the way they kiss on the TV. My dick throbs.

'Killer, don't tell anybody I did that, right?' I say. I trust him. I turn him on his back and blow on his belly like I used to give belly farts to Wee Maggie.

I've got a really funny idea. I take the pearls and put them round Killer's neck. What else? I open the wardrobe and see Measles' First Holy Communion outfit, white and lacy, like a weddin' dress. We're keepin' it for Maggie's turn. One day I put it on Wee Maggie and we said our vows to the TV screen, to be together forever. We may actually be husband and wife. I'm not 100 per cent sure it was legal in the eyes of God – I've not been ordained. There's also the brother and sister thing.

I scrunch the dress up to the neck, like Ma does when she's

puttin' our jumpers on, and wiggle it over Killer's head. When Ma would do that to me, when I was wee, I'd feel like I was never gonna get out of the darkness. Strangled and suffocated at the same time. I'd scream and Ma would slap the legs off me for bein' dramatic. I was always going to be an actor.

Killer looks a geg. Like the chimps in that tea bag advert, dressed as people. I lay his head on the pillow.

'Go to sleep now, my child, God is waitin' on the other side,' I say, like I'm a Priest and he's a dyin' bride in a black and white movie set sometime in the American civil war. Every time he lifts his head up, I push it back down til he just lies there. I watch him. He looks at me from the corner of his eye, with his mouth open and his tongue out. God, his breath smells like dirty trunks.

Boys' noise outside. I juke out and their gang's comin' out of Havana Way entry. They walk over to the gable. Kids come runnin' out of their houses. Like some whistle was blown that all children can hear except me. Everyone from the street together. Boys and girls.

Brill. I can join in cuz everybody's there. And I can make friends with some of the boys maybe cuz, sure as shootin', all of them are goin' to St. Gabriel's. I jump off the bed and stamp my sneakers on without openin' the laces. Ma says if I keep doin' that I'll break the back of them, then she'll break the back of me. But why would you want to waste all that time tyin' and untyin' laces?

I bomb downstairs but slow into a walk outside and sit on McErlane's garden wall. I watch the waste ground jammed with kids. In a wee while, I'll just start playin' without them noticin'.

'What do you want?' says Big Bitch Briege.

So much for my plan. 'Nothin'. Just watchin',' I say. I won't be one of those who begs her. I just wish Martine wasn't

57

here to see. Everybody's lookin' at me.

I look at the boys. None of them will ask me to play. Ma's-a-Whore sniggers and elbows the boy beside him, whisperin', lookin' at me. I've heard what you have to do to join the Boys' Gang. The Tunnel of Death. I'd rather have no friends for the rest of my life than do that. The boys are leavin' it to the girls. Like I'm not really a boy. No Man's Land. Limbo. I put my head down. Maybe Martine will rescue me.

'Ach, go on, yousins, let him play,' says Wee Maggie runnin' into the group. She's back. My heart crashes into my ribs. What would I do without her? If she ever died of TB or was shot or blown up, I would kill myself or join the Foreign Legion.

'Alright, go in,' Briege smirks.

Everybody loves Wee Maggie. I jump off the wall and take her hand. Some of the boys look over and point at me, but I keep holdin' her hand while they're laughin'. I stay back behind the long line and hide, but Maggie's pushin' to the front.

'I thought yous were playin' Rally-Oh!' says Decky, the leader of the boys. He's way older than us, but he still plays with kids. Our Paddy says he's not right in the head. I call him Bony Maronie, cuz like the song, *he's as skinny as a stick of macaroni*. They actually mean spaghetti, surely, which means you can't believe everything you hear in a song.

'We're playin' skips first,' says Briege.

'Skips?' Decky looks disgusted. 'We'll come back then.' He walks away and the boys follow.

I should really go off with the boys, but I don't trust what Ma's-a-Whore will do. And, I'm actually brilliant at skips. I'll show Martine how brilliant I am. And Maggie will be so proud of me.

This is the most excited I've ever felt in my entire life.

Martine will think I'm the best boy cuz I'm not like the others and her and me like the same things.

Oh shit. Our Paddy's back. Walkin' across the street.

'It's your turn, Mickey,' says Wee Maggie.

The rope goes. I have to go. It's my turn. Why did we have to push to the front?

'One, two, three . . .' they call. I don't go. 'One, two, three . . .' I don't go. They stop the rope.

'What's wrong with you?' Briege is really pissed off. Paddy looks over. Briege sees him. She looks at me and smiles. She knows. 'Start the rope,' she says. 'One, two, three . . .' she counts. About a hundred girls join her. I jump in. I have to.

*'I'll tell me Ma, when I go home,*
*The boys won't leave the girls alone.*
*They pull my hair, and steal my comb,*
*But that's alright, til I get home.'*

I skip like I've never skipped before. Shitely. I see Martine's face. She's destroyed. She's so disappointed in me. Probably been waitin' just to see me skip.

I get *out* to look like I'm crap. This whole song is for girls – if it wasn't bad enough skippin' in the first place.

'Take an end,' Briege orders. I don't. 'I said – take an end!' She walks towards me.

'No,' I say. Everybody stares at me like I just stabbed the Pope.

'Wha' did ye say?' She squints her eyes.

'I'm not playin' anymore.'

'Hold on a wee minute. You had yer go and ye got out, so now it's your turn to hold the rope. That's the way it is. Right!' She stabs me with her finger.

'Who says?'

'I say! Everybody knows that. Waster!'

She's right and I know it. I don't know if Martine is lovin' me standin' up to Briege or thinkin' I'm a crazy head-the-ball annoyin' her mate. But at least Paddy can see me bein' cheeky to Briege. R-E-S-P-E-C-T.

'Mickey, come you here, right now!' Ma's voice fills the whole street, she sees I've heard and goes back into the house. Paddy's gone, not even there to see me being cheeky to Briege.

'I have to go,' I say. Everybody knows you have to, if your Ma calls you, so they can't say anythin'. I grab Wee Maggie and pull her with me.

'Ach, I want to play,' she whines.

I pull her across the waste ground to the house.

In the house, I let go of Wee Maggie who bounces on the sofa bitin' her lip with a big frown. I go into the kitchen but Ma's not there. Paddy's at Killer's box. I run out to the yard. 'You're not allowed near him,' I shout. 'Killer's my dog.'

'Shut up, you, he's not even in it,' says Paddy. 'And stay away from that dog box.'

'Away on,' I say. 'I can go there whenever I want. You stay away from it, pimple face.'

Paddy launches, pinnin' me to the wall by the neck. 'Listen, to me,' he says, right up in my face. 'Stay away from there or I'll fuckin' kill you.'

I don't want to cry. My heart is pushin' up to come out my mouth, but Paddy's stranglin' is keepin' it in. I'm tellin' Ma on him, the big bastard. And she'll kill him. And now I'm bloody cryin'. I hate him. I'll get him back one day.

He lets go. 'And stop playin' with the wee girls, fer fuck's sake. You're too old for all of that now. The boys are all laughin' at you. Jesus, they're goin' to murder you in St. Gabe's.'

'Mickey,' Ma calls from the house.

'And stop friggin' cryin' like a wee girl,' he says, lettin' me go.

'I'm not, you big pig,' I say.

'Why do you sound like a girl, anyway? What's wrong with you? Are you gay?'

Our Paddy's turned really evil. I walk with my head down til I get inside. I turn back. 'You were cryin' too when the soldiers beat the shite out of you. I wish they'd hit you harder!' I run, top speed. Ha! That won him. He's goin' to kill me when he gets me but.

Ma stops me in the livin' room.

'Stay away from that Briege McAnally, do ye hear me?' says Ma.

'Yes, Mammy,' says me, cuz I'm a good boy who does what he's told.

'Why's your face all red?' she says to me but looks to Paddy comin' behind me.

I scrunch my face up and give Paddy a dirty look. But I show him I'm not a wee kid by not tellin' on him. Maybe later when he's not here and me and Ma are on our own.

'What's in the bag, Paddy?' says Ma.

Paddy glances down at the bag like he'd forgotten it was there. 'Nothin',' he says, pushin' past her. Ma grabs at the bag. Paddy lifts his hand high, 'Stop it, woman.' And Mammy does.

'Paddy, son, nigh don't be gettin' yourself into trouble,' says Ma.

He ignores her and heads into the street. Ma watches him from the door.

'Mickey, what's Our Paddy up to?'

'I don't know, Mammy,' I say.

'Come upstairs with me, wee boy, I want you,' says she. Paddy gets away with bloody murder *since*.

At the top of the stairs, I can't breathe and my whole head throbs. From the open door you can see Killer asleep on the bed, wearin' pearls and Measles' Holy Communion dress.

'How did . . . ?' says Ma.

'I don't know, Mammy, I swear.'

'Mickey Donnelly, tell the truth and shame the devil. You know fine rightly Killer couldn't've done that himself. I'll send you to the Priest,' she warns.

'I don't know, Mammy, I swear to Almighty God.' I can tell she's not gonna hit me. 'Let's leave him here, Mammy. For a geg. They'll die when they see.' She's not buyin' it. 'We'll say you sent him to bed for bein' cheeky. Or say he made his Holy Communion.'

'You're away in the head, son,' she says. 'You know you can't keep carryin' on like this, don't you?'

I've never put Killer in a dress before, so I don't know what she's talkin' about.

'Yes, Ma,' I say.

'Get him out of that bed, and out of that dress, and ye may pray to God there's not a mark on it or you'll be covered in marks.' Ma does a big long sigh. 'C'mere, sit down first. I need you to be a big boy now, Mickey. What's wrong?' says Ma.

'Nothin'.' I smile and bounce my bum up and down on the bed.

'What did Our Paddy say to you?'

'Nothin' Ma,' I say.

'Tell me, right nigh, wee boy, or I'll get him to tell me,' says Ma.

'No Mammy, don't, please.' I'm so scundered.

'Mickey!'

My throat makes a strange noise. I turn away and pet Killer.

'Do you know how my voice is not . . . I don't sound like the other boys.'

Ma stops breathin'. I pet Killer but gently, gently, gently.

'That's cuz you speak nice, son,' her voice gettin' closer.

'I know, but do you know how I don't, but?' I rub Killer's

wee ear in the special place I know he loves.

'You speak much better than them'ins. And sure, what are ye worried about? Any day now you'll wake up and you'll sound like a big man.'

'Will I?' I look at her. Somethin's happenin' in my brain.

'Of course.' She elbows me in the ribs. 'It's all about growin' up. Boys' stuff. Your voice breaks. Your Da will tell you all about it.'

'Sometimes the boys make fun of me,' says me.

'Who makes fun of you?' says Ma, goin' red. Oh no, the Hulk is comin'. 'Was Paddy . . .'

'It's OK, Mammy,' I say, scared. Ma reverses the Hulk process somehow. She must've caught it just before it took over.

'I'll go round and bust their faces for them.' Ma bounces about like a boxer. Like the Cowardly Lion from the *Wizard of Oz*. I laugh and jump up beside her. I haven't seen her do this in years.

'Put 'em up, put 'em up.' I say in my best Cowardly Lion voice. Ma laughs. My Ma.

'I bet ye they can't do that with their voices the way you can. Eh, son?'

She's right. I was the best in my class. I grab her round the waist and push my face into her tummy like when I was wee. She lets me stay for a good five seconds before she pushes me off by the shoulders. But gentle.

'Mickey, did Paddy say anythin' to you about what he's up to?' says she.

'No. Mammy, sure Our Paddy doesn't tell me anythin', he hates my guts!'

Ma whacks me across the head.

'Awoooahh!'

'Your brother doesn't hate you, nigh, don't be goin'

63

around sayin' that,' says Ma. 'Paddy loves you, he's just got hormones,' says Ma.

'Brain damage, you mean.'

Ma swings for me. 'Stop that, you.'

'Josie, are ye ready?' It's Aunt Kathleen shoutin' from the bottom of the stairs.

'I'm comin',' she shouts to the stairs. She bends down close to me. 'Have a look around for anythin' suspicious that Our Paddy has in your room. A wee mission for ye. You're brilliant at that. And if you find anythin' I might give you a wee surprise.'

I'm lovin' this. 'What like, Ma?'

'Anythin' that shouldn't be there. Clues.' She winks.

'I mean what kind of surprise?'

'Mickey, you head's up your arse,' says she. 'Forget about it.'

'No, I'll do it, I swear,' says me.

'No, don't. I don't know what I was thinkin'.'

'Ach!'

'Nigh, I've got to get back to work.' She pats her pockets. 'Yer Da's not back yet, so you're goin' to have to look after Wee Maggie.'

Me! Holy shit. The world is a-changin'. That's even better than being a detective. 'No problemo, Mamma Mia!'

'Christ the night!' say Ma, shakin' her head. She walks out and down the stairs. I follow.

'Alright, Mickey, son,' says Aunt Kathleen. I give her my biggest smile. Sometimes she gives me money. 'Josie.' She nods to Ma who goes over close and they whisper.

'Nigh, Mary will be in from work soon. I've peeled the potatoes; they're in the big pot at the back of the stove. Keep an eye on them til she gets back. Check on the vegetables in the wee pot, too. Tell her there's steak and kidney pie in

64

the cupboard.' Ma puts her coat on and checks her pockets. 'Nigh, Mickey Donnelly, you look after that child,' she nods at Maggie. 'And I'm tellin' you, don't move from this door or I'll break both your legs. Mary won't be long.' She looks at Wee Maggie. 'You're stayin' in.'

'Ach, Mammy, I'm playing,' says she.

'There's riotin'. Anyway, Mickey's mindin' you.'

My face boils and my body tingles. I've never been so proud of my entire self.

'He's always such a good boy for his Mammy,' Aunt Kathleen says, smilin' at me like *I wish he was my son*. Aunt Kathleen doesn't have any kids. She used to have one but now he's dead. I can't remember why. She keeps a picture of him on her mantelpiece. At the funeral, she jumped into the grave after the coffin went in. I didn't see it cuz I was readin' all the gravestones and thinkin' about bein' born in the past. Everybody says it was really sad to see, but I think it sounds a bit mental.

'Do you have a girlfriend yet, Mickey?' Aunt Kathleen smiles.

'No,' I laugh. I take a double redner and rub my hands between my thighs. I love her askin' though. I jump beside Wee Maggie on the sofa and hold her hand.

'Our Mickey's not like that,' says Ma, annoyed at Aunt Kathleen. 'He's a good boy. Aren't you, son?'

'Yes, Mammy,' I say. She won't tell about Killer, cuz you don't tell people things outside the house.

'Oh, he loves his Mammy,' says Aunt Kathleen, beamin' at me.

Ma lets Aunt Kathleen go ahead of her, looks around the room, pattin' her pockets again to make sure her purse is there. We all know what happens if she leaves it at home. She leans in towards me and I go all tingly. My Mammy loves me.

'And get that friggin' dog into the yard, wee boy, d'ye hear me?' Ma whispers and stands back up. I swing my legs out and let them bang down onto the bottom of the sofa like I used to when I was really wee. Wee Maggie joins in and we laugh. Ma shakes her head and sighs. 'What am I goin' to do with you, Mickey Donnelly?'

'Put me in a children's home?' I say.

'They wouldn't take you,' says she.

I laugh and look at Wee Maggie. Me and her go away with the fairies. I hear Ma leave. I'm a big boy now, who can mind Wee Maggie and the house. And I'm goin' to get my big boy's voice and everythin'.

'Oh my God!' I shove my fist inside my mouth and out again. 'I can mind you now. We can be together forever.' I grab her hands and pull her up and jump in a circle. But her jumps are a bit heavy and she keeps jukin' out the window to the girls. 'Come on!' I shout and pogo like a punk rocker. She laughs and does too.

'I've had a brilliant idea,' says me. 'Shall we get married again?'

'I do,' says Maggie. 'I do.'

'Quick, til we get Killer out of your wedding dress. Unless you want him to be your bridesmaid?'

# 6

'WRAP THE LEAD round your wrist and keep him close,' says Da. Killer's on his first ever official *outside in the big bad world* walk. Da even bought a lead and a collar. 'Pull him in. Don't let him go ahead of you.' Da reaches over me then yanks hard on the lead. Killer's neck jerks like it snapped.

'Watch, Daddy,' I shout and move away. He's so rough.

'He has to learn,' says he. 'A dog doesn't feel it. Look, he's fine.' Killer does look fine now, but still, I don't like it.

Killer sniffs and tries to eat every piece of paper, crisp packet and lump of shite we pass. And pees every 4½ seconds. Walkin' across the waste ground, the kids from the street watch, all wishin' they were me. With my dog, and my Daddy takin' me out, too. I saw Ma nod at Da as we left. A secret. What could it be? I'm thinkin' a present.

Martine! Over by the house shop at the bottom of the Bray lane and the end of the Eggy. I pull Killer left but he won't bloody come, scrabblin' on his feet, pullin' straight ahead. 'Come here, Killer,' I shout. Da looks at me. 'C'mon, wee son,' I say, nicer, to show Da I'm not like him. The wee shit still pulls away from Martine. I have to show her Killer is my dog and I'm super cool. Da's lookin' at me. I know what he wants. I yank Killer hard and he almost does a back flip; my stomach twists, but I yank again. Killer comes to me. It does work, but I hate it.

'Good boy,' says Da. Me or Killer? Da smiles at me. 'We're goin' up to the Bone Hills,' he says, noddin' at the Bray lane. I look over at Martine. Da looks over at Martine and smiles. 'Is that your girl?'

'No.' I hit a redner and tut. Da smiles and changes direction towards Martine. Thanks, Da. Hold on, he's not goin' to scunder me in front of her?

I walk a bit slower now, look around me, not even bothered. Havin' a dog is completely normal, and out with Da is too. My right eye is like Wee Twin McAuley's, twisted round in the socket. Martine is watchin'.

'Stay there, I'm just goin' into the shop,' says Da, leavin' me outside with Martine.

'Hiya, Mickey,' says she.

That's the first time she's said my name. Every single one of the hairs on my head prickle my scalp. I must look like a punk rocker.

'Hiya, Martine,' says me, pattin' my hair down.

'Is that your dog?'

'Yeah,' I say, shruggin' my shoulders like *no big deal*. 'All our ones want him to be the house dog, but he's mine. M'Daddy got him for me.'

'What's his name?'

'Killer.'

'He's so gorgeous. Can I pet him?'

'Yeah.'

Martine's long, goldeny hair falls over her back and nearly touches the ground as she bends down. Killer jumps all over her. She laughs and lifts his front paws so he's standin' up like a human.

'Oh my God, I love him,' she says. Killer is lickin' her face. She giggles. A bit of wee spouts out of him and she jumps back.

'Killer,' I shout, yankin' him hard to show Martine I'm all grown up. 'Bad dog,' I say.

'Ach, leave him Mickey,' says she. 'It's not his fault.'

She's so sweet and gentle. Finally, someone like me. If only they'd let us be together.

Someone comes out of the shop and I look thinkin' it's Da, but it's Briege McAnally lookin' at me like I'm shite. She sees Killer and freezes long enough for me to know she is ragin'. *Yes!*

'Isn't he lovely, Briege?' says Martine.

'Is it yours?' Briege says, almost like a normal human bein'.

'Yeah,' says me.

'C'mon Martine,' says Briege, walkin' away.

'See ya, Killer,' says Martine. 'And see ya later, Mickey. Bring Killer out to play.'

My heart does a high jump and head butts my Adam's apple.

'Yeah,' says me, 'see ya.' I can't believe it. I bend down and tickle Killer. I'm not goin' to play with the girls ever again, but I can let them pet my dog if I happen to be walkin' past when they happen to be playin'.

'C'mon,' says Da behind me and walks towards the Bray. I watch Martine and Briege cross the waste ground, Martine's hair glitterin' in the sun. I'm goin' to write a poem all about her hair. I remember Da and run to catch up.

'C'mon, Killer.' He loves tryin' to keep up with me on his tiny, wee legs. I slow down at Da and walk next to him. His corduroy jacket pocket is bulgin'. He's bought us some surprises to eat at the top. Is that what the secret look was all about? I can't believe it. I know I had to blackmail Da to get Killer, but he still got him. He could have just forgot like he normally does. Maybe Ma's right. Maybe it's all gonna be different this time.

The Bray runs alongside the Bone Hills where big boys go cuz there's a football pitch. I'm not allowed up on my own cuz the Bone Hoppers who live to the right of it are even bigger hallions than Ardoyne boys. But worse, behind it, Prods live. I'm a good boy who doesn't play with hallions and not where he's not allowed. No way.

'How's your girlfriend?' Da smiles.

'Daddy!' I say and laugh and hit a redner, but a nice one. I like it. I puff my chest up and walk with my head up, bouncin' my heels off the ground. This must be what it's like to have a real Da. Like on the TV.

'Have you had many girlfriends, Mickey?' says he.

'No,' I tut, scundered. I should have said *yes*. If only I could think before I open my big mouth.

Drums. Far away. Prods gettin' ready for their marchin' on the 12th July. It's their day, like ours is St. Patrick's Day.

'You know, it's OK, you're old enough now,' says he. 'And like your Mammy says, your voice will break. Do you have any hairs yet?'

Mammy told him. I can't believe she told him. That's what the secret nod was on the way out. I thought I could tell her. Hold on. Hair? Sweet Baby Jesus. He's not goin' to have *the talk*!

'You don't have to tell me if you don't want to,' he says, his hand on my shoulder. I have never been so scundered in my entire life. 'Do you need me to tell you about girls?'

'No, wise up, Da,' I say.

'It's the quiet ones you have to watch, you wee devil,' Da

laughs. 'But you can talk to me, Mickey, son. You can ask me about anythin'.'

'I . . .' I think about askin' about what the boys say to me and Paddy. But Ma told me it's all gonna change soon.

'No rush, son, when you're ready,' says he and gives me a little punch on the arm, which actually hurts, but I don't say anythin'. Maybe next time when we go out I'll ask him some things. We walk, not sayin' anythin', but that's OK. Watchin' Killer is like watchin' a filim. And you never talk durin' a filim.

At the top of the Bray, Da jumps over the railings. I look across to Proddy Oldpark. The band music is comin' from there. I can't get over the railings so I crawl though some broken bars. We climb the last bit on the grass and reach the top where the Brit look-out post stands at the edge like a light-house. It's surrounded by wire mesh as high as *it* is, nearly. On top of the fencin' there's barbed wire. It looks like Our Measles' hair.

The paint-bombed cage is the only colour you can see over the whole of Ardoyne, to the mountains behind. Ardoyne looks like it was made in black and white, like the start of *Coronation Street* I watch with Ma sometimes.

'Do you remember I used to take you up here when you were a wee boy?' says Da, pointin' behind. I frown at the stumps of what I can imagine were swings. I imagine Da pushin' me on one and me laughin'. Maybe it's a memory.

'Yes,' I say.

His hand touches my head and I don't move away.

'Look at this place,' he says, starin' down at Ardoyne. 'Is there anywhere more depressin'? When you grow up son, you get out of here, won't you? Biggest mistake of my life stayin' here.'

'I want to go to America,' I say.

Da's eyes light up. 'Good for you, son. That's it. You think big.'

'I know I'm goin' to America. I'll do anythin'.'

Da looks at me like he's never seen me before. And he likes me.

'Yes, son, do whatever it takes to get out of this . . . Hell. And never come back. There's a whole world beyond those mountains, Mickey. I'm goin' to take you up to Cave Hill one day. You know Napoleon's Nose?'

'You can see him lyin' down, with his nose up like this,' I tip my head back. 'You told me that when I was wee.'

'Not from here. Or up there. But on the way. From a certain angle. Anyway, when you're up there, it's a beautiful view. You can see out to the Lough and the ships comin' and goin'. They can take you anywhere. Anywhere you want.'

'To America, even?' In the old days, they did use boats. I want to get a plane. I dream of gettin' jet lag. It sounds so glamorous.

'I don't see why not,' he smiles. 'Have you thought about how you're going to get the money? You have to be practical.'

I hadn't. Not for one minute. Where would I get the money? Or find another way.

'You can get yourself a job. Start saving. When I was your age, I used to sell sticks, you know, for startin' your fire in the house. I'd collect old wood, chop it up into little sticks, put them in bags and then go round the doors selling them.'

How scunderin'. I'd never embarrass myself like that. Or Ma. But I'm amazed Da actually worked once.

We sit on the edge of the hills and stare at the mountains. Killer is chewin' lumps of grass. I wish they'd stop their bloody drummin'. I pull a clump of grass from the ground and shake the soil off.

PAUL MCVEIGH

Loud laughin' comes from behind. A couple of winos sittin' on the steps of the toilets.

'Stay here.' Da gets up.

'Where you goin'?' I yank Killer to me.

'Just to the toilet. I'll be two minutes,' says he.

'What if Prods come?'

'They won't, Mickey,' he tuts.

I'm scared, but I don't want to spoil everythin'. 'OK,' I say, like I don't care bein' on the Bone Hills by myself. Anyway, I have Killer.

Da heads for the wee hut and I get up and walk to the edge of the hill, shieldin' my eyes from the sun. The wind would cut you here.

I could go to the Philippines first, maybe. My penpal's from there. I haven't heard from him since I wrote to him and he wrote back and I wrote to him again askin' if he was rich.

My Spidey senses tingle. I activate my super hearin'. The only words I can make out are 'fuck', 'bastard' and 'cunt'. Three Hard Men. I look round for Da, but he's gone.

They're gettin' closer. You're supposed to say *Right* and nod up if you pass boys you don't know. If you don't, you could be a Prod, so they'll beat you up. Or you're scared of them, so they'll beat you up. But I hate it cuz I don't sound like them. And my nod feels wrong. And boys always notice and hate me.

Think! I could get out my limp, I mean, who would beat up a cripple?

They would.

I've always known I'd die young, but I thought it would be from somethin' really exotic like Scarlet Fever or Impetigo.

As they get to me, I yank Killer like he's done somethin' really wrong *and* put on a limp. They pass me. A double bluff. Two tactics for the price of one and . . . no boot up the arse for me. Yee Ha!

73

I wonder if in America boys have to say *Right* to each other when they pass. And why can't I do it? It's like every boy in Ardoyne was given some secret code. Was I not at school that day? Or did their Da's tell them? And Da didn't tell me cuz he's useless. He is tryin' today, but. What's takin' him so long anyway? I don't like it.

I look to the toilets. Behind them, a bombed-out cinema. I never even got to go to it. I wonder if it was a Catholic cinema or a Proddy one? I kick at the ground as I walk back to the edge. To the right, I can see the barricades at the top of our street, the tall, corrugated iron walls to stop us killin' each other, and over it, to the Proddy area. So that's what it looks like. Just as shite as Ardoyne. I always thought they'd be richer than us.

Left, more barricades at the bottom of our street and over it into Proddy Crumlin Road. Straight ahead at the top of Ardoyne, the big spires of the Chapel poke the sky near Fartin's street. You can't see beyond that to the Proddy Shankill. I turn to the Proddy Oldpark and realise they have us surrounded. No wonder I'm not allowed to go anywhere.

I turn to look at the mountains, behind the streets. They look like scenery on a movie set. There's a couple of white houses, high on the mountains behind Ardoyne. I wonder what you can see from up there. Somebody said that from Donegal, on a clear day, you can see America. But I've never even been to Donegal. Not even to half of what I see from here.

The mountains surround me on either side, too. Even though I'm really high up, I can't see past them. Keepin' us from seein' out. Mountains are barricades too. Maybe there isn't anythin' else. Just what I can see. But there *is* more. I've seen it on TV.

I'm definitely goin' to travel. I've only gone a few streets away and I know more things. Imagine if I went away. Bein' up here, I can imagine it. I love this view. I'm goin' to come back all the time. With Da. It will be our place. Not even Wee Maggie can come. Da understands me. He understands about gettin' out of here. Gettin' us all out of here.

Where is Da? I walk over to the toilets. The smell of piss fumes out of the open doorway. Only dirtbirds would ever use these. Like the winos who were sitting on the steps. Da's voice comes from inside. I tie Killer to the handrail for the cripples. I suffocate my own self with my arm to prevent invasion of the smell through my nose and mouth. I poke my head in the door, silent as a secret agent. Da's holdin' court, the winos around him. He takes somethin' from his jacket pocket. He's gonna give them our sweets. I can't believe it. They were supposed be for us. Daddy-and-son sweets.

Da unscrews the lid off a whisky bottle. My jaw drops. I shake my head. I am so stupid. As he talks, his hands movin', the winos' heads follow the bottle.

'So, he says to me, he says, he says, *Clear Aff! Ballix to ye!*' Da can't talk for laughin' and the winos laugh too, slappin' their thighs and each other's backs at the hysticalness of my Da, who doesn't sound like himself. He's actin' someone else.

I reverse my head out and step outside. Killer barks and jumps at me. 'Shush, Killer.' Silence inside. They've heard. I untie Killer, but the knot is takin' ages. I can't get it loose. I jump at hands on my shoulder. Winos hurry past me. I don't look up. The stink of drink and piss mixes. *Chanel de Wee Wee* by Lentheric.

'Nice seein' you, boys.' He waves, like they're normal people. 'Sorry, son,' he says to me. 'Got carried away with a few aul mates.'

*Mates?* I look at the whisky bottle stickin' out of his pocket. He follows my eyes.

'How did that get in there?' he says, all annoyed. 'Them

boys playin' a wee joke on me.' He nods his head up. 'Here!' he shouts after them, holdin' out the bottle. 'Do you want to wait til I run after them?' he says to me, and mimes settin' off.

'No,' I say. 'I want to go home.'

He puts his hand on my shoulder and leans down to me. I smell the Polo mints. 'I hope you don't think I was drinkin' in there. I swear, son, I was just sayin' *hello*.'

Lies, straight to my face. Never again will I believe a word that comes out of that man's mouth. I can't believe I was so stupid. Me. Mickey Donnelly, the smartest boy in town.

'Just don't say anythin' to your Mammy,' he says, 'She might get the wrong idea. OK, son?'

As if I'd ever do anythin' to hurt my Mammy. *I'm not you!*

I get the knot loose. 'C'mon, Killer.' I make a click noise in my cheek and lead him across the field.

'That's good, Mickey,' says he, from behind, 'See, he likes that noise, you're learnin'. You're doin' well, son.' I can hear him really tryin'. But it doesn't sound like TV Dad anymore. It's embarrassin'.

I'm glad of the Proddy band now. I listen to the drums to drown him out.

# 7

'WHY DO YOU give a fuck what all those bastards and whores think?' Da shouts.

'Shush, Sean, please!' Ma says, checkin' out the window. That'll make Da worse. Everybody knows that except her.

He goes to the hall and opens the big door. 'I'm not afraid of them. I'll tell them all what I think of them.'

'Don't, Sean, please.' Ma pulls him back into the house. He pushes her into the livin' room and closes the wee door, shuttin' her in here with me.

'There's not one decent human bein' among yous,' he shouts out the street. 'Yous are all animals!'

Ma pulls the door handle, but he must be holdin' it on the other side.

I hold wee Killer like he's a wee baby in his Mammy's arms. Ma has her hands on her hips, starin' at the carpet while he's shoutin' all the things she wanted them not to hear.

When he'd started, she closed the big door to keep the noise in and keep us out. Didn't even notice I was sittin' here the whole time watchin' TV with Killer on my lap. It's cuz sometimes I'm invisible. It's the only explanation. Another one of my amazing powers. I can't control it, but. It just happens.

The wee door comes flyin' open, Da's foot in the air where he must have kicked it. The door hits Mammy in the face.

'Mammy!' I scream. I drop Killer and run to her and grab her round the waist cuz I can fix it.

'Get away from me, wee boy,' she says and pushes me away. She looks at me like she hates me. My Mammy hates me. She must have confused me with Da, everybody says I look like him.

'And you're just the same,' Da says to Ma. Hasn't even noticed the door hit her. 'You're one of them.' He punches the door and staggers out to the path.

'Mammy, are you OK?' I want to cry cuz she's not OK.

Ma hits me. Right across the face, fast and hard. Hard like never before. Wee Killer barks at her. He barks at her like *Leave him alone. Don't do that to my Mickey, cuz I love him.*

Ma kicks Killer in his side and he cries and runs away from her.

I'm not runnin' away, Mammy. I still love you. But that was a bad thing you did to Killer, Mammy. A bad, bad thing.

'Lock that fuckin' dog in the yard,' she shouts and runs into the street to Da. To him. Always him.

It hits me. Harder than her hand.

My Mammy loves my Da more than she loves me.

~

I pull at the paint. Tearin' off tiny strips. What's great is, when you pull a bit off, another bit is ready to come. Sometimes I have to use my fingernails to scratch and scratch til a bit comes up and then I can pull. Like when I pull the wallpaper off the wall under Paddy's bed. Squashed, dark, cold hidin' spots are becomin' my favourite places in the whole world. I think I'm gettin' ready for space travel.

I cuddle up to Killer. He could come to space with me.

Freeze! Someone's comin'. I left the yard door open so I could hear.

'Mickey,' Ma calls. She's in the scullery. She won't find me. 'C'mon, Mickey, yer daddy's gone out.'

I snuggle my face into Killer's ribs. He licks my head – it tickles.

'Come on, Mickey son. You and me can watch TV. Just you and me. I've got a wee surprise,' she says, in her ice-cream voice.

Not even for a wee surprise. And there's nothin' I love more in the whole-wide-world than a wee surprise. Ma must have searched the whole house and couldn't find me. But she knows I didn't go out.

'Where the fuck did that wee boy go?' Ma's in the yard now, right beside me.

I put my hand over my mouth cuz she's talkin' to herself like Nelly Nip-The-Nose who runs round in her nightdress babblin'. A little laugh escapes. The sounds change. Gettin' closer. I hear Ma leanin' on the dog box roof above me.

*Oh, please God, make me invisible again. Please!*

I close my eyes dead, dead tight. So tight I can see stars. I'm in space now. Out in the solar system. I'm an astronaut. On a space walk. I can think out here. It was all my fault today cuz I said somethin'. Then Ma couldn't pretend nothin' was happenin'. Everybody knows that's what you're supposed to do. When am I ever gonna learn to keep my big, fat, stupid mouth shut? I hate you, Mickey Donnelly.

No. It was him. It was him. It's always him. I hate him. He loves scunderin' Ma in front of everyone in the street. Turnin' everyone against her. He makes Ma do bad things. I hate him. I swear to Almighty God, I do. And the next time I see him I'm gonna tell him. I'm gonna say *I hate you, you big bastard. You're nothin' but a horrible, evil bastard and I hate you.* And then I'll kill him. Believe you me. I'll kill him. I wish, I wish, I wish that he would go away and never, ever come back for as long as we both shall live.

The hinges of the dog box roof creak above me. Some force is tryin' to pull me back to Earth. A black hole. Suckin' me in. Forcin' my eyes open. Big light stabbin' through my eyelashes. I can see Ma lookin' at me. I put my hands over my eyes.

*Oh God, please, make me invisible. I'll do anythin' you want. Anythin'.* I'm goin' to piss in my spacesuit. What will they say at NASA?

Concentrate! I'm invisible, I'm invisible, I'm invisible, I'm invisible.

Creak go the hinges and the dark covers me again like a big, cold hug and it feels right. I hear footsteps walkin' away.

'Mickey,' Ma says, in a new voice I don't recognise, 'wherever you are. I'm . . . I promise you . . .' I hear a door close. Ma let on she didn't see me. Cuz she knows I'd be scundered if she made it real by sayin' anythin'. See. See. See. My Mammy loves me. Wait. Maybe she didn't actually see me. Maybe I made myself invisible. Highly friggin' likely. Cuz I am truly amazin'. Incredible.

*Mickey Donnelly, The Incredible Invisible Boy. Son of the Invisible Woman. I will do works of great good around the world. I will destroy the forces of Evil Fathers and Big Brothers. And when I get sent out of the room cuz they're talkin' big people's talk, I'll slip back in and get all their dirty secrets and blackmail everybody to get money enough to get four plane tickets to America for me, Ma, Wee Maggie and Killer.*

Sorry God, I'm only jokin' about the blackmail. I hold Killer's paws together so he's prayin' with me.

'Thank you God, for makin' me invisible. I owe you, Amen.'

*I promise you,* Ma said.

'As you're bein' nice, God,' I look up to the roof of the dog box as if it's Holy Heaven, 'can you make it that Ma doesn't love Da anymore? Can you make it so that he goes away and never, ever comes back? Forever, and ever, Amen.'

I put Killer down and search for his bone with my hands, keepin' my eyes closed like I'm blind. I feel somethin' hard wrapped in material. I unwrap it. Cold, metal. I wipe it clean with the material and wrap it back up. Only someone who gets the special bus to school would leave their fingerprints on a gun. Yes, Briege McAnally, I am talkin' about your Da.

~

I hear one of our bands playin'. People cram through the little gap into Etna Drive. I look at our back gates. Serves them right if they worry about me. Serves them right if I get killed out here. Then they'll all be sorry. I join the crowd and let myself go. The crowd move me like I'm a boat in a river. They can take me anywhere.

Etna Drive is bunged. People linin' the street watchin' the Ardoyne band. I push through to the kerb. Tin whistles. Accordions. Big, giant drums. I wonder if I could join the band? Have everyone watchin' me. I can play the recorder. They taught me 'Kumbaya' at school and I taught myself the theme to *Grandstand* and 'Doe a Deer' from *The Sound of Music*. I can't see any recorders here, but the tin whistle is like it.

'Aul Dickey Mickey!' I'm thumped in the back so hard *I* sound like a drum.

Oh my sweet Jesus! 'Aul Fartin' Martin!' If we lived on the TV, I'd hug him right now.

'C'mon,' he says and runs across the road through the band. Only Fartin' would even dream of it. I can't. I can't do that. His head appears between two drummers. 'C'mon, will ye!'

Like I've been lassoed, my body pulls me forward and I fly into the road through the band. Fartin' can make me do anythin'.

'Our Sinead's away to the caravan to get away from the 12th,' Fartin' says, showin' off. 'Do ye wanna go roun' there? I know where the key is,' says he, bouncin' his eyebrows up and down fast like Groucho Marx.

'Aye, dead on.' I speak different when I'm with him.

Fartin' takes off. I catch up at the bottom of Stratford Gardens. We run together. The kerb stones are painted green, white and orange in a line up the street. Our flag. It's like it's flyin' beside me as I run along.

We slow down together. 'So much has happened. Our house got raided,' says me.

'Big deal,' he tuts. 'Ours gets done every day.'

He's exaggeratin'. 'Well, Our Paddy got arrested and everythin',' I say.

'Our Seamus got interned, sure. They wouldn't even tell us where he was. Turned up weeks later after they dumped him on the Crumlin Road in his trunks.'

'In his trunks?' I pull him to a stop.

'I know,' he says. We stare at each other then bust out laughin'. 'C'mon.'

We stop outside a nice house. Everybody gets them from the Housing Executive when they grow up and they pay your rent and everythin'.

'Do you think your sister will know if we've been here?' I say, as he takes the key from under a leprechaun gnome.

'I'm allowed, sure.' He goes in and I follow. 'Sit down fer fuck's sake.' I squeak on the new sofa cuz the plastic's still on. 'I'm away fer a pish,' says he.

As soon as he leaves I have a nosy. I look under the ornaments on the mantelpiece. Some people hide things under them. I'm a wee bit ragin' cuz he's won all the stories I told. I know – the gun! That'll beat him.

'Donnelly,' Fartin' calls from upstairs.

'What?' I shout up.

'C'm'up here a minute,' says he. I run up to join him. 'In here,' he calls.

The bedroom's full of boxes. 'This is their spare room. They'll probably put the baby in here, but til then Our Sinead says I can stay over anytime I want. She says it's like my room.'

'Class.' It's not fair.

'Here, let's look at this cat'logue.'

I follow him. He sits on the stairs.

'Catalogues are borin',' I say.

'Wha'? Wait t'ye see this,' says he, noddin' and pushin' himself into the wall to make space next to him.

I sit on the stair behind. He tuts and bounces back squashin' me into the wall. It's a bit weird. I don't really understand the whole boys touching thing. If you do, you're gay. But I see them do it all the time. It's cuz I'm not a real boy, I don't know when it's gay or not. *I wish I was a real boy too*, Pinocchio whispers in my ear.

Fartin' puts one side of the catalogue on my legs, the other on his. He flicks through the pages to the women's clothes and slows down. He stops at women in their bras and knickers. 'Look at the diddies on her.'

I'm scundered. I remember me and Fartin' found a dirty magazine in an entry one day after school. We looked at the dirty pictures, shouted *Oh My God!* and threw the magazine up in the air and ran away. Like it could run after us and get us. It ripped. So we ripped it on purpose. We threw diddies and fannies in the air and they were all over the ground. It was a geg. I wasn't scundered. I loved it. Maybe it was different cuz we were outside. We weren't sittin' beside each other, all squashed. Our legs touchin'. My dick throbs. I feel like I just stopped runnin'.

'Look at her. Fuckin' hell!' says he. 'These are the best ones. See-through. It's like lookin' at dirty pictures, isn't it? Ye can see her fuckin' nipples. Like saucers. She's a dirty bitch.'

'Yeah,' I don't know what to say. Martin puts a hand under his half of the catalogue. I stare really hard at the pictures on my side.

'Look at that. Ye can see through this one's knickers,' he says.

'Awooahh!' I say to the elbow dug in my side.

'Yer not lookin'.'

'She's really dirty,' I say. It doesn't sound right when I say things like that. Like one of those bad impersonators you see on the TV. Fartin' doesn't seem to notice.

'See her pubes. Ye can see the dark. Have you got any yet?'

'Aye, a couple.'

'Aye, me too,' Fartin' says, 'That's when ye know ye can wank. Once ye get them. It's called yer puberty. Our Seamus tol' me all about it. Ye get yer puberty an' ye grow yer pubes an' then ye wank an' ye cum an' then you're a man an' then ye can have sex. I bet ye them dirty bitches in the cat'logue have sex with the man that takes the photos.'

'Aye.'

'I bet ye they do have.'

'Aye.'

'That's what I'm gonna do when I grow up.'

I look at him from the corner of my eyes, strainin' them til they hurt. His eyes are closed so I look at him properly. His side of the catalogue is movin' up an' down from underneath.

I feel somethin' in my pants. I put my hand under the catalogue as well. I feel my dick. Squeeze to make it stop growin'. It won't stop and it's gonna show. Fartin's definitely doin' somethin' down there. But he can do anythin' he wants. Nobody would say anythin' to Mad Fartin' Martin, no matter what he did.

I look at the woman with the see-through knickers an' Fartin' knockin' her from underneath. I bet ye if Martin was the photographer he would have sex with her. I can see it. I rub the outside of my trousers. Martin makes a weird noise. I look at him. His eyes rollin' back in his head like a weirdo.

He looks at me and jumps up, throwin' the catalogue onto my knees and runs behind, up the stairs, his keks half way down his legs and disappears into a room. I squash my dick so hard it hurts, hopin' my hard-on will go by the time he comes back.

I hear a toilet flush. Fartin' bounces out behind me. Holdin' on to the wall on one side an' the rail in the other, he lifts his legs clear over my head an' nearly breaks his neck landin' on the stairs. He's so cool.

'Come on, Donnelly. What are ye doin' there? Lookin' at them dirty pictures? Havin' a wee wank there?'

'Nah!'

He grabs the catalogue.

'Ah, Donnelly's got a hard-on,' he laughs, grabbin' at my dick. I cover it with my hands. 'Were you havin' a wank?'

'Dead on,' I say, my face on fire.

'Sure I do it about a hundred times a day,' says he. 'C'mon, let's get outta here,' he says, runnin' down the stairs. He opens the big door. I move my dick flat against my belly so it's not pokin' out and jump down the stairs.

'Hol' on.' He puts his arm out to stop me. His hand touches my hard-on and stays there. We pretend it isn't.

'What?' I say.

'Checkin' there's no Brits,' says he. He pokes his head out further and sticks his bum back til it's against me. My hard-on feels hot against him. He moves from side to side lookin' up and down the street rubbin' on me.

He takes off down the path and I chase after. We run down the street back to the march. In the roads, the band has stopped. Two lines of IRA men in balaclavas, sunglasses and berets. Someone shouts orders like a sergeant major. The men lift rifles I hadn't even noticed.

Fire!

Everyone cheers. So do me and Fartin'. We jump up and down.

Fire!

I don't know really why, cuz you can't see what comes out of the rifles, but I feel like I've just seen fireworks. I know I will see real fireworks one day. And a circus. And a fairground. In America.

'C'mon,' says he, 'We can get in the riots. They let me do a petrol bomb last time.'

They must really like him. He runs towards the IRA men. He sees I haven't followed and holds his hands up *What?*.

I shrug. He shrugs back and ducks into the crowd. I'll show Fartin' next time I'm not scared. I forgot to tell him about the gun. That'll show him. I didn't arrange to meet him again though. Crap!

I don't want to go home so I watch these people instead. I pick out the older boys. Watch them talk. How they move and stand. I watch.

## 8

DA CAME HOME in the night and stole Ma's purse from her coat. The only one time he's ever remembered a key. Measles says that means he planned it. And now we're skint. We were already skint. But that's not the worst. He took the TV. My TV. I don't know what I'm goin' to do. It's the only place I see people like me. I want to die. But at least Da's gone for good. He'd never be able to show his face again. And Ma would never take him back after this.

God got rid of him for me. Just like I asked. But I paid the price. An eye for an eye. A TV for a Da.

## 9

I STRETCH AND YAWN, but quietly, cuz I want to play with Killer before they all wake up. The streaky sunlight is comin' through the special Venetian blinds. I creepity creep out of my bunk and climb down the mini metal ladders, careful not to slip in my socks. I Marcel-Marceau step over Our Paddy's clothes and back out the bedroom door. No sound of movement. 10 out of 10.

I tiptoe down the stairs, turn the handle of the livin' room door and push *slowly, slowly, catchy monkey*. I look upstairs while edgin' my bum in through the doorway, backin' into the livin' room. I close the door carefully. Yes! No-one woke. I jump up and down and do a little Irish jig.

Freeze. A man on our sofa. I'm goin' to wee myself. Or faint. Should I shout? He can't be a burglar cuz we don't have them in Ardoyne cuz the IRA knee-caps them. And would a burglar break in to have a sleep? If he was a homeless burglar he might. He looks homeless with his big beard and long hair. If Da was around it'd be one of his drunken mates. Maybe Paddy's got drunken mates now he thinks he's *it*.

'Alright, kid?' a deep, sleepy voice says. 'Is yer Mammy up?'

'No.'

'I'm Tommy. Yer Uncle Tommy,' says he.

'I don't have an Uncle Tommy,' says me.

'Ah . . .' says he. 'Like a *special* uncle.'

Hmm . . . I try to look all cool while I side-eye the companion set on the hearth. I might need the miniature poker for defence. I walk past him into the kitchen. I get Rice Krispies and pour a bowl. Have I got a long lost uncle? Maybe. Cuz we don't talk to Da's ones. He's fought with them all after he stole from Granny. His own Mammy.

I've heard of *special* uncles who are really your new Da. But my Ma would never in one hundred million years be one of those women.

'Mickey.' I jump. Ma comes in, Uncle Tommy behind her.

'OK, kid?' he says, as he passes me. Ma fires him a look. 'I told yer wee man,' says he, noddin' towards me, 'I'm his Uncle Tommy,' raisin' his eyebrows.

'Right,' says she. 'I'll send Paddy round then. You'll do that message for me.' She winks. He goes out the back door.

Where do big people get the idea that kids don't know they're tryin' to hide somethin'? I mean, come on, like – eyebrows and winkin'? Like terrible actors from a silent movie.

'Where's m'Uncle Tommy goin'?' I ask.

'Oh, he's away home.'

Out our back? Weird. Through the scullery window I watch him in the yard. He lifts up the roof of Killer's dog box, reaches in and puts somethin' in his pocket. I look to Ma who's busy pourin' milk on my Krispies. No more Frosties for us. Bloody Da. I'm not goin' to tell Ma about Uncle Tommy taking the gun. Or on Paddy who must have put it there.

'Go on into the livin' room and watch your cartoons,' she pushes me.

'Sure, Daddy stole the TV,' I say. Ma looks into the sink

and grips it so her knuckles turn white. She's gone somewhere else. I tip toe out back into the livin' room and sit on the floor.

'Mickey, don't you be sayin' to the others about yer Uncle Tommy stayin' here, OK?' Ma's voice walks by.

'Is it a secret?' I ask.

'Yes, it's a secret.'

I love secrets. Especially if I'm the only one that knows.

'Hiya,' Wee Maggie yawns into the livin' room. She comes over beside me and leans her head on my chest. She's gettin' big.

'I'm away down to get a bap for Mary's lunch. I'll be back in ten minutes,' Ma says. She pats her pocket, with her new purse, looks round the room, 'Be yous quiet and don't wake Paddy.'

Bloody Hell. We couldn't make noise cuz of Da and now it's bloody Paddy. I mean, am I the only boy in this house who's normal?

'Do you want some?' I say, liftin' the spoon to Wee Maggie's mouth.

'Aye,' she says and opens her mouth wide.

'Don't say *aye*, say "Yes, please",' I say, in my nicest voice. Somebody has to teach her not to turn out like the hallions in Ardoyne.

'Yes, super-duper please, with a cherry on top.' We both laugh. She is so funny though she's only wee. I aeroplane the Krispies in. I take the next spoonful.

Wee Maggie gives a big yawn.

'Do you want to know a secret?' I say, openin' my eyes dead wide and breathin' in loudly through my nose.

'Yeah.'

'Secret Position, please,' I put the Krispies on the hearth.

We turn to each other sittin' Indian-style, face to face, knee to knee.

'We have a Long Lost Uncle Tommy,' I say.

'Where's he lost?'

'Nowhere. Well, he's turned up found. Brilliant, isn't it?' We grab each other's hands and lock our fingers together. 'He stayed here last night on the sofa,' I whisper. I leave out the bit where he's an IRA man. And almost definitely not really our uncle.

'Where's he now?'

'Away on.'

'Is he comin' back?'

'I don't know.'

'Why's it a secret?'

'I don't know, but maybe he'll be rich and give us pay every week. Wouldn't that be brill?' I gasp, 'Maybe he'll die and leave us money in his will.'

'God!'

Our Measles comes in, still in her nightdress.

'Measles, do we have a long lost uncle? Mickey says we do,' says Wee Maggie.

'Maggie!' I am goin' to kill her.

'Mickey, what are you spoofin' about now?' says Measles.

'We do have cuz I just saw him. He stayed here last night.' Ha!

'Who stayed here last night?' Our Paddy says, comin' in, dressed for football.

'Our long lost uncle,' says Wee Maggie.

'Maggie! Watery mouth! I can't believe your tellin' everybody the secret.'

'Who said it was a secret?' says Paddy.

'M'Mammy,' I say, lookin' at my hands. They feel really itchy. Ma's gonna kill me.

'What's goin' on?' says he.

Measles nods to the scullery then goes into it, followed by

Paddy. The door closes behind them. Who does Our Paddy think he is? Runnin' around closin' doors like he's the King of Siam?

'I can't believe you told them,' I say.

'I didn't mean it,' says she.

'What do you mean *you didn't mean it*?'

'It just came out.'

'God, it wouldn't take us to be in jail together. You'd tout on me in five seconds flat. Have you never heard that *Loose Talk Costs Lives*?'

'No. What does that mean?'

'Wait.' I go over to the kitchen door and put my ear against it. I hear whisperin'.

'Must have been hiding,' says Measles.

'Ma wouldn't let them,' says Paddy.

'What are you earywiggin' for?' I jump at Ma's voice behind me.

'Nothin',' I say.

'Sure look at ye, yer like a beetroot,' says she, squintin'. 'Who's in there?' Ma says, lookin' worried now. 'What's goin' on?'

'Nobody, just Paddy and Mary,' I say.

'They're talkin' about our long lost uncle,' says Wee Maggie.

'Maggie!' I shout. Fuckin' Hell!

'I'm gonna kill you, wee boy,' says Mammy. 'Tell them two to come in here, I want them,' says Ma. She takes off her coat and heads up the stairs.

'I'm never gonna tell you anythin' again,' I sulk.

'Why not?' says she.

'Why not?' My eyebrows on the ceilin', voice squeakin' like a mouse. 'Did somebody give you brain damage in the night?'

I open the scullery door. 'Ma wants yous in here,' says me. I sit on the floor beside the hearth. I want to look as small as possible so maybe Ma won't see me to kick my head in. With every thump of Ma's feet on the stairs my heart jumps.

'Why did you have to open yer big mouth for anyway?' says Our Measles.

'You asked me!' I can't believe I'm getting the blame.

Measles and Paddy slam onto the sofa, hatin' each other. Ma comes in. She sits on Da's chair. This is serious. She smoothes out the material on the arms. We look at each other. Everybody's shittin' themselves.

'Right, I'm gonna tell ye's all somethin' now, and ye's better listen cuz I'm only goin' to say it once. If any of ye's ever get anybody askin' ye's to do anythin' for them – anythin' – ye say, *no*. Right?' She twists her weddin' ring. Da didn't get that when he cleared us out. 'And if they keep on, you tell them to come see yer Ma.'

Even if somebody asks you to go the shops?

'Ye's are not to lift a finger to do anythin' in this district, for anybody. No matter who they are. I don't care who asks ye. You know what I talkin' about, Paddy, Mary. If there's anythin' that has to be done, I'll be the one to do it. Yous are not to get involved,' says she. *Involved*. That means with the IRA. 'D'ye's hear me?' she shouts.

'Yes, Mammy,' we all say, except Paddy.

'Paddy, d'ye hear me talkin' to ye?' She gives him the evil eye.

'Aye,' he answers, lookin' out the window.

'And anythin' that goes on in this house, stays in this house. No goin' around talkin' our business in the street. D'ye's hear me, you two?' she says to me and Maggie.

'Yes, Mammy,' we say. But we all know that anyway cuz of Da.

'So if an uncle comes to stay, ye say nathin'. Ye just keep yer mouth shut about everythin'. That's it. Has any of ye's got anythin' to say?' Silence. 'Right, well, ye's all may get out from under my feet. I need my head showered. Mary, yer bap's on your bed, get yourself ready for work.'

They all get up in silence. Mary heads upstairs. Paddy goes to the kitchen. I stay in my little ball on the floor. Wee Maggie tries to take my hand but I shrug it off. Ma follows Paddy into the kitchen. I follow Ma and listen at the open door. I give finger-on-the-lips to Maggie.

'You're to go round there now. He wants to see ye,' says Ma.

'What did ye say to him?'

'Exactly what I said to you,' says Ma. 'None of them will come near ye, they're well warned. You know who he is?'

'Aye,' says he.

'He gives the orders round here. And any of them so much as look at you, you tell me,' says Ma.

'Aye, Ma.'

'Do you think for one minute I'm jokin',' Ma growls. 'I don't want to know what you've been up to. But it's over nigh.'

'Fine. I don't need to see him. I believe ye,' says he.

'You'll go round there and hear it from his lips, then you'll know.'

Movement. I run across the livin' room, but bang my knee off the arm of Da's chair.

'Aooowwah!' I cry, hoppin' around the room in agony.

'Gabshite,' Our Paddy says, pullin' off his Celtic top. I stop hoppin' when I see the sores and enormous yellow stains of old bruises all over him. He runs upstairs. I limp to the door.

'Where are you goin, wee boy?' says Ma.

'Up to get dressed,' says me. Wee Maggie slides out past

me, up the stairs, not wantin' to get caught in the cross-fire. She's showed her true colours today. Wait til I get her.

'Josie?' That comes from our path. It's Aunt Kathleen.

'Here, Ka'leen,' Ma calls.

Aunt Kathleen comes in. 'What's wrong?'

'Nathin,' Ma says, tryin' to hide her face.

'Josie. Turn round.' Aunt Kathleen sees Mammy's black eye from where the door hit her. 'Is that why you haven't been to work?' Ma looks away.

'Get upstairs, Mickey.' Ma pushes me. 'Go on. Me and your Aunt Ka'leen need to talk. And you can stay up there. You're in trouble, wee boy.'

I want to ask if I can bring Killer up with me, but I think Ma would strangle me. Right, where is that Maggie one til I kill her?

# 10

'She's gorgeous, I'd buck her.'

'Sure you don't even know how to lumber.'

'Aye, I do.'

I know who they're talkin' about. My Martine.

The ones at the back push and the line gets squashed. They're never goin' to get in. They're the ones nobody would ever stick up for. I'm near the back, but I'm not *the back*.

'Everybody knows how to lumber. I'm not eight,' says them.

I don't really. I know it's next up from a kiss and you open your mouth. Anyway, who cares? It's too friggin' excitin' right this minute.

'Hurry up!' I say. It's goin' to start soon. We don't know which one it is yet.

'Mickey, what's a lumber?' says Wee Maggie.

'You're too young,' I whisper.

'It's dirty, isn't it?' says she. I nod. 'Will ye tell me when ye find out?'

'Sure, don't I always,' says me, noddin', with my hands on my hips like *for God's sake*. But I'm not sure if it'll be too grown-up. I have to be her big brother too.

I've got sweets burnin' a hole in my pocket. Can't eat one now or the boys will take them from me. Wee Maggie's so excited she keeps crossin' one knee over the other like she's gonna pish herself.

Martine McNulty. I can't wait to see her. They don't have a car, the McNulty's, but they have a garage. We're all lined up outside it. The people who built these houses must have thought rich people were goin' to live here. But how could they think there was goin' to be any rich people in Ardoyne?

Only about ten houses in the street have garages, but they're knockin' them down soon to build more houses. I'm glad cuz I don't think it's fair that some people get garages and some people don't.

'Right, ye's can go in,' shouts Briege McAnally doin' security. 'Get yer money ready.'

We make our way up the line. It's so brilliant that they're doin' a play cuz without any TV I'm so bored I even played Monopoly. But it's brill Da bein' gone so I'm not goin' to scud it by wishin' we had our TV back. He might come back with it.

Everybody's so happy in our house. No more him arguin' and shoutin' and bangin' the door in the night wakin' us all up. I used to get Ma more to myself when Da leaves us, but cuz he stole everythin' Ma has to work every hour God sends. How exactly does he send it? Post? Telegram? Mule?

I hope Briege's forgot about the skips. She wasn't too bad when I saw her with Killer at the shop. I take my 5p out and hold it hard in my hand. It's nearly me. I need to go to the toilet now too. Really bad.

'That's it. Full up!' says Briege, pushin' my chest.

'Ach!' Wee Maggie starts cryin'.

'There's no more room.' Briege is lovin' every torturin' minute of this.

'It's not fair!' I say.

'Hold on.' She goes back inside and closes the door. If Martine knew, I'm sure she'd save me.

'She's not gonna let us in. It's not fair!' Wee Maggie

whinges. She looks at me like *Do somethin'*. But what can I do? The ones at the end of the queue are walkin' away.

The door opens again. 'OK,' says she, holdin' out her hand. I press my 5p into her palm, hard.

'Wait a minute,' I hear Briege say. I turn to see her arm blockin' Wee Maggie. 'Where's her money?' says Briege to me.

'She's only a wee one,' I say.

'So?'

'Wee ones don't pay.' That's always been the rule. 'She doesn't have any money.'

Wee Maggie looks like when she saw Bambi's Ma bein' shot dead. Right now, if I gave Wee Maggie our secret gun, Briege would be the one getting a bullet in the head.

'You have to get some. Hurry up, or she's not gettin' in,' says Briege.

I don't understand it. She likes Wee Maggie. I look at Wee Maggie and she looks at me.

'Go back and ask m'Mammy,' I say.

'She's not in, sure.'

'Right, I'm closin' the door,' says Briege.

'But . . .' begs Wee Maggie.

'Last chance.'

This isn't about Wee Maggie. Briege is tryin' to get me. Wee Maggie's face is all screwed up, lookin' at me cuz I'm her big brother. And her best friend in the whole-wide-world. Briege pulls the door closed.

'Wait!' I stick my foot in just in time. 'What if I give you sweets?' I take out my sweets and she grabs them with her claws.

'Go on in,' allows the Evil One. And smiles *you'll never beat me and don't you forget it!*

I give her *I hope you choke on them and die! Die! Die!* She lets Wee Maggie in. I grab her hand and pull her beside me. There *are* seats. The lyin' bitch. Just you wait, Briege McAnally. Just like it says on the gable wall – Tiocfaidh ár Lá. *Our Day Will Come.* Me and Wee Maggie's.

Briege closes the door. Anyway, we're in. So really *we* won. At a high price but . . . We sit on two crates they've stolen from the Lemonade Man. Maggie's lookin' at me like I'm her hero. I am.

I hear whisperin' from behind the wooden counter. On the stage there's chairs, an old desk and ripped curtains over the floor.

'Shush,' everybody shushes. Silence. Briege bolts the door and pulls raggedy curtains over the two windows beside the door. Half dark inside. Briege walks to the middle of the stage, her face, dead serious, like when she corners you in the entry to hit you.

'*The Dolls!*' a scary voice of horror announces from somewhere, givin' me the heebee geebees. I squeeze my dick hard. Wee Maggie screams. We turn to each other and link our fingers together, squash them til it hurts, bounce our legs together really fast and rub noses and giggle. I see two boys lookin' at me with horrible smiles. They lean in, whisperin'. I remember what Our Paddy said. Maybe they'll be goin' to St. Gabriel's. I take a redner, drop Wee Maggie's hands and look away.

The girl beside me has her hand up her skirt, pullin' at her knickers. 'Look at *Knicker-Picker*,' I say to Wee Maggie and we snigger. I take her hand again but keep it where no-one can see.

Weird, howlin' wind noises come from behind the counter. A boy comes out in a snorkel jacket with the hood zipped up hidin' his face. He walks across the front of us, but he's walkin' with wind blowin' dead strong against him. An explorer, maybe.

'Who is it?' somebody says and everybody whispers. Right enough. What boy would be with the girls? A mystery actor.

He's shakin', shiverin', his teeth chatterin'. He unzips his hood and pulls it down. He's wearin' a balaclava mask. He gasps for breath, staggers, falls on both knees and screams in pain. He falls forward onto his hands then lies down flat. Not a twitch. He's a goner. Friggin' beezer. It's only started and already somebody's dead.

Silence. The girls come out from behind the counter in single file. Their faces white with big, red circles on their cheeks. Walkin' like robots. Legs straight. Arms straight. Stoppin' and startin'. Clumpin' right, clumpin' left. Half bent sometimes, like they're broken in the middle. I've never seen anythin' like this in real life, ever. They must be *The Dolls*.

Gigglin' beside me, but there's nothin' funny about it. The Dolls stop at the dead body. What are they goin' to do? Wait. The Explorer moved. He groans, strugglin' to get up on his hunkers. He rubs his eyes and as he opens them, the Dolls freeze on the spot like in 1, 2, 3 Red Lights. He sees them. Sweet, scary smiles are frozen on their faces. Somethin' really bad is about to happen. I am completely shittin' myself.

He moves towards them. Their little girly Doll smiles have fooled him. Me and Wee Maggie grab each other and let out little screams. The Explorer reaches out his hand in slow motion. His hand gets right close to . . . Martine. I nearly didn't recognise her. She's gorgeous. And has a garage. And acts in plays. I'm officially, completely and utterly in love.

The Explorer's hand touches the Martine Doll but nothin' happens. Martine doesn't move. I was sure she'd come alive.

'I wasn't scared. I knew nothin' was gonna happen,' I say. *Knicker-Picker* looks like she believes me. The Explorer's right up in the faces of the other Dolls, but they don't move. He gives up and walks over to the windows. He pulls a curtain across and looks out. Light comes into the dark and shines on the Dolls. They come alive.

Screams from everyone. Like opposite vampires. Who thought of that? What friggin' genius? Could it be the actor? Let's face it, the rest couldn't. Not even my angel, Martine.

Then, from the corner, somethin' moves. A shape risin' from behind the counter. It's evil Briege. She has her face painted white too, but with black circles on her cheeks, not red like the others. All the Dolls look at her and bow. Oh my Sweet Jesus! Mary, Mother of Perpetual Sucker! I can't take much more. Briege . . . she's . . . she's . . . Queen Of The Dolls. My eyes feel like they're double the size. I've got goose pimples all over my arms and legs. The Queen points at the Explorer, her mad eyes say *get him*. The Dolls clump towards him but he's still lookin' out the window.

'They're gonna get you,' I scream. But he doesn't turn round. He can't hear me all the way up in the North Pole. He turns round as hands grab his neck. He gurgles and spits as he's strangled. Dolls surround him, their deformed hands with fingers stuck together like one fat finger, snappin' against their thumbs. They nip him as he falls in slow-motion death.

'Help!' he moans. Girls scream. He collapses in a lump. The Dolls step back, leavin' a space in the middle. The Queen clumps into the centre and raises her arms above her head. She drops to her knees, opens her mouth, wide, and shows us her big, fangy teeth. She falls forward attackin' the Explorer's stomach with her mouth. Jesus Christ, she's eatin' him! The Dolls join in. They munch and growl and tear strips off him. He screams. We scream. The Explorer gives a big, giant scream and sits up, lookin' straight at us. He holds out his hand, like we're there in the snow with him, like he's here in the garage with us. But he's not. *We're* not. There's nothin' we can do.

He falls down dead.

The Dolls smile. They wipe their bloody mouths on their sleeves and their bloody hands on their dresses. They line up behind the counter and slowly sink down, like they're all in a lift down to Hell.

'The End!' the scary horror voice shouts.

Everybody goes ballistic. Bouncin' up and down, screamin'. The Dolls come out and the Explorer stands up, they stand together and bow. We clap and clap. The actors look at each other smilin'. Me and Wee Maggie stare at each other. How lucky are we? And how cool, for seein' this. Imagine bein' a real actor. Everybody would love you. That's it. I have to be an actor. That would get me to America. To Hollywood.

'Right, everybody out, we have to tidy up now,' says Briege. Everyone rushes out to be the first to tell the ones who didn't get in.

'That was brilliant, wasn't it,' says Wee Maggie.

'It was the best thing I've ever seen in my whole *entire* life,' I say.

'My whole *entire* life, too.'

'And we saw it together.' I give her our special look, the one we're not allowed to give anyone else, and she gives it me right back. We walk outside and the kids in the street come runnin' over.

'I'm gonna be an actor when I grow up,' I say. Wee Maggie completely believes me and her face lights up like a sparkler.

I'm goin' to wait here. All day, if it takes me. Til I see Martine comin' out and tell her how amazin' she was. I should go get Killer first so she'll stop and like me and I'll tell her at the same time that she's amazin', and with all of that goin' on, you never know what could happen. I want to see who the mystery actor is too.

Decky comes out. The leader of the boys' gang. I didn't

see him in there. I never thought he'd watch plays. Was he the actor? Leader of the boys and leader of the girls together like *Grease*?

'That was brilliant, Decky,' I chance. He actually nods. 'It's the best thing I've ever seen.' I follow him. He doesn't tell me to clear off, so I leave Wee Maggie and walk beside him. 'The way they got him? That was brilliant.'

'Aye,' he nods.

That's the most he's ever said to me. I can't believe it. Maybe I could mess about with him today. Maybe we could be mates. In St. Gabriel's too. But I can't think of anythin' to say. 'I could watch that again, right now.' I try to read what his face is sayin'. He spits on the ground.

I follow him to the corner. I can't go with him unless he says somethin'. We bang straight into a Brit patrol. I don't look at them. Decky spits on the ground beside them. I stay a bit behind.

'I wish I could be in the next one,' says me. I can't believe I just said that.

He stops, lookin' me up and down. 'With all the girls? Like that wee fruit in there?' he laughs. 'I suppose, the way you get on.' He walks to the corner of the Eggy. 'Are you followin' me?' He turns.

I freeze. Improvise. Practise your skills. 'Goin' to the shop,' I say, like *catch a grip, why would I want to follow you for*?

'Aye, right,' he says, out of the side of his mouth. He doesn't believe me. So I run across the road to McQuillan's new house shop. This is proper actin'. Like you really do it. They said on the TV it's called Method Acting.

I stop at the door. I have no money. Shit. I look over and he's still there. I search for the 10p that I don't have. I put on the look of *Where's my money?* And follow that with, *It's not there! Shock! Horror!* And then finish up with *Fuck me,*

*I've lost it.* When I look up, he's gone. The old, 'look – one, two, three'. It's very hard to pull off. But to a Look Master like myself, it's tea and toast. And in facto, isn't look-masterin' really just acting? And I've been doin' it all my life.

'Whaddye want?' Mrs McQuillan says.

Nobody likes the McQuillans cuz they're gyppos, except they've got a house. And nobody's been buyin' anythin' from them cuz they smell. Everybody says that everythin' you buy will taste like their smell. I don't care what everybody says, the McQuillan's have always been nice to me, and Mammy likes them.

'I've lost my money,' I lie. Act, I mean.

'Ach, have ye, son.'

'I was at the play up in the garage and it must have fell out when I was sittin' down.'

'Ach, son, ye have to be careful with money.'

'I know, Mrs McQuillan.'

'How's your Mammy?' she says, like Ma's dyin'.

'OK,' I say.

'Must be hard with your Da gone?' she says. Ma would go mad if she knew there was talk, she'd pull this house down, and she wouldn't need the bulldozers down the street. 'You didn't have 10p, son, did ye, ye can tell me?'

Shit. She found me out. 'No, Mrs McQuillan,' I say. 'I'm . . .'

'Shush, don't say any more,' Mrs McQuillan looks like she's about to cry. 'Here, son, take these, your Mammy's been good to me often enough.' A 10p mix-up.

'Thanks, Mrs McQuillan.' Unbelievable. I've always thought she was dead-on, but not Ardoyne's Mother Theresa.

'And tell yer Mammy, she can always be on the list.' My Ma would never be on anybody's list. 'I saw Minnie goin' in,' she whispers. 'Now, you look after your Mammy.'

I run down the street past the gable. There's only one Minnie. Minnie the Tick Woman. Ma doesn't get tick, so what's Minnie doin' in our house?

I burst into our house and Ma near shits herself. She crumples somethin' in her fist and puts it under her leg.

'Alright, son?' smiles Minnie in her squeaky wheeze.

'Is everythin' OK, Mammy?' I say.

'Listen to Granda,' Ma laughs. Minnie joins in with a wheeze. 'Go on out nigh you, we're talkin'.'

'Can I just get some water please, Mammy?'

'He's awful nice. He's a credit to you, Josie,' says Minnie.

'Hurry up, well,' says Ma, squintin' at me. 'And close that door,' she shouts after me. God, grown-ups are daft. Seriously. With the door closed, I can go right up to the door and listen even better.

'. . . every Friday,' says Minnie.

'Can I drop it round to you?' says Ma.

'No.'

'It's just I hate them knowin' my business,' says Ma.

'Sure, amn't I here nigh?'

'Yes,' says Ma. 'But please, Minnie, if you don't mind.'

'If I let everyone come round, Josie, I'd get no rest,' says Minnie, her squeak gettin' sharper. Killer starts barkin' out the back. I think she's in dog range. 'I'd be up and down from the door every two seconds. And there's those, I know you won't believe this, but there's those who wouldn't turn up.'

I burst in. 'Sure I'll bring it round to you, Mrs Maloney, and sure I could do your messages for you while I'm there.' I beam her the biggest smile I've got. 'Go on, Mrs Maloney, a lady like you shouldn't be runnin' up and down the street carryin' bags of shoppin'.'

Minnie giggles into her hand like one of those women from

old filims. I beam over to Ma. Shit. I've given away that I was listenin'. I wish I would think for one minute.

'Isn't he a wee dote? An absolute credit to you. A credit.' Minnie leans over and pinches my cheek. 'As a special favour to you, Josie, but don't let anyone else know.'

'Well, we can all keep quiet then.' Ma nods and smiles and keeps her smile frozen, turnin' to me.

'Well, that's me. No rest for the wicked,' squeaks Minnie, cuppin' my cheek with her hand. 'I'll be seein' you then, won't I? A wee gentleman.' She turns to Ma. 'Aren't you lucky?' She smiles again and wheezes her way out the door.

Ma's arm on my back guides me with her to watch Minnie out the door. She looks right and left. Only kids on the street. But someone will be watchin' from their window. Ma closes the wee door.

Whack!

'Mammy! That was sore,' I shout. And I just bloody helped her.

'Well, you shouldn't have been listenin', wee boy,' says she. 'Now, listen you, watery mouth, if you say one word to the rest of them I'll kill you stone dead.'

'Wise up, Mammy,' I say. 'I'm brilliant at keepin' secrets, you could tell me anythin'.' Oh crap. Uncle Tommy. 'I promise you, Mammy. Cross my heart and hope to fry,' says me.

'Be careful what you hope for,' says Ma. 'Nigh go on out and play.'

'Do I have to?' I kick the sofa. Ma slaps me across the legs. 'Mammy, will you stop that,' I shout.

'Well, you stop kickin' my good sofa,' she warns. 'The money man's dead. You break that sofa and we'll use you to sit on. Go on before I hit you a dig.'

'Put 'em up, put 'em up,' I say like the Cowardly Lion, to make her laugh.

Ma whacks me across the head.

'What was that for?'

'I just felt like it.' She pisses herself laughin'. I do too.

She laughs so much she falls on the chair. I jump on her lap. 'Jesus Christ and his Holy Mother,' she moans.

It's nice bein' here. I stick my head on her shoulder. I can't get down to her chest now, where I like it.

'Fuck me, wee boy, you're a bag of bones,' her voice deep and out of breath. 'Get up, your boney arse is stickin' into me.'

I jump up. I don't want to. I wish I was small.

'Here, go and get yerself somethin',' says she.

'No, Mammy, I don't want anything,' says I.

'Why?'

'Cuz. Minnie,' I say.

She laughs. 'It was just a one-time thing, son.' Cuz of Da takin' everythin'. I hate him. 'Yer Ma's always alright, son. But if you don't want the money, I'll give it to Paddy,' says she and heads for the door. I follow her. She can't really be goin' to give it to Paddy.

'Where is he now?' Ma looks up and down the street. 'Pa . . .'

'Ma!' I shout.

'Shush. You'll wake your Da,' says Ma. Her face drops and turns white. 'Yer Aul' Ma's away with fairies.' She twists the weddin' ring on her finger. She does it all the time now. 'Here.' She holds out her hand flat with a coin in her palm, like it's Holy Communion. On Sunday the new Priest changed the law so we can get it in our hands like that. Aul Aggie says he's the Anti-Christ.

'Thanks, Ma.' I grab the money and run. I turn back, 'Do you want to go to the shop for me, Ma? Seein' how I've come into a bit of money. I'll give you somethin' for goin'.'

'You're some pup, Mickey Donnelly,' she laughs.

'I'm no Donnelly, Ma.'

'No, you're no Donnelly, son, you're an O'Connor . . .' She smiles her Ma smile. The one you try hard for. 'Be back in half an hour for your supper. Don't have me callin' you, or all you'll be gettin' for dinner is a dig in the gub.'

'Mmmm . . . my favourite!' I lick my lips and rub my belly. Ma laughs.

I run to the entry. I turn to do a little dance for her but she's gone inside. I look over at the gable. Wee Maggie sees me. She's ragin'. Shit. I ran away and left her. I do a little dance for her. I hold the money up in one hand and the 10p mix-up from McQuillan's in the other and she runs at me like a baby rhino.

Behind her I see a boy leavin' the garage. It's Helmet Head, the new boy who joined my class with the brilliant stories. He was the actor in the play. I bloody well knew I hated him. I'll have to bump him off to get in the next play.

## 11

I'M BORED. WHAT did people do in the old days without TV? I'm desperate. My whole body won't sit still. Ma and Measles are at work. Wee Maggie's playin' with the girls at the gable. Our Paddy's out collectin' wood for the bonfire they're buildin' in the waste ground. I can't risk him seein' me with the girls. I don't really want to play with them, but I want to find out about the plays. I hate Briege anyway. Could I collect wood?

I pretend the window is the TV. Martine's sittin' on the wall watchin' the older boys at the bonfire. I wish we could play together, just us. We'd laugh. And just stare at each other. Maybe sing songs too. Like 'Hopelessly Devoted to You'. If only I could get rid of Briege.

I know. Take Killer for a walk and dander oh-so-casually by the girls. Then I can take him round to show the new people in the new houses. I run out to the yard. 'Come on, Killer. Come on, wee boy. Good dog.'

He bounces after me and we run out over the waste ground. At the girls, I stop and pet him while he jumps up and down barkin'. I wind him up by pretendin' I'm goin' to attack him.

'Martine, yer wanted,' her Ma shouts. Damn! I run towards her house, like I was goin' that way.

'Hiya, Mickey,' says she. 'Hiya, Killer.' She pets him so I stop.

'Hiya,' I say. 'What you doin'?'

'Just playin'. Are you not?'

'I have to take Killer for a walk.' I roll my eyes and tut. 'Cuz he's my dog, I have to look after him.'

'You're so lucky,' says she. Martine McNulty thinks *I'm* lucky. 'Who got him for you?'

'My Daddy.' I want to lie and say Ma, but everybody knows Mas don't buy dogs.

'Where is your Daddy?'

I hit a redner. I can't believe she asked. 'He's in America,' I say, 'tryin' to get work. He'll send for all of us when he can.'

'Oh, that's brilliant,' says she. 'But you're not going soon?'

Holy Battered Sausages! She doesn't want me to go. 'Well, we probably won't go. He'll probably just bring back loads of money for us to be rich.'

'Martine. Right nigh!' her Ma shouts.

'See ya later, Mickey. Bye, Killer.' Martine runs off into her house.

*Oh yes. Oh yes. Oh yes-sir-ee.* I do a little skip. I try the *Wizard of Oz* dance. I see the boys and stop. I put on the dander I did with Ma's-a-Whore and yank Killer to me. I sneak a glance and see some of them starin'. So, so jealous. Ha! I turn into the new estate. I don't need them. I can make new friends in the new estate with my dog.

I hear somethin' shouted after me but I don't even listen.

This doesn't even look like our street now. Like its own little private world. I take corners and twists, like Tron on his motorbike. It's like a maze. I could get lost in here and I only live two centimetres away. Down here they don't leave their doors open like we do, though Aul Aggie in our street has started shuttin' her door. She says she keeps it shut even when she's in the house. It's the talk of the street.

Everybody's movin' to Ardoyne cuz we don't pay the TV license. And nobody mugs you or burgles you – except your own Da! – or breaks our laws cuz the IRA shoot your knee-caps off. If you do it again you get *Put Out* of the district and if you come back, you're dead.

I sit on the wee wall of a new house and watch kids playin' with the sand in another new buildin' site. A new wee boy's at his door lookin' at me. 'Come on, Killer. Jump up. Jump up.' I hold my hand out and bounce it up. Killer follows to catch it.

'Bad dog! Get down,' I shout at Killer, checkin' the new boy who's makin' his way over kickin' a stone.

'Is that *your* dog?' says the new boy.

'Yeah.'

'He's class,' says he.

'He can do all these tricks,' says me.

'Can he?'

'Aye, but you have to give him biscuits. He's one of those special dogs like you see in the Pedigree Chum advert. We've got a bit a paper tellin' you how special he is.' I saw that on TV.

'Aye, right,' says he, laughin'. 'You're a right snob.'

I don't like him so I walk away. It's cool to leave first, so I win.

'What school d'ye go to?' he calls after me.

'I'm goin' to St. Gabriel's,' I shout over my shoulder.

'Ye mean St. Gabe's. You *are* a snob,' he laughs. 'I'm goin' there.'

I want to talk now. I don't want to win anymore. I turn back but he's gone in. He could have been a new mate for school. *St. Gabe's.* I must stop sayin' St. Gabriel's. I don't want to go there. I want to go St. Malachy's. It's not fair. Maybe there's a way. Think, Mickey. It's your new mission. Yeah, *Mission Friggin' Impossible.*

I cross into Brompton Park entry and through the broken railings into my old school pitch. Kids are playing all sorts of PE games like school. It's the Summer Scheme. Brill! That's what I can do. All summer. Me and Maggie can be goin' to the Summer Scheme every day. I can't wait to tell her. I look at all the kids playin' and laughin'. And boys and girls together. Yes, this is definitely where I'm comin'. Everythin's goin' to be brilliant.

I let Killer off the lead for a wee minute. I shouldn't but he's such a good boy, he comes when I call him. 'C'mon, Killer, good boy.' I crawl through the hole in the wire fence and come out into another No Man's Land.

I thought it was called No Man's Land like the Bray is called the Bray. There's no sign on it or anythin', but everybody knows its name. Then they called this No Man's Land, too. It's where no man lives. Between us and the Prods. I'm not allowed here, even though it's right next to my old school. Ardoyne doesn't make sense.

The old Flax Mill is now the army barracks, with a huge look-out post spyin' on us. Ma worked there when she was a wee girl before the Brits took it over. There's always riotin' here.

The sun comes out and the broken glass sparkles. The waste ground looks beautiful. Like an ocean floor scattered with treasure. I cup my hands round my eyes, puttin' on my special *treasure-seekin' binoculars.* I look for any cracker coloured bits. Sometimes I take bits home and put them in my shoebox under Paddy's bed. It's the box where I put the letters from my pen pal. I should write to him again. Maybe my last letter got lost in the post. Maybe I could go see him one day. Maybe he'd help me escape.

As I'm binocularisin', I see a beautiful bit of red glass. I lift it and look through it. Ardoyne turns from black and white to colour, just like in the *Wizard of Oz*. A Brit patrol appears through the doorway cut into the tall corrugated iron barricades of the border. Nobody ever goes through it. Ever. The Prods would kill us for enterin' their land. And if we saw anyone comin' into our side, we'd kill them.

'Here, Killer.' I pat my thighs. I put him back on his lead and run across the road in front of the barricades.

The Prods live behind them across the Crumlin Road in the Shankill. The Kingdom of the Prods. That's where they found John McTaggart.

John McTaggart was drunk in town and he got into a Shankill Black Taxi instead of an Ardoyne one. They look exactly the same but you get them from a different place. John McTaggart opened his mouth. Loose talked. Said where he lived. The taxi man threw him out on the Shankill Road and shouted to the Prods, 'He's a Taig'. John McTaggart was taken to a burnt-out house in the Shankill and they dropped breeze blocks on his head til he was dead. Just behind there.

'Come on, Killer, let's go home, wee man.' I head back to my old school.

Two Jeeps appear from Old Ardoyne, movin' like snails beside the soldiers. On the corner of Etna Drive, a few boys stand guard, watchin' the border, guardin' our side. Some older boys join. I feel butterflies in my tummy. I don't like gangs of boys and I have to walk past them to get back home. There's nowhere to hide cuz it's No Man's Land. The crowd is gettin' bigger, some pacin' up and down like the lions in Belfast Zoo. They see me. I'm between them and the Brits. I can't move. I don't know where to go.

Shoutin'. Some big boys put balaclavas on over their faces. *Riot*. Men join the crowd pushin' wee ones to the front. They're only about my . . . *Fartin'! Fartin's at the front!* What's he doin' down here? He's mental.

*BANG!* Shootin'.

Fartin' better watch himself. A police Jeep speeds down Flax Street, then another. They stop and Peelers jump out with riot shields.

Shots again. From different places. I don't know if it's them or us. *Move Mickey*. Killer barks. 'It's OK, wee son.'

A petrol bomb hits a Peeler's shield and it goes up in flames. So does the Peeler. The crowd cheers. Peelers flap at their man on fire and put the flames out. There'll be murder now. A Brit runs past me. A Peeler shoots a rubber bullet into the crowd. He can't do that, Fartin's there. They're only kids at the front. The crowd run down Etna Drive, but the shootin' hasn't stopped. The Peelers and the Brits run after them, shootin' rubber bullets at their backs.

This is my chance, while the riot is on the run. More shots. *NOW. MOVE IT.*

I loosen my hold on Killer's lead to wrap the length around my wrist and keep him close.

A sound so loud my body vibrates. I become smaller. Wind blows me to the ground.

Crash. Crash. Smash. Windows explode one at a time like glass dominoes. Chimneys fall. Alarm bells and sirens all at the same time. Deafenin'. I try to get up but my head is too heavy.

I'm in the sea. Crawlin' on the sand. My treasure. My lovely red glass. I must get my treasure. I push myself up to sittin'. Cryin'. Is that me? I don't know why I'm cryin'. I don't feel anythin'. Nothin' at all. Then I do. A warm feelin' travellin' down my legs. I must be bleedin'. Ma'll kill me. I can't see blood. Oh no, why couldn't it be blood? Now I really cry.

I get up. I hobble. I feel dizzy. Sick. People are comin' out of their houses. I can't let them see I've wet myself. People will see. A man appears mimin' words. No sound is comin' out. He shakes me.

'Son?' I can hear him now. 'Can you hear me? Are ye OK?'

'Yes, Mister, just let me go,' says me.

'What's this?'

'I wet myself,' I cry.

'No, your head,' says he.

I touch around my head, feel warm, thick stickiness. My hands are red. I'm so stupid. He didn't even know I'd pissed myself. And I told him. Stupid, stupid, stupid! I hate you, Mickey Donnelly! I hate your guts!

Three men with balaclavas runnin' at me. The man holdin' me hides his face. I copy him. You can't tell on what you don't see.

'What the fuck are you doin' down here?' one of the Balaclava Men shouts. Two hands grab my shoulders. A Balaclava Man has me.

'Look at your head. Get down home now, Mickey.' He knows me. IRA men don't know me. Long Lost Uncle Tommy?

I know who it is.

'Now, Mickey!' Our Paddy shouts, but I can't move. The man who was helpin' me runs.

Killer. Where's Killer? I had him . . . I can't . . . I'm pulled along the tarmac by Paddy, but I'm draggin' my legs. I'm goin' to tell Ma on him, she said . . .

'Run!' another Balaclava man shouts. 'He'll be alright.' I'm let go. Paddy walks backwards, away from me, turns and runs. The piss is gettin' cold on my legs.

Barkin'. 'Killer!' I scream. Where is he? 'Killer!'

There, in the middle of the road, lookin' at me. Behind him I see a Saracen comin' up Flax Street on its way to the barracks. I run but fall. Pain stabs my knees. No sound again. Heavy head. Killer looks so tiny. I can see he's barkin'. 'Killer, come here.' Am I even makin' sound? I pull myself up. The Saracen comes right up behind Killer. Can't he hear it? A few kids appear at the bottom of Flax Street and throw stones and bottles at the Saracen.

Bodies of Brits and Peelers lyin' on the waste ground. A man with no shirt staggers bleedin' towards me with his arms out like somethin' from a horror filim. 'Killer!' He's still there lookin' at me. Stupid dog. 'Run!' The Saracen's gettin' closer to him. *Move, Killer, go back, please!* I telepath.

*You shouldn't have brought me down here, Mickey.*

Killer? You're telepathin' again.

*You're not allowed down Flax Street. You know that you're not allowed here on your own. And you know you're not supposed to take me out of the house without askin'. And now I'm in Flax Street. And now I'm goin' to get run over.*

The Saracen's movin' slowly. Killer's got plenty of time to get out of the way. Why doesn't he? 'Get out of the way!' I can't walk in a straight line. A useless drunk like Da.

*Mickey, it's comin' to get me.*

The man who tried to help me is comin' back.

'Mister, get my dog,' I shout, 'Please, Mister, my wee dog's there.'

He runs for me. 'Not me. My dog!' I cry. The stupid man.

'Killer!' Thank God, he hears me. He moves to me, but his back legs aren't workin'. What's happened? What have I done? The Saracen roars. 'Killer!' I can walk straight. I speed up. I point to him and the man who is comin' for me turns and sees Killer. He puts his arm over his eyes.

I turn to see the Saracen swervin', but Killer is hit on the side, lifted off the ground, spun. He lands at the side of the road. He moves. He's not dead. 'I'm comin'!' *Whatever it* takes. *I'll get the best doctors in the world, we'll fix you,* I telepath. I reach him and lean over. Should I lift him? I don't know what to do. Killer looks right at me. Right in the eye. He wants to tell me somethin'.

*Help me, Mickey, can't ye see I'm dyin' here?*

His eyes close. No, Killer, don't go to sleep. If you bang your head you don't go to sleep cuz you never wake up again. Remember I told you, that's what the woman said to me when I fell off the swing at the Waterworks.

*But I didn't fall off the swings, did I, Mickey?*

'No. It was the bomb. And the Saracen,' I say.

*Cuz you took me out. And you let me go.*

'It's all my fault.'

*I love you, Mickey.*

'I love you too, Killer. I'm so, so sorry.'

*It's you I'm sorry for.*

Why?

*Who are you gonna play with now?*

Killer closes his eyes. He wants to go a wee sleep. I close my eyes too.

Dark.

Words.

Spinnin'.

Hurtin'.

Fireworks.

Shush.

'Where do you live, son?'

'Mammy?' I open my eyes.

'What's your name?' says the man. I can hear.

I walk past him.

'Mammy.'

I'm a good boy.

And my Mummy will love me.

I run and it hurts.

I'm dizzy. Sick. Spinning.

In my street everyone's out. I blink. My eyes roll back in my head.

I'm at our back gates. How did I get here?

Concentrate. Hand through. Open latch. Sneak in.

I need to wash face. Remove evidence. Water. Killer's bowl. It's the only way.

I wash my head and face, the water turning red. I empty it down the drain. I look at my reflection in the metal bowl. There's no blood.

Wee Maggie comes to the kitchen window. 'Maggie!' I shout-whisper and wave. She sees me. *C'mere*, I call with my arm. I hide behind the yard wall.

'What's wrong?' she's scared.

'Did you hear the bomb?'

'Aye, it was a big one. Everybody's out,' says she.

'I was there. I was right there. Look what I done.' I show her my trousers.

'You'd better get in to Mammy,' says she.

'Ma will kill me if I go in like this. She'll know I was down there. You've got to get me some clean shorts or trousers.'

'How can I get them out?'

'Maggie, you've got to get them,' says me. 'And don't say nothin', even if you get caught. Say anythin', but don't tell, quick!'

Wee Maggie runs back inside. The piss is stickin' my trousers to my skin. Bendin' down, I can really smell it. I kick off my boots and pull my trousers off over my feet.

'Mickey,' I hear whispered. Maggie comes with a plastic bag.

'Keep dick,' I say.

I peel off my pants and put the clean ones on and the new

shorts. I shove the wet stuff into the bag and put it in Killer's dog box. My stomach flips, but I can't think about that now.

'Is Paddy in?' I say.

'He just went upstairs,' says she.

My stomach flips again. I can't go to my room.

'What've you done?' says Ma, steppin' into the yard.

'Nothin',' I say. Does she know? I look at Maggie. She shrugs.

'No use lookin' at her. It's written all over yer face. What have you been up to, wee boy?'

'Nothin', Mammy, I swear to God.' Please God, help me. I'll do whatever you want.

'That's a sin before God, yer a wee liar. You're goin' up to see the Priest, I'm not jokin' ye.' Ma frowns and comes for me. 'What's that on our head?' I touch my head and I can feel warm goo. 'Get in here til I look at ye.' Ma walks into the house and I follow.

'I was runnin' down the Bray, Mammy, and I fell and I didn't want to tell you cuz I knew you'd shout at me.' I try to sound like I'm four. 'Didn't I, Maggie?'

'Yes, Mammy, he did. I saw him,' says she.

'Did you take her up there with ye? I'll break your neck, wee boy. She's not allowed up there. And ne'er are you. You've no sense. C'mere til I have a look.'

I walk over. She puts her hands through my hair.

'Awoah!' I say, more to get her on my side.

'Look at ye. You're bleedin'. You stay away from there, wee boy, do ye hear me? I'm sick tellin' ye. You'll have to go round to Mrs Brannagan and get some dumbbell stitches.'

'Ach, Mammy! Do I have to?'

'Yes, ye do. Go round right nigh and say yer Mammy sent ye.'

'Sake!' I say, kickin' the floor. 'Can Wee Maggie come with me?'

'No, she can't. Now, go on, get round there.' Ma twists her weddin' ring. 'And nigh I'll have to take her to work with me, wee boy.' Ma pats her purse in her pocket, grabs Maggie and heads into the livin' room. 'And before you ask, you can't take Killer.'

Another bomb goes off inside me. Through me. Inside my head is that noise you hear when the TV programmes finish at night.

'Where is that dog?' Ma asks.

I can't speak. My arm rises all by itself. I don't even tell it too. I point out at Killer's box.

'Go the back way, it's quicker.' Ma leaves and Maggie follows her.

I walk out the yard door, lift up the roof of Killer's dog box and climb inside, closin' the roof behind me. I'll go round to Mrs Brannagan's later.

I smell Killer on the scrap of carpet he slept on. I hug the old blanket I covered him with when I first got him and suck the corner where it's rough.

Whenever I close my eyes I see zombies, covered in blood, in No Man's Land. No Man's Land. Where the dead live. They're coming for me. I keep my eyes open in the dark.

# 12

THE ENTRY BEHIND Jamaica St. stinks. It's used as a rubbish dump. I wish Wee Maggie was here with me, but I can't tell her about Killer. She can't keep a secret. Look when I told her about Uncle Tommy. But she knows somethin's up cuz I wouldn't let her come with me.

Concentrate boy!

Up the short, steep hill of the big, bumpy Eggy field. It's empty. It's so big. It's covered in jaggie nettles and wet-the-beds. I'm not allowed up here, but I've never wanted to come cuz on hot days, when there's wavey-world over the tarmac, the Eggy smells of dead. I wonder how many of the bumps are just field and how many have dogs and cats buried in them. I heard there's people buried too. Touts. Grassers under the grass. I don't know if there is or not, but I've never heard of a secret that wasn't true.

Everyone thinks Killer squeezed out the back gates somehow. That he'll find his way home. I scratch my dumbbell stitches, which aren't really stitches at all. They're skinny plasters. Mrs Brannagan says there'll be a scar. I'm glad. I'll never forget then. Even when I'm all grown up.

I made a lollipop-stick flier like Ma's-a-Whore showed me, but like a crucifix. Holdin' it in prayer hands, eyes to the ground. No thinkin' of anythin' else. The funeral starts . . . now.

Slowly, I march across the field til there's a dip between two mounds. I kneel, layin' the crucifix gently, gently on the ground. With my fingers, I dig at the soil, fingernails stuffed full brown. I spit on my hands and wipe them on my jeans. Of course, they're just goin' to get dirty again. See. You should be goin' to St Gabe's, you're so stupid.

*Concentrate Mickey! Can you not even do that? For Killer.*

I dig. Two hands like paws. Diggin' like a dog makes a hidin' place for a bone.

When the hole is Killer-sized I sit up, take a slow, deep breath and knot my fingers together. Eyes closed, I see Killer lyin' dead in Flax St. I see me kneelin' over him. I pick him up and hold him in my arms like he's a little baby.

'I'm sorry, Killer. I'm really, really sorry.'

Killer's dead eyes open. *Are you really, Mickey?* he telepaths.

Yes.

*You have to tell Ma the truth.*

No. I can't. She'll kill me. They'll all hate me.

*Then you'll have to tell God.*

I thought he knew everythin'.

*You have to go to Confession.*

I can't tell.

*You have to, Mickey. Unless you wanna go to Hell. That's the way it is.*

Will God forgive me?

*Yes.*

Will you forgive me?

*Yes, I will. Then I'll rest in peace.* Killer's dead eyes close.

Goodbye, Killer.

I open my eyes and imagine him in my arms. I lay him in his grave and fill in the hole. I put the lollipop crucifix into his grave and bow my head.

'Oh God, please take Killer into Heaven with you. He can guard it. He'd bark to let you know if anybody's climbin' over the gates, just like he did for us. If you let him in, and promise not to send me to Hell, I do solemnly swear I'll go to Confession.'

I pull out some wet-the-beds and place them beside the crucifix. I stand up and genuflect to the grave and bless myself. 'Amen.'

~

I pass the shop on the corner of Fartin's street with the poster in the window. *Loose Talk Cost Lives.* Isn't Confession 'loose talk'? But Priests can't tell anyone. I saw it in a filim. Montgomery Clift wasn't allowed to tell, even though the man was a murderer!

I look up Fartin's street. I wish he could come with me, but I have to do this alone. On the Crumlin Road, I check both ways. Way down the road, our ones are smashin' the windows of a city bus, hijackin' it, too far away to be trouble for me. I run across to the Chapel.

I bless myself with the cold water in the wee font. Inside – cold silence. Why is it always dark in here, even when it's warm and sunny outside? Marble and gold, chalices and candlesticks. Like a palace. Or a filim set.

Down the aisle I check the Priest names outside the Confession huts, lookin' for one I don't know. I always say the same things in Confession: 'I was cheeky to m'Mammy' and 'I said a bad word, Father'. I never have anythin' really bad. Except today.

It's dark in there and the wee shutter he opens to talk to you has a grill so he can't see you, but he can recognise your voice. I could put on an accent, use my actin' skills, but if he wants he has a wee curtain he can look out when I leave.

The new Priest is makin' a bee line for me.

'Ah, Mickey Donnelly, how are you?' says he.

'OK, Father.' Does he remember the name of everyone in Ardoyne?

'So you've finally come for our wee chat then?'

'No, Father, well . . . I mean, I have to go to Confession,' I say, bowin' my head.

'OK, Mickey, follow me.'

He walks up the altar steps before I can answer. My stomach twists as I follow through a door behind the altar and down a corridor of dark brown, shiny wood. It smells of polish and old sofas. The floorboards creak, like in scary filims. No good tryin' to sneak around in here. He directs me into a room and closes the door behind us. He sits on a big, dark wooden chair with carved arms and red velvet cushions. A wooden throne.

'Now then, Mickey, let's talk. Sit down.' He points to a pew and a small wooden chair. God must love wood. Ah, Jesus – carpenter – wood. Got it.

'Are you ready to make your Confession?' says he.

'Are we not goin' into a Confession box?' says me.

'Och, well, I don't like using them, I prefer to sit with people in front of me. I think it's very old fashioned to put people in a scary, dark room, as though sin was something to hide from.'

'I've never done it this way before,' says me. I look at the floor. I really don't want to look at him. It's bad enough havin' to tell. But havin' him see me . . . Can I make a break for it now?

'Well, if it helps, you can turn your chair around and face the wall or close your eyes,' he says.

I turn my chair *and* close my eyes. Deep breath. I know my lines.

'Bless me Father, for I have sinned. It's been . . . ' *about two months* '. . . two weeks since my last Confession. I've said some bad words, and I've been cheeky to m'Mammy.'

'Well, are you sorry for saying those bad words?'

'Yes, Father. And I'm goin' to try really hard not to say them again,' says me, to show him I was a good boy once.

'And what about this being cheeky?'

'No, Father, I'm not goin' to be cheeky again,' says me. I'm a good boy, see?

'Well, you probably will, Mickey. None of us are saints. We all make mistakes. I sin and have to go to Confession too,' says he.

I near have convulsions. 'Really?' I turn and open my eyes. He smiles. I believe him. I turn back, closin' me eyes again.

'Let's just say that you're going to try really hard not to be cheeky. And if you are then you'll make it up to your mother. You love your mother, don't you?'

'Yes,' says me.

'And you wouldn't want her to be sad, would you?'

'No.'

'Well, you make it up to your mother and help her around the house. She doesn't have an easy time of it, what with your father not around.'

'No,' I say. Bloody Ardoyne smoke signals. Ma will hate that he knows.

'And is that what your mother wanted me to talk to you about?' says he.

'No, well, sort of, I was messin' about in Chapel that day. But it wasn't my fault. My mate was makin' me laugh.'

'So, it wasn't you, it was your friend?' says he.

I know from school this never works, even when it's true. 'It was me too,' says me.

'Now that's better, isn't it? It wasn't that hard to tell the truth, was it? And don't you feel better now?'

'Yes.' I feel better cuz he's bein' so nice. I rub my hands between my thighs and wriggle on the cushions.

'Now, is there anything else before I give you your penance?'

'Yes, Father,' says me, swallowin' ten gobstoppers covered in sand.

'Take your time.'

In the silence, I open my eyes. I see my reflection in the window in front of me. My frown. I lick my fingers and press down my cow's lick. Underneath my face, letters dance, jumpin' over each other like a Disney cartoon. Two hands enter, fingers dancin', kickin' the letters. The letters from *LOOSE TALK*. The hands come either side of my face and cover my mouth.

I'm not goin' to let them stop me. I promised. And I don't want to go Hell.

'I did a very bad thing, Father,' I mumble.

'Go on.'

'I can't, Father, it's too bad,' says me. I look for somethin' I can throw up into.

'I'm sure it's not as bad as you think.'

'It is, Father. It's really, really bad.'

'Well, think about it. Maybe you're not ready to tell me. You can always come back,' says he.

Yes, yes, come back.

No. I don't want to do this again. 'Can I whisper it?' I say.

'Yes,' says he. Screechin' on the floor as his throne moves closer.

'I took our wee dog Killer out without tellin' m'Mammy. I brought him down Flax Street where I'm not allowed. And then there was a bomb and he got hit by a Saracen and got killed and it's all my fault.' I look at the window to try to see his face behind me but I can't.

'Oh Mickey,' he sighs. 'It wasn't really your fault.'

'But I wasn't allowed to take him without tellin' Mammy and I wasn't allowed down where the bomb was,' I say. He's wrong. It is my fault.

'OK, Mickey, OK. So you didn't do what you were told. But it was a terrible accident. You're not responsible for that. Is your mother blaming you?'

I go white like a zombie. I wish I was dead. I feel dead. Dead but full of feelin's. Bad feelin's. This might be what Hell is like. I want to run.

'Mickey?' I hear in the distance. 'What did your mother . . . You haven't told her,' says he.

'How did you know? Did God tell you? Am I goin' to Hell? Am I?' says me, heart thumpin', the taste of metal in my mouth.

'No, Mickey. God didn't tell me, and you're not going to go to Hell. But you know what you have to do?'

'Confess,' says me.

'Well, yes, but . . . What do you think will happen if you tell your mother what happened?'

'She'll kill me. And not just her. My brother and sisters will too.' I start cryin'. They're goin' to hate me so much. And not messin' either. Hate me deep down and forever. Like I hate Da.

'I know it seems that way but they won't kill you. It will be hard for them to hear . . .'

'They will. You don't know them, Father,' says me, hardly able to understand my own words through the blubberin'.

'But Mickey, you know you're not going to get any peace until you tell them. I could help if you want,' he says, puttin' an arm on my shoulder.

'No, Father, please don't make me,' I say, turnin' to him. 'Please don't make me tell them. They'll hate me. They all hate me anyway.'

'Who hates you, Mickey?'

'Everybody. Everybody hates me. And they'll all hate me more.' I can't help cryin'. 'The wee girls all hate me, I'm not even allowed to play with them, anyway, and wee boys hate me, call me names and make fun of me.' I cry into my hands.

'What names do they call you?'

'I don't want to say. It's bad.'

'You can tell me anything,' say he.

'No, I can't.' I shake my head in my hands.

'When I was young the boys used to call me names too.'

I catch my breath. 'Did they?'

'They would shout, in the street, in school,' he says.

I try to stop cryin' and look at him. 'You're just sayin' that.'

'It's the truth,' says he, noddin'. 'Do you know what they used to call me, Mickey?'

'What?'

'They used to call me gay and a Ginny Anne.'

'You?' I can't believe it. He's doesn't sound gay.

'Yes.'

'Why?'

'Because I was different.'

'I'm different,' I say.

'I can see that,' he says. 'It's OK to be different. It gets easier as you get older.'

'Because your voice drops, and everythin'?'

'Yes, partly.'

'It's because I like different filims and actin' and . . .'

'You like the theatre then?'

'I saw a play in a garage.' I think about Martine and hit a redner. 'And I love brilliant actors in filims.'

'Wait there,' he says and leaves.

I look out the window at the green grass and trees. Trees

are lovely. I only see them from far away on the mountain-side.

'Here you go,' he says, the door creakin' closed behind him. He hands me a big, thick book. 'Actors of stage and screen,' he says.

I take the book. It looks too grown-up, but if I'm really grateful he might forgive me or give me less penance.

'Thank you, Father, this is great,' I say.

'Look Mickey, there's much to discuss here. A lot has come up today. I've house calls to make. Come up again, we can talk more then. I can see you're not ready to tell your Mammy about your dog yet.'

'Can I have my forgiveness from God now, because I've confessed?'

'Yes, Mickey, but part of your penance is that you have to consider tellin' the truth. Pray to God for strength and guid-ance.'

'OK, Father.'

He mumbles prayers. I take a deep breath. Out the window, blue sky. Not a cloud. Like my soul now. Clear. No clouds. And blue. And my soul is blue cuz I'm a boy. No bein' stupid anymore.

'Amen,' says he.

'Amen,' I answer.

Father holds the door open. 'Come and see me again soon and we can talk more.'

I nod as I pass him. I didn't hear what my penance was. I'll say ten Hail Marys and ten Our Fathers on the way home. I've gone to Confession and that was the deal. But I'm not tellin' our ones. No way.

Down the altar steps, I run along the aisle to the doors.

'Runnin' in Chapel, Michael Donnelly. Tut, tut,' says some aul doll. 'Wait til I tell your mother.'

You can't get away with anythin' in Ardoyne. And I don't even know her and she knows me. Wait! Someone might have seen me in the bomb with Killer. Someone might tell.

I check no Prods are waitin' to get any of us comin' out of the Chapel. Black tyre smoke bubbles from the bus that's now on fire. Our ones dance on the pavement wavin' scarves like rags to a bull, tryin' to get the Prods to come out from the other side of the street. Two Jeeps screech out of the Shankill and our ones run to the barricades at Flax Street. I run across into upper Ardoyne.

~

'*We are the Ardoyne girls,*
*We wear our hairs in curls,*
*We wear our knickers to our knees,*
*If ye please . . .*
*We never smoke or drink,*
*That's what our parents think,*
*We are the Ardoyne girls.*'

The girls are at the gable showin' off to the boys who're buildin' the bonfire. Why don't boys sing? You weren't allowed to like singin' in Holy Cross. Boys are only allowed to sing if they're at a football match.

The bonfire is for the Feast of Our Lady. Everybody in Ardoyne says *bone*fire, but Mr McManus told us they're actually called *bon*fires. I'm the only one who says it right. I used to think people only hated bad guys. People who were wrong. But they hate you when you're right too.

The bonfire's on the waste ground in front of the knocked-down houses. There's fencin' round the waste ground now. They were goin' to start buildin' more new houses, but the

IRA stopped them til the bonfire's burnt.

The boys have built a wee hut like an Indian tepee made of wood. Our Paddy tells them all what to do and they do it. He's the Big Chief. He never comes home, he even sleeps in the tepee. He says it's in case ones from the other streets come to steal the wood for *their* bonfire.

Stayin' away from Paddy means I can't have anythin' to do with the bonfire when everyone else in the whole world is part of it. But I don't care. Who wants to run round the streets collectin' dirty old wood and rubbish in a half-wrecked wheelbarrow nicked from the buildin' site, just to sit inside a stupid, smelly, bonfire tepee with boys?

I wish Killer was here. I miss him. I miss Wee Maggie too. I'm afraid she'll be able to telepath me and find out about Killer, so I hide from her. I've thought about tellin' Ma, like the Priest said, but no way.

Paddy talks to some boys and walks with them down the entry. Two stay behind and keep dick. I run across the waste ground then zigzag through the new estate to the entry and hide behind the bins. I watch Paddy and the older boys. The way they walk and stand and laugh and spit and smoke. Nothin' like me at all. And nothin' like I want to be either. Our Paddy's the worst. We haven't been in the same airspace for more than a second since the bomb. Since Killer. But I've watched him. I don't know if he saw Killer with me in the bomb. I was hopin' I'd be able to tell by starin' at him.

'What you doin', Mickey?' a voice from behind I recognise.

'Jesus, Wee Maggie, you scared the shit out of me!' says me.

'Why are you're hidin' in the bins?' says she.

'I'm not,' says me. 'I was just tyin' my lace.'

'No you weren't. I've been watchin' ye.'

'Since when?'

'I watched ye up the Eggy too. What were you doin'?' says

she.

She's been bloody followin' me. 'Just playin' a game,' I say. My whole head is throbbin'.

'Was it a game about Killer?' says she.

I lean back onto the wall. How does she know? How . . . telepathy! I knew it. I snap a look at her. She's reading my mind.

Think of a brick wall. That's what they do to block out those kids in that film *Village of the Damned*.

'You're not tellin' me somethin',' says she.

*Think of a brick wall. Think of a brick wall.* I've got to get away. Improvise.

'Yes, I'm not tellin' you that I don't want to play with you anymore. You're too young. I'm a big boy now. I'm going to big school. And you're a wee girl,' says me. 'I'm not your friend anymore.'

She stands still. Frozen like the Dolls from Martine's play. Starin' at me with mad eyes, just like one of those kids from the filim. She's tryin' her telepathy. To get over the wall.

'That's why I'm hidin'. I'm hidin' from you. Cuz I didn't want to have to tell you to your face. But there. Now you know. Now, go away and leave me alone and stop followin' me like a weirdo.'

I run away. Through the maze of the new estate where nobody knows me. Run til breathin' feels like a knife slicin' in my chest. I want breathin' to cut me open and this bomb to get out of my chest. I hate you, Mickey Donnelly. I hate your guts.

## 13

'WHAT THE FUCK are you doing in there?' Our Paddy shouts, lettin' the roof fall out of his hand and whack the wall behind. He reaches into Killer's box and pulls me up by my T-shirt. I hear rippin'.

'Watch my good T-shirt. I'm tellin' Ma on you!' I shout. 'Awooahh!' my legs crack against the wood as he drags me out. 'You're hurtin' me!'

He leans down to my face. I don't look away. I hate him. Just as much as Da. I don't care if he saw me with Killer. He'll be in bigger trouble than me.

'What were you doin' in there?'

'Nothin',' I say.

'You are a fucking weirdo.'

'No, *you* are,' says me.

'Did you touch anythin'?'

'No,' I say.

He looks past me into the box. 'Stay out of there from now on. If I catch you even lookin' in there again I'm going to ram my fist down your throat.' He grinds his fist into my cheek.

I shake my head to get his fist off. 'Leave go.' I pull on his hands.

'And don't you ever say a word about what happened, do you hear me?' He stabs his finger in my face. 'People can get put in prison. They can get killed.'

Good. So I can blackmail him if I want. I'm going to get him back for this. He hasn't said anything about Killer. He musn't have seen. The power is mine.

'You can get killed, Mickey. For opening your mouth. Do you understand? You gabshite. And don't leave the street. If I see you about those places again, I'll kill you myself.'

What's it got to do with bloody him anyway? He can't make me. He won't even know what I do. I'll show him. I might even join the IRA and be better at it than him and get to be his boss.

He lets me go. I see his grip bag on the ground. I walk to the kitchen door. He lifts the grip bag and unzips it.

'Get away, Mickey.' He points to the kitchen. 'I mean it.'

'You're not my Da!' I shout and run like shite through the house and out.

~

I throw away the old dead ones and put some fresh wet-the-beds beside the crucifix on Killer's grave. They look nice. If I can't be near him in his dog box, I can be up here. I know I'm not allowed on the Eggy, but I can't see anyone around. The glue-sniffers are in the old factory, not here on the field.

Flowers aren't enough so I'm going to catch a bee in a jam jar so Killer can watch it fly round and round. Like him havin' his own goldfish.

Ticklin' on the back of my hand. A creepy crawly. I jump and shake to get it off me. I don't want any of them wee friggers gettin' in my ears. Gives me the heebie-jeebies even thinkin' about it. This boy in our street, an earywig crawled inside him through his ear. It laid eggs and they hatched and the baby crawlies came out and ate his brain. Now he lives in Purdisburn Loony Bin. Fact!

I sit on the grass beside a clump of brown and cream little bee flowers. They look like nothin', but bees love them. I put some in the jar for the bee to eat. I'm gonna be really nice to the bee. Take care of it. I already put a hole in the lid with a knife so it can breathe.

Loads of bees everywhere. I watch a big fat one as it moves from one flower to the other. It knows I've spotted it so I look around like I couldn't give a frig. *Just you sit right there.* I hold the jar far away from me in case I miss. I don't want to get stung. Jimmy Carville told me he got stung once and his head swelled up. He had to have an operation or his head would've exploded. Fact!

Pounce. Got it. The bee buzzes loudly, really losin' the bap. I slide the lid under the jar carefully and pick it up, quickly screwin' the lid on. I can feel the buzz when the big bee bangs off the glass. Once, this kid came down our street with six bees in a jar. Up close, the noise of the six bees fuzzin' off the glass made me feel sick. You could tell they hated bein' trapped, squashed so close together. You just knew they were goin' to end up killin' each other.

I place the jar beside the crucifix and surround it with wet-the-beds. 'There you go, Killer. Isn't that nice?' He doesn't answer. 'He'll keep you company when I'm not here. Shall we give him a name? Billy the Bee?' Can't call him Billy, only Prod's are called Billy. 'We'll have a think, eh?'

I pick the grass. A blade. Like a sword. I reckon if I was a super hero I'd have this as my weapon. No-one would expect it. 'En garde!' I'd say. Villains would laugh when I pulled it out. I'd watch their faces drop as my blade of grass grew into my special sword that could cut through anythin'. Though no-one uses swords anymore. They just use a gun and shoot you. I could join the IRA and learn to shoot.

I wonder if they're trainin' Our Paddy in special secret camps down in Armagh. If I joined I could go to their rifle ranges and shoot at cardboard Brits. I'd love that. I'd be brilliant at it. Some things you just know.

If I was in America, I wouldn't even need to join the IRA to do that. I could go to the fair, like they have in filims. America has everythin'. Imagine. You'd get to shoot just by payin' the rifle range man. The Rifle Ranger.

When I get to America, I'm goin' to get a job at a fair so I can shoot all night after people have gone home. I'll get dead good and the Rifle Ranger will say, 'Hey Mickey, God damn it kid, I've never seen anybody shoot like that. Not in all my born days. Hot Diggity Dog!' And then he'll bring this man to see me shootin'. The man will say, 'I want you for the Olympic Team.' And I'll say, 'No problem, Mister, but I have to shoot for Ireland, not America.' And he'd say, 'Okay, we couldn't let a talent like yours go to waste and besides, we God damn love the Irish people.'

I'll win Ireland's first Olympic gold medal. And they'll make a filim about me. Especially if I collapse at the last minute cuz I'm secretly dyin'. Everybody would love a filim about an Olympic gold medal winnin' cancer boy who died when he shot his last winnin' cardboard man in the heart.

When I get to America.

'Sorry for spacin' out, Killer. I'll come again. I love you. Amen.'

I get up and walk towards the old factory. I used to think that there was loads of chickens in the egg factory makin' eggs, but somebody told me that the eggs were brought here and the factory just put them into boxes. But then how did they get the eggs to the egg factory, if they weren't in boxes already? That's one for *Arthur C Clarke's Mysterious World*.

I head for the hole in the factory wall where a window used to be. You can see inside. I'm not allowed up the Eggy, but I'm specially not allowed in the old factory. I climb through and stumble on bricks. It stinks of knocked-down wall, piss and glue.

Noise. Freeze. A ghost? They say it's haunted. I edge further into the room, over the bits of broken ceilin', like someone from a horror filim you shout 'Don't do it!' at. There's a hole smashed through the back wall. I can see deep inside. It's dark but the missin' slates in the roof lets in lines of light like you see comin' through clouds in holy pictures of Heaven.

Glue-Sniffers. I can smell. Three lumps take shape on a broken wall. Two girls and a boy. The boy and a girl in a ra-ra skirt are kissin'. The other girl has a plastic bag over her face. Even from here the smell is disgustin'. Sniffin' must do somethin' amazin' or why would you stick that? People say that glue-sniffers are dirtbirds, but that doesn't stop them. Maybe sniffin' glue makes you not care what people call you.

Glue Girl passes the bag to Ra-Ra Girl. I never thought glue-sniffers would share things. Maybe they're nice. Not like people say. The boy slips the hand on Ra-Ra Girl and moves his hand up and down her fanny. She puts her hand between his legs and rubs too. I like watchin'. Them not knowin'. I feel a crampin' between my legs, in the place I always forget is there, between my bum and my willy. I pulse it like a slow heartbeat and feel my willy bounce.

Helicopters. Low and loud. They have these special machines that can detect you through walls by the heat comin' from your body. I saw it on *Tomorrow's World*. I want to keep watchin' but don't want the Brits in the helicopter seein' me in here. And I'm not supposed to be here, they could land and arrest me. I tiptoe away, climb through the window hole, out onto the path.

Walkin' the Eggy field, the helicopters chop above, spyin'. Somebody's always watchin' you in Ardoyne. At least they know I've left the factory and I'm not doin' anythin' bad. They fly off over Jamaica Street.

Up the field towards the Bray. I think of the day Da took me up there. Da and me and Killer. Only me left.

I hear a noise and turn. Teresa McAllister. She's a dirtbird. Nobody likes her. And not me. She lives way up our street and we don't mix with themin's. She's wearin' a ra-ra skirt like one of the glue-sniffers. Not *like* – it's the exact same one. Teresa McAllister *is* Glue-sniffin' Ra-Ra Girl that Glue Boy slipped the hand on. I'm gonna tell everybody. The boys. I could tell them. They might like me then. Not that I even care.

'Alright, Mickey, whaddaye doin'?' she asks.

'Nothin',' I say, kickin' some grass.

'C'mon and sit down with me,' she says, sittin' on a bump. That could be a dead dog.

I don't have anyone else to play with and nobody can see. I'll never say I played with her. I sit near her, but not on the bump. She slides over beside me.

'D'ye want some?' she says, passin' me a glue bag.

'I don't do it,' says me, rubbin' my hands on my knees.

'Why not?' says she.

'I don't like it.'

'I bet you've never tried it,' says she.

'Aye, I have,' says me.

'Prove it.' She pushes the bag into my hands.

There's no way round this. It can't look like she's braver than me when she's just a girl. 'OK, then,' tryin' to sound like a glue-sniffer. 'You first, but,' I say, givin' her it back so I can see how.

She grips the top of the bag and pulls the handles out over her fist, like a magician with a hanky. Her fist opens and she puts the openin' over her nose and mouth, breathin' in and pushin' the air out of the bag from the bottom with her other hand. It stinks. She passes it to me.

'What does it do?' I ask.

'See, I knew you hadn't done it.'

'It was ages ago,' I say.

'You get dizzy and you go out of it, away far away.' She laughs and lies back on the bump. 'You'd better do it.' She hands the bag over.

I want to be far away. Out of it all. And maybe I could be friends with the cool St. Gabriel's boys if I can do it. I put the bag over my face and hold my breath. I push the bag towards my mouth and breathe a little in.

'See, I told you I've done it before.' I pass the bag back.

'C'mere and help me up.'

Lyin' down she looks even fatter than normal. I crawl over. I'm dizzy. Woo. I try to pull her up. Jesus, she's heavy. I swear to God she weighs a ton. *Two Ton Tessie*. Fat people shouldn't lie down cuz they look fatter and you can't get them back up again. I laugh.

'What are you laughin' at?' She laughs too.

My head is throbbin'. Heavy. But light and dizzy too. Funny.

'You have to help too,' I say.

'I am.'

I put all my weight into pullin' but she doesn't even budge. The effort is makin' me dizzier and spacier. I stop tryin', and as I do she pulls me down on top of her. I put my hands out to stop my fall and they land on her diddies.

'Fuckin' hell!' I shout. She's wettin' herself. She wraps her arms round me, tight. My first feel of diddies. She keeps laughin'. So I stay there. And give them a squeeze. She wants me to lumber her. But I've never done it before. Little kisses, yes. If she lets boys slip the hand she's not gonna be a little kisser.

I don't like her. I mean, I'd never have her as my girlfriend. No way! But if I go away now, she'll tell people I wouldn't lumber her. You have to lumber a girl even if she's ugly, cuz if you don't you're a big poof. But if I said that I lumbered Teresa McAllister everyone would sleg me cuz she's an ugly stinker. You can't win. I guess at least I'd know how to actually do it.

'D'ye have a girlfriend?' she asks.

'Yes.'

'No ye don't. Who?'

'Jackie O'Halloran.'

'Who's that?'

'I met her at this roller disco up the Falls.'

She'll never know that's my old teacher, Mrs O'Halloran, cuz only boys went to my school.

'How did ye get way up the Falls?' she asks.

'M'Da drove me.'

'You're a wee liar.'

I am. I thought she would believe me.

'Anyway, ye haven't got a girlfriend in Ardoyne, have ye?' she says.

Does that mean you're allowed two girlfriends as long as they live in different places? It's hard keepin' my face from hers lyin' on top of her. She's not as bad lookin' as I've always thought. I mean, if she wasn't Teresa McAllister, like. If I didn't know her, she'd look alright. She must fancy me. Nobody's ever fancied me.

I move my hand down on her leg. I want to try as many

things as possible. I could do anythin' I want cuz it's just her. Teresa doesn't say anythin'. I move my hand up her leg and touch her fanny.

'Fuck off!' She laughs and pushes me off. I make a funny face to say it was just a joke. She laughs even more.

'Look over there.' I point. She looks and I put my hand on her fanny again.

'Fuck off!' she shouts, laughin'.

I pull my hand away and pull a face like *Who was that? What happened there?* She thinks this is dead funny. I check if anyone's comin'. It's a bad thing I'm goin' to do, but it's an even badder thing to be caught doin' it to a dirtbird.

'Somebody's comin',' she says.

'Where?' I say and look around panicin'. She grabs my dick.

'What do you think you're doin'?' I jump up and start to sway. She laughs her head off. She thinks everythin's funny. Does she ever stop that laughin'? I feel dizzy. My head thumpin'. What am I doin'? Killer. I came here for Killer. What's just happened? It's the glue. It must have been the glue. I'm a good boy.

I stagger off. I can hear her followin' me. I juke round. She's runnin' after me. She thinks this is a game. 'Go away!'

I clear the field. On the path my head clears and I can run properly, across the bottom of the Bray, past a burnt-out car that's been hijacked. Some boys are flyin' down the Hills usin' the bonnet as a sleigh. They'd never let me play with them. And anyway, Teresa would only catch up and scunder me.

How could I do that? What is wrong with me? She'd better not tell anybody I slipped the hand on her or I'll kill her. I'll just say she's a liar. Who would believe her anyway?

I did get to slip the hand but. Only on the outside of the

knickers. But still. I've touched a fanny. I wish I could tell the boys. They'd think I'm like them. But I'd never tell anyone I sniffed glue. That'd make me a dirtbird.

~

From the corner of entry I watch Wee Maggie play with the girls. I wish I could play with her. She doesn't even miss me. I can't believe she hasn't tried to make up with me. I've stepped out twice to make sure she knows I'm here. I'm sure I could tell her about Killer now. I know I could trust her. We're best friends. And special brother and sister. I telepath to her. *Come here. Maggie. I'm sorry.* It's not workin'. Have I broken it? Is it gone forever?

I step out and cough loudly. She looks over. I look away. She definitely knows now to come over. But she doesn't come. I don't care. I kick the wall. I run right through the girls lookin' straight ahead so they can see I don't even care about them. Ha! Straight into the house. I hear Ma in the kitchen. She must have a break from work.

'Mammy!' I shout. 'It's your favourite son.' My face drops when I see a man with a plastic bag over his hair, with two tiny streams of black gloop drippin' down his forehead.

'Are you a hairdresser now, Mammy?' I say.

'Yes, son, that's right,' says she. How many jobs does Ma have?

'Alright, Mickey?' he says.

How does he know my name? 'Yeah,' I say. Ah. It's long-lost Uncle Tommy, the IRA man. He's shaved off his beard.

'Go on now, out you go,' Ma says, pushin' me. She stops to get her purse from the hearth.

'But Mammy, I don't want to play outside anymore.'

'Here's 10p. Go and get yourself a mix-up,' says Ma.

This must be the only time in my entire life I don't want a 10p mix-up. 'Can I not stay with you?' says me.

'Mickey, get out before I lose the bap,' says she.

I kick the floor. 'Sake!' I feel her hands push me but I try to stick my feet to the carpet. She pushes me out the front door and shuts it.

'I hate this house,' I shout in the letter box.

I want Killer. I hear the girls singin' some stupid song. I see the boys all shoutin' and buildin' their big stupid bonfire. I kick our front door and run. I'm dead when I get home. Not that Ma will even be in tonight. She's never bloody in anymore. Always workin'. Bloody Da. It's all his fault. If I ever see him again I'm goin' to kill him. So help me God.

# 14

'ARE YOU SURE you don't mind, Mickey, son?' says Minnie the Tick Woman.

'Don't sweat it, Mrs Maloney,' I say, like an American.

'Don't sweat it?' She giggles into her hand. You'd swear there was a hanky in it and she was a Southern belle in Tennessee. I turn left and stamp, like a Confederate soldier. 'Not that way,' she giggles. 'You'll have to go to the shops up the top of the street to get the meat.'

I'm not allowed up there, but it's too late to tell her now when I'm in the middle of a performance. I spin on my heels like Michael Jackson and head the other way.

'Make sure you tell him it's a fiver, too.' Aul Sammy is famous for tryin' some way of doin' you. Pretendin' you gave him a pound note when it was a fiver, is one of them.

I salute Minnie. She giggles and I run off 'Meep Meep' like Road Runner.

'*Don't sweat it, honey.*' Rizzo says that to Sandy in *Grease*. I love *Grease*. We had it on pirate. It was inside the Betamax when Da sold it last year. I used to watch *Grease* all the time. Rizzo is the best one in it. She's so funny and she has the best two songs – 'Sandra Dee', which is the funniest song I've ever heard, and 'There Are Worse Things I Could Do', which is the saddest song I've ever heard. I cried at that bit every single time. And at every episode of *Little*

*House on the Prairie*, *The Littlest Hobo* and sometimes *Flipper*.

When I get to the border of the new houses, I pass Martine's house. I look through her window but can't see her. 'Clear off!' her Ma shouts. I didn't see her sittin' on the sofa. She's goin' to think I'm really ignorant. I speed-walk away.

I walk past the girls all playin' together, Evil Briege rulin' the roost as usual. Martine's leanin' against the fences at the back of the new Jamaica Court. It's the only one of the new street names I know. She sees me. How did she know to look? We must be connected. Maybe we're growin' a telepathic connection. I smile and wave. Martine checks Briege then looks to me and smiles too.

*Right, don't blow it Mickey. Let her see you be cool.* I dander like I've rehearsed. Like an actor. There's only two cool ways to go up the street – run or dander. Runnin' is cool cuz ye must be doin' somethin' important to run, or you're runnin' cuz you're in trouble. Both make you cool. Danderin' is cool cuz that means you don't care about anythin' enough to get there fast, or you're not scared of nothin' enough to run from it. Just walkin' is definitely not cool. The uncoolist way to get anywhere. Now I know why they say 'act cool'. It's about actin'. Everything. And I'm goin' to be cool always from now on.

Down the entry I see Our Measles sittin' on a wall with her mates, smokin'. 'I see you smokin',' I shout, and wag my finger.

'Aye, well, I see you walkin' like John Wayne,' she says. Her mates laugh.

I bloody hate John Wayne. Da does a bad impression when he's drunk. He should leave the actin' to the experts – me.

'More like John Travolta,' I say and do the *Saturday Night Fever* walk. They all wet themselves. I'm a hit.

Measles runs over. 'Where you goin'?'

'The shops for Minnie,' I say. 'But it's really for Mammy.'

She squints. 'Don't you hang around up there. Come you straight back.'

'OK,' I say and do an encore of my John Travolta for her and her mates.

'You're walkin' like you've shit yourself,' shouts Measles and her mates laugh with their hands on their fannies, legs crossed. They're so loud. Wantin' people to look at them. I walk on. 'I've seen your dirty trunks,' Measles shouts. She has. She washes them by hand in the kitchen sink. Measles is showin' off to her mates. I can't let her win me but.

'Yeah, well, do your friends know Ma uses your aul knickers as a dishcloth?' I shout and run.

At the end of Jamaica Street I check she hasn't run after me. I check I haven't lost the fiver either. One day, when I grow up, I'm goin' to have a fiver of my own and I'm goin' to spend it all on sweets.

I check there's no Prods or gangs about in Alliance Avenue and cross to the corrugated iron barricades. There's a tiny little door to the Prods. You're not allowed to use it. You'd be murdered. They've started callin' them *peace lines* which really makes me laugh cuz actually this is where people come to kill each other.

Aul Sammy's shop is next to it. Painted black. Metal sheets nailed on the door. And painted black. The windows are thick, with wire inside them, so the broken bits stay stuck to it. Oh, and they're painted black too. It looks like the entrance to Hell.

'Right?' I say, like I don't hate Sammy's guts.

'Aye, how's yer Ma?' says he, like he really hates mine.

I've only ever been up here with her. 'OK,' says me.

Mrs Maloney told me to give the note to Sammy. Like I can't just get her the messages myself. I mean, does she think

I'm 4½? Right. Six big potatoes. No problem there. I kneel down and feel through the sack of potatoes. I get her the biggest ones. Bigger than my two hands. *He* wouldn't have given her the biggest ones. I put them in the clear plastic bags he has beside the box. I could steal some. What could I use them for? Concentrate, Mickey!

*You have five seconds before we shoot* – steak and kidney pie . . . 4. Eggs, yes. 3. Fairy liquid, aha. 2. Peas, sure thing. 1. Steak and kidney pie. *Zero.* Yes! Saved. I will not die today. *Lasers down, boys. Fingers off the triggers fellas.*

Dr. Whites. *DR. WHITES!* Boys don't buy *them*. That's why she wanted me to give Sammy the note. How can I give him it now? Why didn't I just do what I was told? Ma says I never listen.

'What are ye lookin' for?' he spits.

'Nothin',' I say, goin' purple.

'Suit yerself.'

A man comes into the shop hobblin', with someone behind him. I hide back down on the floor playin' with the potatoes.

'For fuck's sake, son, what are ye lookin' for?' snaps Sammy.

I have to tell him. But I'm scundered. I steal some of his bags down my keks to make him pay. I walk over to the counter and put the note down and point to where it says . . .

'Dr. White's?' He spits and rubs it into it the floor with his shoe.

I nod, my stomach squeezed by a giant's fist. He gets his pole from under the counter, reaches to the top shelf behind him, snags a packet, pullin' it down. Instead of puttin' the Dr. White's straight into a bag, like he would if Ma was here, he puts them on the counter and looks at the man who just came in. The bastard's makin' me pay for not lettin' him help me. I know people. I know their evil ways.

Now I see who's behind the man. Ma's-a-Whore. Watchin' me squirm. That must be his Da. He had his knees done and was put out of the district years ago. They must have allowed him back or he'd be dead.

With a massive redner I put my fiver on the counter. Sammy sorts out the change from the til, chucklin'.

'That's a fiver by the way,' I say. Ha! That won him.

He looks at me like he'll slit my throat and slams the change down on the counter. I give him a big dirty look, lift my messages and leave.

I squeeze past the soldier crouched down in the hall. One of my bags catches on his rifle.

'Alright, kid? Do ya wanna 'ave a look fru 'ere?' says the soldier. *Fru*, that's funny. 'Have you seen one of these before? In your house, maybe?'

He's obviously new cuz they only ask you that when they get you away from everyone, tryin' to make you tell on your Da. Ma's-a-Whore comes behind me. He could tell the IRA I'm a traitor cuz that Brit talked to me. Report me to the Incident Centre. It's like our Police Station as we don't use the real Peelers cuz they're all Prods.

'Why don't you go back where you belong?' I say, with a big dirty look, just to prove I'm no traitor.

There's another Brit crouched inside the hall of the sweet shop two doors up. Why are they on their own? You never see just two. They're definitely new. I should really wait til Minnie gives me some change for goin' to the shop, but I want some sweets now. Hmmm . . . a couple of sweeties. She won't notice if I bought just a couple.

'Donnelly buys fanny pads!' I hear Ma's-a-Whore shout. I turn to see him laughin'. How could he scunder me like that in front of a Brit? That's not right. I'll report *him* to the Incident Centre!

His Da comes out and they cross the road to our street. I hang back in case he's told his Da what I said about the Ma the last time we fought. They could be waitin' round the corner to get me.

The bell above the door goes as I push it open, past the other Brit.

'What can I do you for?' asks the Sweet Shop Man, as he comes from out the back, not lookin' at me but clockin' the Brit in his hall.

'Will you give us a Refresher and two Black Jacks, please?' I say.

'Please, is it?' He smiles.

I put the 3p down, grab the sweets from on top of the newspapers and head out to the hallway. I peel the wrapper off a Black Jack and chuck it in my gub. The Sweet Shop Man comes out with grills for his windows. That means riot. How does he know? I look around. I'd better get out of here.

Crossin' to the top of our street I see boys playin' football. Ma's-a-Whore is shoutin', pushing one of the smaller ones, his Da gone. Could be waitin' for me. I turn right into the entry at the back of our street.

Shots. I hear runnin'. I look back. A man runnin' down the entry towards me. I step face first into the back yard wall of a house. Head down. *Don't look.* The running goes by. I look right to see him running to the bottom of our street. He jumps and climbs up over someone's back gates. I look left to see one of the new soldiers lyin' in the middle of the road. His head in a puddle of blood. I wonder which one is dead?

Soldiers run towards me. I speed walk cuz I can't run with all the messages knockin' off my legs. Fast as I can. I don't look back.

'Kid!' Shoutin' behind me. 'Hold it, kid!'

I stop.

'Where did he go?' a Brit says.

'I . . . that way,' I say, noddin' towards the cut-through to Etna drive. I remember my acting. 'I swear.' I frown and nod. They run towards the cut-through and I keep going.

I can't wait to tell Fartin' I saw a soldier get shot. Well, nearly. And I helped the IRA. He won't get over it. He's not the only one who's in the middle of it all. And I can't wait to tell Martine and all the others. I mean, it's not as excitin' as Briege's Da bein' in jail, but it's nearly.

As I pass our back gates I see movement through the gaps in the wood. I peek through to watch Ma. She's up in the yard. What's she . . . it's not Ma. It's a man. He takes off his bala-clava and wraps it round something and gives it to Our Paddy who puts it in Killer's box. He glances back and I duck. It's the man who's not really my Uncle Tommy.

❧

'What kept you, son? I've been waitin' to get the dinner on,' says Minnie.

'There was shootin' up the street,' say me, frownin'. Minnie steps out and looks around scrunchin' up her eyes and face. 'I saw a soldier dead. It'll be on the news, I bet you.'

'Oh, Holy Mother of God,' she wheezes, grabbin' her heart.

I follow her in and put the messages down on the kitchen floor.

'God, son, I'm awful sorry you got caught up in that. Your Mammy would go mad if she knew I sent you up there.'

I'm just about to say it's not your fault but instead I act all worried and scared. 'I know, Mrs Maloney, the dead soldier was right in front of me and everythin'.'

'No,' her squeak gettin' sharp.

'I swear. I saw the blood comin' right out of him onto the ground.'

'Sweet Heart of Jesus.' She crosses herself and puts her hand on her heart and sits on the sofa. Maybe I've gone too far.

'Here's your change,' I say, emptyin' my pockets to prove I'm not stealin'.

'There's 50p son, don't say anythin' to your Mammy, will you?'

Dead on! 'Thanks, Mrs Maloney.' I get out quick in case she changes her mind. I could put that towards savin' for America.

She comes behind me to open the door.

'Tell yer Mammy she was short this week and to drop the rest round as soon as possible.'

Hold on. It's not all paid back? How much does Ma owe?

'Mrs Maloney, can you put this 50p with the other money. Off what Ma owes you.'

She smiles, takes my cheeks in her hands and bends down so her nose almost touches mine. She's so close I can see the lines all around her lips, like a cat's bum.

'There's not many like you, Mickey Donnelly,' says she. 'Does your Mammy know what a good son she has?'

~

I hit Etna Drive entry by grabbin' the wall with one hand and swingin' round into it. A wee girl's comin' at me. It's Martine. Walkin' straight towards me. I've got to say somethin'. Our first time with no-one else around in my whole long-legged life.

I kick a bit of broken glass as I walk. I glance up then *shock, surprise, what do you know?*

'Hello, Mickey,' she says, and her actual voice is like smiles.

'Hi-ye!' I say, dead cool.

'What happened to your head?'

I frown, pattin' down my cow's lick. I feel my cut. But that was ages ago.

'I was in a bomb,' I say, turnin' to the side to give her a better look. 'But don't tell anyone.'

'The big one? Oh my God! Let's see,' she says, all fluttery like a butterfly, a flutterfly, a . . . She touches my scar. Touches *me*. I breathe in through my teeth as if it really hurts.

'Sorry, was that sore?' she says.

'Nah, it's OK,' I say, bein' brave. 'You can touch it again.'

'If that was me I'd be cryin' my head off,' she says, her blue eyes sparkling.

'I saw you in the play the other week. You were brilliant,' says me. She smiles. 'Really, really beezer.'

'No, not me. Briege was the really brilliant one.' She looks at her shoes and white ankle socks.

'No, you were miles better,' I say, and Martine smiles even bigger. 'A hundred miles better,' I add and she smiles even more. 'It was the best real life actin' I've ever seen. You could be on the TV, and I should know cuz I've watched more TV than anyone in the whole of Ardoyne.' I nod, yes.

Martine has a big redner on. Like I get. She's all cut, scundered and doesn't know where to look. And nor do I now cuz I see what I've made her feel. I can't think of what to say so I touch my scar again and do my *God this really hurts* breathin'.

'Is it really sore?' she says, takin' a hand from the pocket of her lace-lined, beautiful, blue-checked dress. She so, so, gently, touches my forehead. Boys noise in the entry. Martine sees them. 'C'mon, over here.' She flies off. I follow her as she runs behind the Highfield Club. It has a grilled, fenced cage surroundin' it. You have to buzz to get in. All the clubs have them now cuz the Prods keep bustin' in and shootin' everyone.

Martine's leanin' against the fence. She's got her back to me jukin' round the other side.

'What are you doin'?' I ask.

'Just seein' if anybody's comin',' says she.

Must be in case Briege sees her with me. I check round my side and the boys have gone. We look at each other. I look at the ground.

'C'mere a wee minute, Mickey,' she says. Even though I'm nervous, I do, cuz I want her to know I'll do whatever she says. I'd do anythin' for her. I'd even eat Weetabix. 'Mickey, can I ask you somethin'?'

'Aye.' I hope it's about space. Or Egypt. Or America.

'Do you promise not to tell anybody?' she asks.

'Cross my heart and hope to fry.'

'But you can never tell anybody,' she warns,

'I swear to God.'

'No, you'll tell.' She shakes her golden hair and I swear there was glitter comin' off it.

I squash up my face, really, really hard and lick my finger. 'I swear to Almighty God,' I say, makin' the sign of the cross over my heart. I look her dead in the eye. She looks from side to side and leans over to me.

'Do you know how to lumber?' she whispers.

Shit. I'm supposed to know cuz I'm a boy. Fuck it. I should've done it with Teresa McAllister up the Eggy.

'Yeah. Do *you* not?' says me.

'No,' she looks away. 'Will ye show me?'

'You mean, show it. Like, do it?'

'Aye.'

*Ha-lay-lu,*

*Ha-lay-lu,*

*Ha-lay-lu,*
*Ha-lay-lu-yah,*
*Praise be the Lord!*
Thank you, Jesus!
'But ye can't tell anybody,' says she.
'Away on! I wouldn't do that,' says me.
'Swear it again.'
'I swear.' I cross my heart.
'On Wee Maggie's life.'
'I swear.'
'Killer's life too.'

I put my hands on my guts. I feel sick. I've already lost them both. Can I not just have this brilliant thing, God?

'Mickey?'

'I'm not feelin' well.'

'It's cuz you don't want to swear, you don't really mean it.'

She must want to be my girlfriend. She's so close that I can feel her breath on me.

'I do. I promise. I swear, on Killer's life too,' says me.

'OK.'

Her arm brushes along mine. I get goose pimples where it touched. Then my whole body tingles and my balls roll backwards like they're goin' up inside me. That's never happened to me before. Is that my puberty? Is that love?

'Show me. What do we do?' says she.

'Now?' Shit. What was I thinkin'? 'I can't. Not with my head like this. It's killin' me.' I do all this pain actin'. I scratch my cut again tryin' to make it bleed. 'And I just saw a Brit get shot dead.'

She backs off. 'Oh my God! The one from today?' says she.

'Yes, I'd better get home. I haven't even told my Ma yet.'

That was a close shave. I wish I could have come up with a different excuse though cuz I don't want to go home. I want us to play. And sing and laugh and maybe do baby kissin' stuff.

'But really soon,' says me.

'When?'

'Soon,' says me.

'OK, soon then,' she says and kisses me on the cheek. She runs off. I watch her beautiful, long, ringlety hair floatin' behind her. I breathe in deep.

Lumber her. Me. Martine's goin' to be my girlfriend. Everyone's goin' to be so jealous. And they'll all want to be my friend. The boys and the girls.

Now, all I need to do is find out how to lumber. Is there any other way? Other than Teresa McAllister.

# 15

'Y ER GETTIN' ON my friggin' nerves, wee boy,' says Ma.

I bang my body off the arm of the sofa. My face burnin' hot. 'Ach, Mammy, I don't want to.'

'Get out and play or I'm gonna bring ye in for the rest of the day,' she snaps.

'Good,' I say.

'Aye, in bed,' she says.

I do a really loud tut.

'Are you tuttin'?' she shouts.

'No.' I kick the carpet. She heads out to the yard with bucket and brush. 'Sake!'

'What did ye say?' she turns. 'Did you *sake* me? Are you sakin' me?'

'No.'

'I'm tellin' ye now,' she screams, '. . . one more word out of ye and I'll sake ye up and down them stairs with this brush.' Ma disappears back into the yard. I see her fags on the hearth. I'll show her. I nick one and stick it down my sock. I take two matches from the box.

'I hate you!' I shout. I hear Ma runnin' in and I leg it outside.

'Wait til ye come back here, wee boy. I'll break yer two legs!' Ma screams down the street after me. Jesus. Not even funny. I'm glad I stole a fag now.

I hide in Havana Street entry. I can't stand seeing Maggie playin' with the girls. And I don't want to see Martine til I know how to lumber. I hate bein' out on my own all the time. But Ma's in such a stinkin' mood. I don't know why. I can't believe she won't let me stay in and help her. She's never even home anymore and the one time she is, she's like this.

I run a match along the wall and light up. It tastes disgustin'. I practice breathin' the smoke out of my nose while suckin' in another draw. The older boys do it. I've watched. I'll be cool if I can smoke in St. Gabriel's.

'Here, wee boy?' A voice comes from behind me.

I drop the fag and look round, slow, in case she knows me. I don't want to be dragged round to Ma for smokin', like Aul Aggie up the street did to Our Paddy.

'What?' I say. No, I don't know her.

'D'ye know where the Henrys live?'

'Aye. They live in our street,' I say. I see the *Loose Talk Costs Lives* poster on the wall. Shit, I shouldn't have said that. But she doesn't look like a Prod to me.

'Whereabouts?' she asks.

'I can't remember. You'll have to ask somebody round there,' says me, just in case.

'Does yer Mummy know ye smoke?' says she.

'No, my Ma ran away with a soldier,' says me.

'If you're Ma heard you sayin' that she'd slap the head of ye.'

'Oh she does that anyway, Mrs.'

What's wrong with Mammy? I'm worried about her. *I know.* I'll spy with my little eye. I run round the back of our house, duck behind next door's fence and watch through the gap.

Ma's attackin' the ground with the yard brush. It sounds like she's sandpaperin', takin' a whole layer of ground off. Maybe that's what we should use on Our Paddy's spots.

Screech – the teeth-gnawin' noise the bucket makes as it's dragged across the ground. Scrub, scrub, scrub. No-one cleans like my Ma. She's like two men and a wee lad. You want to see her muscles.

Ma puts her hands on the top of the brush pole and rests her head down on them. A wee break. She must be wrecked. She looks up, leans the brush on her chest and twists her weddin' ring on her finger, starin' into space. Ma's spacin' out like me. Mammy thinks too. I never realised. I wonder what goes on in there. I don't try to telepath cuz her brain would be like Fort Knox.

'Fuck!' she shouts, soundin' like a man. She makes a fist and thumps her leg.

'Mammy.' It comes out as a whisper. Lucky she didn't hear. She's cryin'. My Mammy never cries.

She starts scrubbin' the ground again, dead, dead hard. She empties the bucket and brushes hard and fast. The water heads down towards me. I jump back. When I look up Ma's gone back into the house.

Is Da back? That must be it. He's done somethin'. I'm gonna kill him if he's done anythin' to my Mammy. I run round our front. What if he's in there and he's drunk and he hits me? *Don't think.*

But what if Ma's still pissed off with me for earlier and *she* hits me?

*Don't think.*

I go up our path. I cough loudly in the hall and start whistlin' to let her know to stop cryin'. She'd hate me seein'.

'Mammy,' I say, openin' the wee door. She must be in the scullery. Maybe *he's* in there with her. 'Mammy,' I say, creepin' in.

'What?' she shouts, turnin' from the sink. She's hand-washin' our clothes.

'Nothin', Mammy. I was just lookin' for you.'

'Don't be hangin' round here, I've got too much work to do.'

'I'm sorry I was cheeky, Mammy.'

She doesn't say anythin'. Probably cuz we never say sorry in our house. We just pretend things didn't happen.

'Mammy, do you want me to help you?' I ask.

'No, go you on out, ye'll only keep me back,' she says and sticks her head in the cupboard under the sink, searchin' for somethin'.

This is the dodgy bit. By ignorin' her she could actually explode and blow me to smithereens. But I've got to find out what's wrong.

'Mammy,' I say, dead quiet. 'Mammy.'

Still doesn't hear me. *God, please make her turn round. Please.* Baby step nearer. I didn't tell myself to, my feet just did it all by themselves.

*Hello, brain, excuse me one wee minute, but who's in control here?*

Baby step forward. I must be on automatic pilot.

*Hello, Captain Brain, this is Commander Donnelly of ground control. Could you switch off the automatic pilot and take charge?*

No response. Another step.

*Proximity Alert! Danger! Collision Warning!*

I'm standin' right over her. I hear her heavy breath. I see my hand goin' out as I bend down towards her. I'll stop if I tell myself to. If I hear one word . . .

*This is your last chance to back up and out of there, Captain.*

It's no use, I'm a Kamikaze. I touch down on the runway of her back and hear myself say, 'Mammy.'

'What?' she screams. She puts her fists either side of her head and they shake. I don't know if she's gonna hit herself or me. She grabs her hair on one side and pulls it, lookin' at the floor. My stomach goes roller coaster. I step back and knock into the chair, hands coverin' my face. I peek through my fingers. She lets go of her hair and stares at the ground.

What is wrong with Ma? Da isn't even here.

'I could do the brass. Couldn't I, Mammy?' I say. 'And then I wouldn't be in your way.'

She looks at me. She's so sad. She bites her fist and breathes hard. Once, twice, three times.

'Get some newspaper from the coal hole. While you're in there, see if there's any mice in the trap,' says she.

Brilliant. I bounce out like I'm on springs. See how I can make my Mammy happy.

I'm really glad there's no mouse in the trap. If there is, you're the one that has to dump it. Or worse, if it's alive, you have to kill it with the poker from the wee companion set on the hearth.

I grab an old newspaper from the top of the pile, the Brasso and cloths. I don't know why they call this the *coal hole* cuz your coal bunker's in the yard. And it's not a hole either, it's a wee room. I'd love to have the coal hole to myself. Like it was my room. Imagine havin' your own room.

'Mickey!' I jump at her shout from the scullery. 'Bring them in here and do them.'

See! You don't need to say *sorry*. That's sorry. Everythin's goin' to be OK.

I spread a *Republican News* on the table with the cloths and the Brasso. We never read it, but when they sell it at the door you have to buy it or they look at you. I get the ornaments from the mantelpiece. And the companion set. The brass plate things that hang in the livin' room and the leather thing with the brass shape of a horse on it too. I don't know what the frig it's supposed to be, but Ma likes it.

I Brasso the ornaments. Ma will see how quick I am. Faster than the speed of sound. It's a good time to ask. Now that she's a bit better. 'Mammy, is m'Daddy back?' I check.

Her head snaps. 'Why, did ye see him?'

'No.'

Good. Beezer. Fab-a-rooni. Class. Magic. Brill. We can stay happy, can't we, Mammy? Time to shine the brass up. Rub dead hard. Hard so my arm hurts. Shine it up good.

Wait, so why was she cryin'? *Maybe cuz you said you hated her. That's not very nice, Mickey, is it? Your own Mammy. Imagine makin' your Mammy cry. Are you happy now? Every time you open your mouth, somethin' bad happens. Keep your big mouth shut!*

I've polished about half already. When I get them all done she'll really love me.

*What if the others find out you made Ma cry?*

They'll kill me.

*Faster, faster. Harder, harder, harder.*

I'm nearly finished. Think about somethin' else. Martine. Martine.

*I'm gonna lumber Martine.*

*The best lookin' girl I've ev-er seen.*

I wouldn't slip the hand on her but. She's not a wee dirt-bird. How can I find out about lumberin'?

'Mickey?' says Ma.

I jump, droppin' the lid of a tiny brass teapot on the glass table. Freeze. Is she gonna kill me? Did she hear what I was thinkin'? 'What?'

'Have ye done all of them already?' says Ma.

'This is the last one.' I breathe. 'Is there anythin' else you want me to do?'

'No sure, I'm finished.' She picks up her purse.

'Here, go and get yerself a wee somethin' in the shop.'

'No, it's OK,' says me.

'Wha'?' she screams, actin', makin' me laugh. 'Fuck me, our Mickey sayin' no to money.'

'Mammy!' I laugh, takin' a redner.

'Our Mickey, who'd sell his Ma to the Prods for 20p?'

'Aye, away on, Mammy,' says me. '25p, maybe.'

We laugh.

'Ye cheeky wee get!' She goes for a slap and I dodge, *Easy-Peasy Japanesey*.

'You're gettin' slow in your aul age, Ma.'

Ma kicks me on the shin. 'Awooah!'

'I've still got a few tricks up my sleeve,' she laughs. We laugh. Laugh and laugh like I've never seen my Mummy laugh before. I'm a good boy. She makes my heart hurt happy. My Mammy loves me. We don't say that in our house either.

Knock at the front door. We freeze. She nods for me to ask.

'Who's there?' I shout.

'Is yer Mammy in?' says a man's voice behind the door. Mammy mouths *no*. She points to the door. If it's the *Republican News* Man you have tell them to their faces or else they know your lyin'. Ma hides in the scullery.

'M'Mammy's not in, Mister,' I say, like I'm about six and a half.

'Tell'er she was short last week and Minnie says to send it round. Yesterday.'

What, like get in a time machine? 'Yes, Mister, I will.'

I wait in the hall til he's gone up the street.

'Mammy,' I say. She comes out of the scullery. 'Here, Mammy.' I hold out the 10p. 'For the house.' She goes bright red like I do.

'Your head's a balloon, wee boy. Now, away to Hell's Gates with ye before I change my mind and take it back.'

I bullet through the scullery and out into the street. 'Unda-lay! Unda-lay! Eee-bah! Eee-bah!' I'm Speedy Gonzales, me. 'Yee ha!' I should really go to McQuillan's cuz it's only fair after she gave me that free mix-up. But Toner's Saloon is my favourite. I could save some of the money to give Teresa McAl-lister to show me how to lumber, but I reckon she'd do it for free.

'Hello, son. How's your Mammy?' says Mrs Toner.

'OK.'

'God, you're gettin' grown up, aren't ye, now?' she nods.

'Yes,' I say, puttin' on my older-boy voice. I wish I had one I didn't have to put on. Wouldn't it be great if you could buy one from the shop? I probably wouldn't be able to afford it. But I could order one from the catalogue and pay it off weekly. Or I could loan the money from Minnie the Tick Woman.

Now I'm a big boy, will Mrs Toner let me buy a fagarette? 'And can I have a single?' I say, lookin' down at the counter.

'You're too young to be smokin' you, away on to that with you.' She flicks her hand.

'I was only jokin' you,' I say. 'A 10p mix-up, please.'

She side-eyes me, not sure if she believes me, but she gives me the mix-up. 'Thanks, Mrs Toner.' I grab the sweets and run out.

I bang into someone. It's the new Priest. What's he doin' way down here?

'Hello, Mickey.'

'Hello, Father.'

'How are you?' says he.

'OK,' I say but don't look at him.

'How's your Mother coping?' says he.

What? Without Da? Sure, we love it. Everybody's happy when he's not here. 'OK, Father,' I say.

'Well, tell your mum I was asking for her, will you, and say I'll call in soon.'

'OK, Father, thanks,' I say, turnin' to escape.

'Michael, have you thought about what we spoke about,' says he.

My stomach twists. Killer's wee face.

'I . . .' says me. I'd forgotten. How could I? How could I forget even for one minute?

'Come up and see me, Mickey,' he says.

'I will, Father,' I say.

'Have you looked at the book I gave you?' says he. 'Lots of tips on how to be an actor.'

'Really?' I put it under the bed and forgot about it. 'Father, I have to get back. Ma's waitin' on me.' Is it a really special sin if you lie to a Priest?

'OK,' he smiles.

I run down to the house.

*Killer, I'm sorry. I'm goin' to go up to your grave today.*

I burst through the door. Aunt Kathleen and Ma stop talkin'.

'I just saw the new Priest up the road and he said he'd call in soon,' I say.

'He's lovely that new Priest,' Ma says.

'Not bad lookin' either,' says Aunt Kathleen.

'God forgive you and pardon you,' Ma says, but her face wants to smile.

'I'm sure he's not that way inclined, anyway,' says Aunt Kathleen, with a cheeky smile.

Ma shakes her head, *shush*. She must mean cuz he's a Priest and they aren't allowed to do dirty things. I jump on Auntie's knee.

'Fuck ye, wee boy, you're gettin' too big to be jumpin' on me like that,' she laughs.

I slide off to the ground and lean into Mammy's legs. My *listen to the gossip position* since I was nought.

'Go and make me and your Aunt Kathleen a wee cuppa,' says Ma, nice as pie. Like actually askin' and not like *do it now or I'll kill you*. 'I've heated some soup in the pot for you,' she shouts after me.

I put the kettle on. Whisperin' from the livin' room. I tippy-toe to the scullery door and listen.

'I don't know what I'm goin' to do for money. I can't work any more hours. The children are rarin' themselves,' says Ma.

'Any word?'

'No,' says Ma,

'Aye, well God's good. Ye never know, he might be dead in a ditch somewhere,' says Aunt Kathleen.

'Fuck off now, Ka'leen,' says Ma.

'But c'mon, Josie love, you can't still . . . you have to move on.'

'In the eyes of God we're still married. I can't . . . After all these years.' Snifflin' sounds. 'It's hard, with the kids. Our Paddy, I don't know what to do with that wee boy. I never see him. And when I do, he won't look at me. I know he's up to somethin', but the IRA have promised me they won't involve him. And I'm still payin' that bloody TV and video off, never mind the rest of it. New uniform for Maggie and Paddy. At least Mickey can have Paddy's old one.'

I bloody knew it. You'd think just once, startin' a new school and all, I could have my own bloody clothes.

Thud! 'Aoowah!' Door right in my face.

'Serves you right for listenin',' says Ma. 'Where's the tea?' The kettle's boilin' away. Ma tuts and pours the boiling water into the tea pot. I stand behind her. 'Here, there's soup here for you.' She ladles some into a bowl.

'I don't want any,' says me.

'Eat some friggin' soup. You're skin and bones gettin'.' Ma carries two cups and the teapot through. The scullery door closes.

I listen.

'Aye, I don't know what I'm goin' to do. Paddy's got another year before he can leave school, so there's only my money and the wee bit Mary gets,' says Ma. 'I don't have 2d to rub together.'

I pour half my soup back in the pot so there's more to go round.

'What about Minnie?'

'Sure I haven't paid her the last lot,' says Ma.

'Jesus Christ,' says Aunt Kathleen. 'Be careful, you don't want them comin' down on ye.'

*I can't believe how selfish you are, Mickey Donnelly.* Mammy's distracted and all you can think about is a stupid uniform. I have to find a way of helpin' with money. I pour the rest of my soup back into the pot.

'Mickey, have you finished your soup?' Ma shouts.

'Yes, Mammy.'

'Go on out and let me and Aunt Kathleen talk then.'

'Alright, Mickey son,' says Aunt Kathleen, as I walk in. 'What time is it? I've a blow-dry booked at five, for darts tonight,' says Aunt Kathleen.

'Sure, Mammy can do it for you,' says me. 'She does hair-dressin' now.'

'What are you sayin' nigh?' says Ma.

'Aren't you doin' hairdressin', Mammy?'

Ma and Aunt Kathleen look at each other, Ma laughs. 'He was hidin' here the other night. Had to cut and dye his hair for him, for disguise.' Ma stares out the window, twistin' the ring on her finger.

'Do you know *Uncle Tommy*?' says me, winkin'.

'Who's Uncle Tommy?' says Aunt Kathleen.

Ma laughs. She nods at Aunt Kathleen. She laughs too.

'Get out you and close that door after you. And don't you be sayin' anythin' in the street.'

I close the wee door and listen in the hall.

'And your Mickey, Jesus, what's goin' to happen to him?' says Aunt Kathleen.

*What does she mean?*

'I'm distracted,' says Ma. I knew it. She is distracted. 'He's always acted the maggot. He's still such a baby sometimes. My head's away. He doesn't have any friends. Doesn't bother with the other kids.'

'And the way he is,' says Aunt Kathleen. Silence. 'Do you think he's . . . ?'

'Shut up, K'leen. Don't you dare. If he'd've gotten to St. Malachy's maybe he'd've been alright,' says Ma. 'School starts in a couple of weeks and what'll . . .' Silence. Whisperin'.

'Mickey!' she shouts and I jump six feet in the air. 'If you're in that hall, I'll break your face.'

I run out to the street. I don't want Mammy worryin' about me. I thought she didn't want me to play with them in the street. It's so confusin'. The girls are all playin' Queenio at the gable. And my Wee Maggie too. I have to try for Mammy, don't I? So she won't worry. So even if Briege scunders me in front of everyone. It's for my Mammy. I can play with my Wee Maggie again too.

At the line of girls, I slow beside Wee Maggie. She looks at me. I don't recognise her look. Our thing. It's gone. I've killed it. I want it back. I want Wee Maggie back.

'Can I play, Briege?' I say.

The ball bounces and no-one goes for it, so it rolls down the line. Briege gives me her evil smile. Wee Maggie looks scundered for me. Silence.

'Go on, Briege, let him play.' Martine. I hadn't seen her. She's backed me up. Not Maggie.

Briege squints at Martine. She doesn't like it. The rules are, if you're backed up, that's it, you have to be let in. No-one crosses Briege though.

'Alright then,' says Briege.

I have to not get the ball for the first couple of goes now. Stay back and not be seen.

Sheila's *on*. She throws the ball and we all run towards it. Everybody screams and pushes. Briege got it. If she's near it, you have to let her. We all go back and stand on the kerb.

'*Queenio, Queenio,*
*Who's got the ballio?*
*I haven't got it,*
*In my pocket.*'

Sheila looks along the line and smiles at everybody. I look along the line and see Martine near the end. She isn't even playin'. She's puttin' a little plait in her hair. She can do that. Nobody would ever say anythin' to Martine.

'God, I nearly dropped it there,' someone says. We all laugh. I laugh loudest and longest to make nice.

'God, I nearly dropped it, too.'

'*I haven't got it,*
*Down my knickers,*' someone sings.

We all piss ourselves. Everybody's bluffin' dead good, cuz they don't want Briege to get caught and turn nasty.

'Is it you?' Sheila points at Lizzy.

'*I haven't got it,*

*In my pocket,*' Lizzy sings, showin' her hands.

'It was me,' says Briege.

Everybody laughs and shouts 'Yeah!' and Briege holds out the ball. You're supposed to get a couple of guesses, but there's different rules for Briege McAnally. She goes up to the gable to be *on*. She throws the ball over her shoulder and we all run.

Wee Maggie got the ball. I run over and stand beside her. I'm her big brother. My sister's a winner. How cool does that make me? I look to Martine and she looks at me. This is good fun. I don't know why I get things in my head.

'*Queenio, Queenio,*

*Who's got the ballio?*

*I haven't got it,*

*In my pocket,*' we all sing.

Briege turns round. We all try to fool her. Wee Maggie's all excited cuz she'll get to be *on*. Sheila's on the other side of Maggie. I see her lookin' at Briege.

'*I haven't got it in my pocket,*' Sheila sings, noddin' down at Wee Maggie.

'God, it's really hard. Yous are too good at this,' says Briege. They all smile cuz Briege's tellin' them they're good.

'Is it . . .' she looks along the line, '. . . you?' She points at Wee Maggie, like I knew she would.

Maggie can't believe it cuz when there's so many playin' you never guess who's got the ball. Maggie looks at me, and I don't know what to do. I shrug my shoulders and sort of smile like *ah well*. I should do somethin'. Maggie's lookin' at me like, *I don't understand. What did I do wrong?* I want to tell her it's not her fault.

Wee Maggie looks away like *you're no use* and gives the ball back to Briege, who gets to be *on* again.

I hate Briege McAnally. And she's gonna pay. Believe you me. Nobody cheats my Wee Maggie. No-one hurts her. I won't let anyone. I'm bubblin' inside. Like a witches cauldron of hate. I'm gonna do it now. I'm gonna tell her. The big white letters on the gable dance for me. *Our Day Will Come!*

'Briege,' I say.

'Wha'?'

The words don't come. So I stare at her and she stares at me. It's a Stare Out. I can see her tiny, flea-sized brain, tryin' to figure out what I'm up to.

'Who the fuck d'ye think yer starin' at, fruity boy?' she spits.

Martine would have heard.

'I'm starin' at you!' says me. I'm doin' this for Wee Maggie.

'Oh, ho, ho!' She sucks in air through her teeth. 'That's it for you, Donnelly. Never again. Yer out for good.'

'You think you're great cuz yer Da's in jail.'

I've detonated a bomb that's made the whole world freeze.

'What did ye say about my Da?' Briege shouts, breakin' the spell. I don't answer her. I don't feel so brave now. 'You've a cheek to talk about anybody's Da,' she says big and loud. 'Sure, everybody knows yer Da's a fuckin' nutcase who runs round the street screamin'. And he's an alcoholic.' She takes in her audience.

'No, now, I wouldn't think so,' I shout. 'My Daddy's in America. He's over there workin' to get us money and he's goin' to send for us all to go and live with him.' I fold my arms to show I've won.

'My Ma says your Da hangs around town with all the alchos, lyin' on the pavement beggin' for money.'

I can't believe it. How could he do that to us? I want him

DEAD! No, I don't want him dead, I want him rubbed out like he never existed. And now she's won me. He helped her win me.

*Accessing databanks.* She *thinks* she's won.

'Aye, well, what about *your* Da. You think he's in jail cuz he's this big IRA man, but he's in jail for stealin' a bag of sausages!'

Some laugh. Some are shocked and stunned. Briege looks like I just punched her in the face.

'I tell ye what, I'm gonna tell my Da on you and you're gonna get killed. You're fuckin' dead, Donnelly. I'm gonna get the IRA on you.'

'Mickey, come you here, right now!' Ma shouts. When did she come out? Aunt Kathleen's walkin' up the street, lookin' over. 'Do you hear me callin' ye?' she shouts.

I give Briege a big dirty look.

'You're dead, Donnelly.'

I run over across the waste ground to Ma.

'Get in here, wee boy.' I don't answer her as I duck past in case there's a slap on the head. I sit on the chair where the TV was and start swingin' my legs. I friggin' hate Briege McAnally. I want to kill her.

'What was she sayin' to you?' Ma's stayed at the door lookin' over at the gang.

'Nothin'.'

'Stay away from her. I don't know why ye wanna hang about with the wee girls for anyway. You're gettin' too old for that.'

I bloody only played with them for Ma. I can't believe it. Wait. I'm so stupid. Of course she meant wee boy friends not wee girls.

What's Briege gonna do? She's gonna get me killed.

Wee Maggie comes in. She heard all that about Da. I'll make it OK.

'C'mere,' I hold out my arms.

'Why do you have to spoil everything?' says she. 'I hate that you're my brother!' She runs out.

From the window, I watch Wee Maggie join Briege and the girls as they walk into the entry. I get cramp, right in my heart. I see myself reflected in the window. Another me. A ghost me. Maybe I just died.

# 16

F ROM OUR WINDOW I see a line of boys, arms arched, leanin' forward with their hands against the gable wall, makin' a long tunnel. Ma's-a-Whore has become the new leader of the gang. He stands, arms in the air.

One of the boys, Rat, from the new houses, is crouched at the end of the tunnel lookin' in, havin' second thoughts. I'd be havin' 162,000 thoughts, but they would all be the same one – 'No friggin' way am I goin' in there!'

'Go!' shouts Ma's-a-Whore and slaps Rat on his legs.

Rat runs. The boys cheer. Cheer sounds like fun. This isn't. They kick and punch as he runs up the line. After he passes them, the boys run to join the end so the line doesn't stop and they get to hit him again. The Tunnel of Death. Just to play with them. You'd have to be brain damaged to choose that.

Sorry, Mammy, I'm always going to be on my own until I get away to America.

'*Somewhere over the rainbow,*
*Way up high . . .*'

Somewhere over the Atlantic away from our street and everybody in it.

'Do you hear me talkin' to you?' says Ma.

'Yes,' says me.

'Well, come on then.' Ma's at the door but I've no idea

why. I leave the window and follow her out. I daren't ask or she'll kill me for not listenin'.

'Put these vouchers in your pocket and don't lose them,' says Ma.

I squash them right down to the bottom of my pocket.

'Take them to the Pope John Paul Youth Club and collect the food. Mary will cook somethin' from whatever you get. I'll walk you down half way.' Ma grabs my shoulders. 'Don't hang around down there, after that bomb, do you hear me?'

'I won't, Ma.'

'What's wrong with your face?' My bloody face always gives me away.

'Nothin',' I say. Ma squints at me then drags me after her. Thank God she has somethin' on her mind.

Ma nods at some women hangin' around the corner. They stop talkin' and nod, arms folded. I look back and they start talkin' again, now we've passed. I give them a big dirty look.

'What are you doin' the day?' asks Ma.

Ma never asks me that. 'Ammm . . . don't know.'

'You miss wee Killer, don't you?'

'Yes,' I say. Oh God. Does she know somethin'? That's the first she's brought it up in ages.

'Well, God's good, son. You never know.'

But I do know. I'll go up and see Killer later. We walk in silence.

'Mickey, I've got extra work in the Shamrock at night. It means I won't be gettin' home to very late.'

'Ach, Mammy . . .'

'Mickey, you're goin' to have to be a good boy, nigh. You're my good boy, aren't you?'

'Yes, Mammy,' I say. I wish I could get a job and help.

'Don't have me worryin' about you, son. Do what Paddy

and Mary tell you. One of them will always be in to mind yous at night,' she says, stoppin' at the end of our street.

I hope it's not Paddy.

'And son, try to get out of the house and make some friends,' says she. She spits on her hand and pats down my cow's lick. I lean into her hand.

'OK, Mammy,' I say.

'Now, go on and no hangin' around about here,' she says, checkin' No Man's Land and the barricades where Killer died.

I watch her walk up to the chippy. She turns and sees me still there and waves her arm *shoo*. I wave. I take off over to the entry at the side of my old school.

Across our pitch, kids are dodgin' cones and hoops. Obstacle race, I bet you. I love the obstacle race and always came first or second on School Sport's Day. It's the only thing I'm any good at in sport. And runnin'. But they're not really sports, are they? Runnin' and dodgin' obstacles?

I see kids runnin' with their legs tied. I want to cry. Me and Wee Maggie won't be winnin' the three-legged race again this year. Never again. I've never even been to the Summer Scheme on my own. Without Wee Maggie. I could but. And people don't know me there. I could maybe meet new friends. Make Ma happy. I love the Summer Scheme. I can go get the food after.

Inside my old school it's madness. Everybody's runnin' around hysterical like they're on fire. I don't know any of them. They come from everywhere to do this. Cuz it's free. Kids from the Bone, Ardoyne, Old Ardoyne – everywhere. And the new ones from the new estates. I can be anybody. They don't know anythin' about me, and our street. I run up the corridor and shout as well.

I run into the hall and run round in a circle. This is brilliant.

'Right, everyone gather round,' some hairy Bigfoot-lookin' man is sayin'. 'Here's what's goin' on today.' Jesus, he smells too. 'There's storytellin'. If you want to do that, stand over in this corner. Arts and crafts, stand over here. There's a trip to Cave Hill.'

Cave Hill. *The* Cave Hill. Where you can see out of here. Or was that just another lie from Da?

Everyone's buzzin'. Millions put their hands up. A trip out of Ardoyne. I will kill anyone who gets in my way.

'There's only room for ten in the minibus. Stand over by the main doors and Pierre will choose who can go,' says Bigfoot.

Pierre. A foreign one. I remember last year. They come to help out at the Summer Scheme. People think they're mad cuz they're always smilin' and happy. I think they're mad cuz who in their right mind would want to come here? You'd have to be mental, definitely.

I have to go on this trip. I can find out where he's from and run away to his house if it's really bad in St. Gabriel's.

We're all crowded round Pierre. 'Me!' Everyone bounces up and down, arms in the air. No girls at all.

'Yes.' He points his magic, wish-grantin', foreign finger, 'Yes, 3, 4, you, you, 7, 8, 9. One more . . .'

'Me, Pierre, me!' I scream his name like I've heard it on the TV.

He laughs. 'You speak French?'

'Bibliotheque!' I shout. It means library. I remember it because I imagined Jesus jivin' at the disco.

Some of the boys hate me, but they're just dead jealous. Pierre taps me on the head. He picked me! Nobody ever picks me for nothin'.

'And what eeze your name?' Pierre asks me.

'Mickey.'

'Bonjour, Mickey.'

'Bonjour, Pierre.'

He laughs. I love him so much. We're best friends already. He's the coolest teacher I've ever had.

In the car park, the bus driver opens the back doors of the minibus, fag hangin' from his mouth. The boys near kill each other to get in first. I walk, actin' like the Fonz, turn to Pierre and shrug *What are they like?* noddin' at the boys, and get in last. Pierre locks the door behind me, shakin' his head and laughin' at me through the little window. He jumps in the front.

'I've heard the views are very beautiful, no?' Pierre asks.

'Aye, it's alright,' someone says.

Da must be tellin' the truth if Pierre's heard it too.

Off we go, and everybody's up to the high doe. All the ones at the front are turned round in their seats, pointin' at us.

*'The back of the bus is in the huffs, Bar-ney Boo!*
*The back of the bus is in the huffs, Bar-ney Boo!*
*The back of the bus is in the huffs,*
*Because they can't sing like us.*
*Inky Binky, Bar-ney, Boo-oo-oo!'*

See, boys can sing. Have I found my people?

'What the fuck does *Inky Binky Barney Boo* mean, anyway?' a wee boy says, and we all laugh. He's right. I've never even thought about it before. 'Right, everybody here!' He calls us into a huddle. He's our leader now. I get there too late to hear what he said but I'm in the huddle, arms round two boys in front of me. I've never felt so like a boy. Touchin' another boy.

Singin' starts, two words before all of us *back of the busers* join in.

*'Oh, ye canny throw yer granny off the bus,*
*No, ye canny throw yer granny off the bus,*
*No, ye canny throw yer granny,*

*Cuz she's yer Mammy's Mammy,*
*No, ye canny throw yer granny off the bus.'*

I'm in the *back of the bus gang*. We're all together. Mates. And people are lookin' at me like I'm supposed to be here. See, if I went where people don't know me, then everythin' could be alright. I always knew it.

We cross Cliftonville Circus. Down the Westland. We've crossed the border into a Proddy area. You know cuz of all the Union Jacks and the red, white and blue painted kerbs. You never, never, ever go down here. Five minutes drive from my street and I've never been down here in my whole life.

*ALL TAIGS ARE TARGETS* is painted on the wall. Taigs are what the Protestants call us Catholics. So that means me.

We turn a bend and have to slow cuz of a ramp. Teams of men rush the minibus from each side, planks of wood and metal bars in their hands. Hands go round eyes against the glass windows like they're wearing goggles to see in. Eyes dart between us. I take in everybody at once. No Celtic or Cliftonville football club gear. Thank God. Nothin' to tell them we're Catholics. Will the driver run them over or stop?

We stop. The driver winds down his window. A baldy, tattooed man, sticks his head in. We all look at the floor.

'Where you going?' says Baldy.

'Takin' the kids from the summer scheme up to Cave Hill,' says our driver, tappin' a fag on his ciggy box, cool as you like. Like we're not all about to die.

'Where you comin' from?' says Baldy.

Our driver takes a long drag of his fag. This is it. 'Shankill,' he says.

'Shankill Community Centre?' says Baldy.

A face comes over baldy's right shoulder. 'Know it well, who do you know there?' the man smiles, his eyebrows and hooked nose dip as he does.

I get a cramp in my stomach. I push my fist into it.

'Billy,' our driver says. Nearly every Prod is Billy, I think. And Ian. Like millions of us are called Paddy and Mickey.

I look round and every single kid is shittin' himself. At least it's not just me.

'He's a lying bastard,' says Hook Nose, his face twistin' into somethin' hateful.

Baldy scans the bus slowly. I cross my legs to stop the wee that is pushin' its way out. I hear a sniffle but don't look to draw attention.

'Drive on,' says Baldy.

'Wha'?' Hook Nose shouts, arms up.

Our bus moves slowly.

'Let them go,' Baldy shouts, pushin' men back with his arms. They part for us.

'What the fuck are you doin'?' Hook Nose shouts, lookin' from Baldy to us. He spits on our windows. I watch it ooze down. Spit comes from all sides from faces squashed in hate.

Our driver puts his foot down and we speed off to the end of the road. Out the back window, I see the men have gathered round Baldy who saved us. A Prod saved our lives. I wish I'd looked at him more. I want to remember him.

I feel light headed. I feel stupid. I feel like I could do anything. I feel like I'm on glue! I look round at my gang and I want us to sing again.

'*Stop the bus, I want a wee wee,*' I sing without thinkin'. The whole bus joins in.

'*Stop the bus, I want a wee wee,*
*Stop the bus, I want a wee wee,*
*If ye don't stop it now, I'll do it on the floor.*'

Me. Me. Me. They joined in with *me*. I started somethin'. Everyone's goin' mental. I'm playin' with boys. And I can do anythin' I want. I climb over the seats and lean over the front, close to Pierre. The driver's cigarette is shakin' in his hand and the ash is fallin' on his trousers. Not so cool anymore. And Pierre doesn't look too good. It's funny cuz us kids are havin' a laugh and the big ones are still shittin' themselves.

'It's OK,' I pat Pierre on the shoulder. 'You'll be out of here soon. Back home in France.' Talkin' makes Ma better sometimes. 'So, how come you speak good English?'

'We learn English in school. Do you learn languages at your school?'

'No. But in big school I probably will. I'm goin' soon and I'm definitely goin' to do French.' I've never thought of doin' that before but I definitely will now.

'That is a very good idea. Then you can travel around the world when you finish school,' says he, lookin' a bit livelier.

Travel round the world. Not just America. He's thinks I can. Then why can't I? And I could go to his house and be his friend.

The minibus pulls in and parks up. We all rush to the back door.

'You must wait. I open zee door,' says he.

We all pretend to wait but we're edgin' in front of each other, laughin'. The *Napoleon's Nose Gang*. One specky eejit climbs over a double seat and falls in between, legs stickin' up in the air. Everybody shouts 'Nah!'

'Help me!' he cries.

That just makes everybody laugh even more. Dumbo! Doesn't he know to keep his mouth shut? I should help him up, but if I do, that'll make me his mate. I'm in the gang now. The back door opens and everyone jumps out. I wait behind a bit. When no-one can see, I help Joe 90 get up.

'Thanks,' says he.

I don't say anythin' back. I don't even smile cuz I'm not goin' to be friends with someone like him. I jump out and take a look along the road. The boys are runnin' up the hill, like wild animals, the noise they're makin'. Hallions, the lot of them. I want to be part of the gang, but I'm not gettin' on like that. Not in front of Pierre.

I stop to look at the enormous white house facin' where we've parked. It has big, giant windows, nearly the size of the house. I wonder what it would be like if our family lived on Cave Hill. In a big house with money.

No flags here. No painted kerbs, broken windows, knocked-down houses, burnt-out cars, dog dirt. No waste ground. No broken glass. No smell of gas. No police. No soldiers. No barricades. And no gangs. So rich people don't have the Troubles. As well as havin' everythin' else. It's just not fair.

'Come on, Meekey.' I turn to Pierre's voice. They're up the hill. They'll all watch me now cuz he shouted down. I bet I look cool down here by myself. I could *cool dander* up there, but it would take too long. It'll have to be cool runnin'.

'That was very fast? You are a good runner, no?' says Pierre.

'Yeah,' I say, out of breath, to show how fast I must've been.

There's about three or four boys hangin' round Pierre. Big licks. I hear one of them tellin' him about space. I know millions about that. I bet you I know more about space than all of them put together. I want to show him how much *I* know. But I'm not joinin' themin's. Wise up. Wise the bap. Catch a grip. Catch yourself on. I'm not just goin' to be like the rest. I'm better than the gang.

'Well, Meekey, you are a loner, yes?' says Pierre.

'No, I'm not!' Does he think I'm a weirdo?

'Like is happy on their own. Strong. Adult.'

I take a big redner. A loner's good. Not like you've got no

friends. I'm goin' to be on my own all the time from now on. But where people can see, so they know I'm a loner.

Should I be a loner? Or be in a gang?

I look at Pierre and he smiles at me like I'm his mate, not just like he's a teacher. I'm more grown up than the rest of them. I walk alongside him with the licks, but I'm not one. I'm here cuz Pierre asked me to, by talkin' to me.

'So this is Napoleon's Nose,' Pierre says.

'Napoleon was from your country, wasn't he?' says me.

'Yes, very good, Meekey.'

'It doesn't look like Napoleon's Nose,' says a stupid one.

'Not from here, while you're on it,' says me.

''ow do we see it?' asks Pierre.

'You have to see it from down there. He's lyin' on his back, like this,' I say, 'with his nose stickin' out.'

We walk to the edge of the cliff. I slow down with baby steps and stare at my feet. My heart beats fast and my head swims. There's no barrier or anything. Nothin' to stop you fallin' over. I raise my head and my mouth drops open. Goose-bumps. So Belfast isn't completely surrounded. There's a way out. There's Samson and Delilah, the huge yellow cranes at the docks I've seen on the news. Belfast Lough. And big ships. Leavin' here. I take a big breath.

The boys start a game of Chasies behind me. I've got Pierre all to myself. He's lookin' at the view and I'm lookin' at him but pretendin' I'm not. He's got shorts on and his legs are gorilla hairy. A bit like the wipe-yer-feet mat outside our front door. I've never seen hairy legs before. Daddy and Paddy don't have them.

He reaches down and scratches his leg. It makes a cracklin' noise. When I grow up, I want really hairy legs. I'd be a real man then. Nobody could call you gay if you had hairy legs. I'm goin' to scratch mine all day. And wear shorts. Even in the winter. I'll show everybody. I want him to scratch his leg again.

I stare really hard at his leg, just above his right knee. Superman eyes, laser beamin' that leg. If he doesn't play ball, I'm goin' to laser beam his leg right off at the knee. Kneecappin' of the future. The IRA would love that. No need for guns. No fingerprint evidence.

He did it. Scratched his leg. I must never, ever doubt my powers. I am Super Human. That's why I'm different. I came here from somewhere else. Maybe another planet, even. When I was a baby, it was said that I was special, the King of Kings, so the ordinary King wanted me dead. He put me in a basket and floated me into space and I landed on Earth, in the River Lagan, where I was found and taken in by a poor family from Ardoyne.

Pierre looks at me. I look up at him. He smiles.

'Ouch! I think I've been beetten on the leg.' He twists his leg round to see his calf.

I bend down on my knees and look dead close at his leg. 'I can't see anythin'. Your legs are too hairy. You should be in the zoo!'

He laughs. I rub my hands on my jeans and look at my Tony Tiger patch I sewed on all by myself at the start of the summer. 'They'rrrre Grrrreat!' says Tony. I can't stop starin' at his hairy legs. I want to touch them. The bottom of my belly sinks in. Somethin's going on in my pants.

I feel scared or somethin'. Lookin' up, Pierre has a strange look on his face. I shouldn't have been starin'. He looks back to the others. Somethin' has changed. He doesn't want to be my friend anymore.

Rain. Out of nowhere.

'Everyone! Back to zee bus!' Pierre shouts and runs along the path, callin' us with his arm.

I watch everyone run down the path. I turn into the rain. They're all runnin' to the minibus so they don't get wet. Ha! If the ones in our street could see me now. They wouldn't call me names. Here I am – Mickey Donnelly, on his tod, standin' on Napoleon's Nose, a step away from death, hands in his pockets, gettin' wet and stayin' cool as a cucumber. I'm a loner. Like from the filims. And I don't need anybody.

I stand right on the edge of Napoleon's Nose, fling my arms out of my pockets and watch some old bits of gunk and paper fly out of them and away into the sky. I want to fly with them. My chest fills with excitement like I want to jump. I hold out my arms, spread out my fingers, clench my legs hard and stand, *We Shall Not Be Moved* in my feet. I wish they were all watchin', everyone in the world.

Me, the loner. I don't need them. Boys or girls or gangs or friends. Up their holes with big jam rolls! I don't care what anybody says.

I bend down and in the wet dirt on Napoleon's Nose I write – *Mickey Donnelly was here.* It's already washin' off before I stand up. I don't care. Cuz I know I was here. And I'm goin' to other places too. I look out to the Lough and there's a ginormous ship headin' out to sea. Out of here. Goin' anywhere you want. Like Da said. He was tellin' the truth about here. About the view. About the ships. But I still hate him.

I take a big breath and blow hard at the ship. To give it some extra wind to get out of here quicker. I'm goin' to get out of here one day.

'Come on, Meekey!' I hear shouted from down the path.

I walk super-duper slow. They can all wait.

∼

'Where've you been?' says Mary.

'Nowhere. Why?' says me.

'Where's the food?'

I check my pockets. Dizzy. I'm dizzy. I hold onto the side of the sofa. The vouchers are gone. The bits of paper that flew out of my pockets on Napoleon's Nose.

'What have you done, Mickey?'

'Nothin',' I say.

'It's all over your face.'

'I haven't done nothin',' I say.

'Mickey!'

'I'll go get the food now.' I run out of the house.

What have I done? What are they goin' to eat? Where can I get money? Minnie. I could go to Minnie. But how can I pay her back?

Mrs McQuillan's house shop. She said Ma could go on the list. Ma will kill me. But not if she doesn't know.

I run up to the shop. *Think, think, think Mickey.*

'Hello, Mrs McQuillan. Can I get some stuff?' says me.

'Yes, Mickey, certainly son. What you want?'

'A steak and kidney pie, and some potatoes, and a tin of peas.'

There must be a way of payin' for them. Must be. On the floor, there's bags of sticks. Chopped up and in clear plastic bags for the fire. Like Da said he used to sell. I still have the bags I stole from Aul Sammy's shop in my secret box. And I can steal more. Could I *Swap Shop* them for food? That wouldn't get much.

Sticks. Wood. Plenty in the burnt-out houses. Look at the bonfire. And the egg factory. Chop chop. The hatchet Uncle John left behind Killer's dog box.

Eureka!

'Now, Mrs McQuillan, you strike me as a smart business

woman who knows a good deal when she sees one,' I say, like an American sales man.

'Mickey Donnelly, stop actin' the maggot.' She shakes her head and laughs, but I know I have her.

# 17

'This is my last one, Killer.'

My hands are full of splinters and they hurt like anythin'. I spin the bag of sticks until the top is twisted, then tie a knot. In the wheelbarrow with the rest. I was thinkin' if I didn't want to keep my new job a secret I could start my own business. *Mickey's Stickeys* or *Mick's Sticks*. I reckon the first lot I've made will pay for the food and a little to sneak into Ma's purse. Then I can help pay Minnie. Then save for my ticket to the US of A.

Everybody needs sticks for their fires to get hot water. Well, not everybody. If you're rich you could turn on the emersion heater. All the new houses have them. Emersions. We'll have one when they knock our old house down and give us a new one.

It's taken ages to do twelve bags. That poor wee hatchet of Uncle John's won't take much more. Its head nods when I chop.

Nearly gettin' night so better hurry up.

'Good-bye, Killer. Be a good boy.'

The goldfish bee is dead at the bottom of the jam jar. I hope his ghost is with Killer. I leave the jar there so it can be his grave, right beside Killer's.

The glue-sniffers are here today for the first time in ages. I've been watchin'. Waitin'.

I push the bonfire wheelbarrow over the Eggy field towards the egg factory. It's not easy over the bumps. The wheel sticks where the out-of-shape barrow rubs the wheel on each turn. The bonfire boys battered it to death with an enormous hammer when they'd finished with it, then dumped it in the burnt-out houses.

Outside the hole in the wall, I set the barrow down and climb through, makin' some noise in the rubble so they know someone's comin'.

'Teresa?' I shout.

'Who's that?' Glue Boy shouts back.

'Mickey Donnelly. I'm lookin' for Teresa McAllister,' I say, as deep as I can.

Whisperin'. 'C'mon in,' Teresa shouts.

'You come out here,' I shout back.

'Nah, you come in here,' her voice sendin' creepy crawlies runnin' over my skin.

I make my way over the broken bits of wall, pipes and metal boxes. That light is comin' through the roof in lines, same as last time. God's light. Shinin' on the Children of the Glue.

''Right?' says Glue Boy.

'Aye,' I say, actin' like an Ardoyne hard man. I need to try out my character for St. Gabriel's.

I sit down beside Teresa. Glue Boy puts his hand on her leg.

'Get off you. *She's* yer girlfriend,' Teresa says and points at Glue Girl.

Glue Boy puts his hand on Glue Girl's leg. I don't know if she minds or not. It's hard to tell cuz I can't see her face through the glue bag.

'So, Mickey Donnelly, whaddaye want?' says Teresa.

'De ye wanna go for a walk outside?' I ask.

'Nah, it's my turn. Here, gi' us that, you!' she says, grabbin' the bag from Glue Girl.

I don't know Glue Boy. He's not from round here. He looks a real weirdo. But rough.

'What's yer name again?' he asks.

'Donnelly,' says me, cuz hard men don't use their first names.

'Mickey Dicky, that's what,' laughs Teresa.

'Here,' he pushes the bag in Teresa's hand towards me, 'your turn.'

'Nah!' I say, all hard. Maybe cuz he doesn't know me he might believe I am a real Ardoyne one. But I can hear me and I still sound nice.

'Whaddyemean, *nah*!' Glue Boy says. 'Ye've never tried it.' He gives me the evil eye.

'Aye, I have. Haven't I, Teresa?' says me.

'I don't know,' she shrugs.

She's makin' me pay for last time. 'OK, then, give it to me, well,' I say.

I take the bag off Teresa. They watch. I put the bag over my face and take some. And again. 'There ye go. I tol' ye I've done it before.' I pass the bag to Glue Girl.

Light head. Like when I stand up too quick. Glue Boy smiles. Somehow he knows I feel it. He puts his hand on his girlfriend's leg and the other on Teresa's.

'Fuck aff you! I told ye, didn't I?' She pushes him hard and he falls back off the broken bit of wall he's sittin' on. Teresa's laugh turns into a huge cough. She spits up phlegm.

*Isn't she lovely*, sings Stevie Wonder in my head. You'd need to be Stevie Wonder to wanna go anywhere near Teresa. But this is for Martine.

Teresa sits on my knee, puttin' her arm round my neck,

hangin' onto me like I'm Rod Hull and she's Emu. Only Emu's better lookin' and my hand's not going up her bum.

Glue Boy puts his hand on Glue Girl's face and turns it to him. Her eyes aren't even open. He starts kissin' her. He opens and closes his mouth like a fish. That must be lumberin'.

'C'mon then. I'm not sittin' here like a fuckin' eejit.' Teresa leans forward, closin' her eyes and openin' her mouth. I open my mouth but keep my eyes open. She locks on like a spacecraft dockin'.

She opens and closes her mouth. I do the same, movin' my head round so I can see the others. Glue Boy's goin' in and out too. He puts his hand up Glue Girl's skirt. She puts her hand between his legs. I can see the outline of his dick, stickin' out. My dick twitches. I want to watch them.

Yuck! She just put her tongue in my mouth. God only knows where that's been. My tongue pushes hers back into her mouth, but she thinks that we're havin' a tongue fight. I see a tiny Luke Skywalker in my mouth, holdin' my tongue lightsaber. In her mouth Darth Vader is holding hers. Our lightsaber tongues lock. She makes this funny noise. I think she likes it. She grabs my dick. It's gettin' hard but she's stranglin' it to death.

Jesus, this is awful. Sorry, Jesus, sayin' your name while bein' dirty. There can't be any more to learn. I don't care if there is. Sorry Martine. I push her off.

'I've got to go,' I say.

'Where?' says she.

'To Ma's chippy, to get our dinner,' says me. Improvising never lets me down.

'Ach, stay another wee while,' says she.

'If it was just for me it'd be OK, but our ones'll kick my shite in,' I say, really gettin' into character now. I can really act on glue. 'But here, sure I'll get Ma to gimme extra chips and I'll bring ye's some up.'

'Aye, fuck, dead on,' says Glue Boy.

Teresa's buyin' it but she still isn't movin'. I push her off and stand up.

'Right, well, I'll see ye's later on,' says me.

'Aye,' says he.

'I'll walk out with ye,' says Teresa.

'Nah, it's OK, I've gotta run.' I hurry to the light of the Glue Hole and climb through.

'Wait, Mickey,' she shouts.

She's right behind me. *Fuck a big giant duck!* How can someone so big move so fast? I jump through the Glue Hole, out to the concrete path.

'I've gotta run,' I shout, not lookin' back.

'Whose sticks are these?' says she.

Shit, shit, shit! I have to go back over to her.

She reaches out of the Glue Hole and puts her arms round my neck. I close my eyes tight and dive in, tongue first, so she can't get hers into mine. I mouth 'I don't like this' as I lumber her. That cancels it. I break off, grab the barrow. 'Awooah!' my hands hurt. I push with all my might.

'Here, don't forget the chips!' she shouts.

∾

Briege, Roisin and Sheila are at the bottom of our path. Must be callin' for Wee Maggie. I push past them into the house.

'Right?' says Briege, the Great Evil One. Davros of the Daleks.

'Right?' I play along like we don't hate each other's guts.

Wee Maggie comes to the door and gives me a dirty look.

I go into the coal hole and check Ma's coat pocket and her purse is there. I put in the money that was left after I paid Mrs McQuillan what I owed. I can't believe I got so much. Next time, I'll pay some to Minnie. I hold a 10p and think about a mix-up. But mix-ups just aren't the same without Wee Maggie. I could give it to her so she can get one. Maybe it will make her remember when we were best friends.

I squeeze next to Wee Maggie, who's still at the door.

'Are ye comin' out?' says Briege.

Me? What's goin' on? She can't have forgot. Unless she's been hit in the head with a rubber bullet.

'Why?' says me.

'We're playin' at the gable. Rallio. Are ye playin'?' says she.

I look at Wee Maggie, who looks like she's been electramuted. She can't believe it. *I* can't believe it. Somethin's not right. Fishy fingers. But I want to get to Martine now I can show her how to lumber. And if we're goin' to be together, I'll have to get on with her best friend.

'Well, are ye comin?' says Briege.

'Aye, in a wee bit.' I play it cool.

'Hold on,' says Sheila and goes to Briege. They gaggle together, whisperin'.

Wee Maggie comes behind me and pulls at my shorts. 'What's goin' on?' she whispers. It's the first thing she's said to me in ages.

Sheila comes back. 'It was gonna be a surprise, but we're goin' to Martine's garage to practice a new play. And we need a boy. D'ye wanna come round or not?' says Sheila.

Me? God! My dream come true. I knew it'd happen one day. A play. Martine's garage. Wee Maggie grabs my hand. 'Awoaahh!' Jesus, she has the grip of a wrestler and she's squeezin' the splinters in my hands. Her face is like thunder. Can she only think about herself? She's just jealous

cuz she thinks they're *her* friends now. She's not gettin' that
10p.

'Is Martine gonna be there?' I ask.

Briege looks at me. I feel my face on fire.

'Aye. C'mon, if you're comin',' Briege says and leaves.

I shake off Wee Maggie's hand and follow them down the
path.

'I need to go to my house first. Yous go on round to Martine's and I'll meet ye's in the garage,' says Briege and leaves
with Roisin.

Me and Sheila walk to Martine's house. I look back, Wee
Maggie looks ragin'. She waves *c'mere*, to me. I shake my head.

At Martine's, I stand back while Sheila knocks the door.
After we've rehearsed the play, I can take Martine away and
show her how to lumber. And Briege won't say nothin' cuz I'm
not just *in* the gang, I'll be big in the gang. Me and Martine
will be the King and Queen of the Prom.

'Is Martine in?' Sheila asks Martine's Ma who looks me
up and down. What does she want? A picture? Am I wearin'
somethin' belongin' to her?

'Martine. Yer wanted,' her Ma calls up the stairs.

Martine comes down the stairs and sees me. She goes red
like me. Blushin'. Cuz she's in love.

'Are ye comin' round to the garage?' says Sheila.

'What for?' she asks.

'For the practice,' says Sheila.

'What practice?' says Martine.

'Did ye forget?' says Sheila, like *You're such a dopey dick
but so God-damn gorgeous all we can do is laugh about it.*

'I've got to stay in for a wee bit cuz we're waitin' for the
doctor cuz our Barry has German Measles,' says Martine.

'Well, can we have the keys to your garage then and we'll
meet ye round there when ye can come?' says Sheila.

'Mammy, can Briege and themin's practice in the garage for a wee while?'

Her Ma gives her the key, but she doesn't look too happy about it.

'Here.' Martine gives the key to Sheila. 'I'll see ye round there.'

I give a little look back as we get to the entry. Martine's watchin'. I give her a big smile and thumbs up and nod sayin' *Yes, Sir, I Can Boogie.* We slip into the tiny entry and out the back of the houses to the garage. Sheila opens the lock and we go inside.

'Right, let's tidy up while we wait. You clean up on the stage,' says Sheila.

Me on stage. I walk to it slow. Like I'm in Chapel on the way to the altar. It feels like loads of people are watchin' me. Up close, I can see the stage has been made with crates tied together. Martine's Da must have made it for her. Imagine havin' a Da like that.

Sheila's not doin' a pick of work, standin' with her arms folded. Lazy wee pig. I'm gonna clean the stage really good before Briege comes back. She'll see how I'm brilliant, and how much better I am to have around than Sheila.

'Is Helmet comin'?' I ask. God, I hope not, cuz I want the main part.

'He's away seein' his Ma on his holidays,' Sheila says. I haven't seen him about for ages. Normally I would hate him cuz he can afford a holiday, but I actually feel sorry for him cuz after they've seen me act he'll never get another part again.

I step onto the stage. A cold, tingly wave makes its way up my legs and arms. This feels right. This is where I belong. I hear someone come in. Briege. With a smile on her face that I don't like. Briege's Ma appears behind, her arms folded over her apron like she's in *Coronation Street*. A huge man fills the doorway.

My tongue has turned into a sponge suckin' all the wet out of my mouth. My heart goes like a dinger.

'What's yer name, son?' the big man says, in a gravelly voice, the way Da sounds with a hangover after smokin' 200 Park Drive.

*Can't answer. Systems down.* Briege and her henchwomen stand with their arms folded, starin' at me with big smiles. I should have known.

'Girls, it's time for ye's to leave.' The man sits at the back where I sat to watch the play.

'Can I not stay?' Briege asks her Ma who looks at the man.

'This is not a game, love. Off ye go now,' he says.

It's not a play. It's not a game. What is it? Somethin' very, very bad.

Briege leads the girls out. At the door, she gives me a smile on only one side of her mouth, like that Charleen in *Dallas*.

'Stay close and let me know if anyone comes,' says Briege's Ma, closin' the door. She stands beside the man. They both stare at me. I shuffle to the edge of the stage.

'Where are ye goin'?' the man says. 'Stay where ye are.'

I stop dead.

'Right, now,' says Briege's Ma. 'Tell the man what ye shouted all over the street.'

A sound happens in my throat. If my Ma was here . . .

'Tell the man!' she shouts.

My lips open. 'I . . .' is all that comes out. I can feel a wave goin' down me now. My head emptyin', my chest, arms, legs. I could faint on stage. I'd be good at it.

'What's yer name, son?' says he.

I still can't speak.

'Tell me yer name!' he shouts.

'His name's Mickey Donnelly,' Briege's Ma says.

'Paddy Donnelly's brother?' says he.

Oh no! Every time I met a new teacher at school I'd hear that. Followed by *hope you're nothing like him*.

'Yes,' I croak. I clear my throat with a cough. I could pretend I've got TB.

'D'ye know who I am?' says he.

'No, Mister,' says me.

'Do ye know why I'm here?'

'No, Mister.'

'Now, we've been tol' ye've been actin' the big lad . . .' says he.

*Me!* I can't believe that someone thinks I'm that good at it. I've only been rehearsin'.

'A Ginny-Ann more like . . .' says Briege's Ma. She shouldn't be allowed to say that. It's not fair.

'Who do you know in the IRA?' says he.

'I . . .' Wait, is this a test? Are they seein' if I *loose talk*? 'No, Mister, sure I don't even know anybody who's in the IRA,' says me.

'Ye know who's in jail but, don't ye?' says the Briege's Ma.

'No, I don't even know anybody in jail,' says me.

'And ye didn't shout all over the street in front of everyone that my husband was in prison for stealin' sausages?' she says.

I look down at my feet. All I can do is wait for this to be over.

'Well?' says he.

'Yes, Mister,' I say.

'Don't ye realise that ye could get into serious trouble for talkin' out of turn?' he says.

'Who told you that anyway? About the sausages?' she asks.

'About the IRA. Did ye hear it in the street?' he asks.

'Or did ye hear it in yer house?' Briege's Ma says.

I always thought I'd be brilliant if I was ever interrogated. That I could be a hero.

'D'you hear me talkin' to you?' says he.

*Say nothin', Mickey.*

A long silence.

'Mr McAnally is a soldier,' says he. 'A man who has fought hard for his country and who's sittin' in jail for it. And, for your information, Mr McAnally is in jail for robbin' that factory cuz he was sent there by the Irish Republican Army,' says the man.

They wanted him to steal sausages? Why? Were they hungry? And could they not just buy them from the butcher's like everybody else? There's no way I'm ever gonna join the IRA if that's the kinda missions you get sent on.

'Now, son, this is how it works. The first time we have to talk to you, it's a wee chat, like this. The next time we'll come to your door and it'll get serious. Do ye understand what I'm sayin'?'

They call it a community beatin'.

'Yes, Mister,' I say.

'Just keep your mouth shut in future. Remember that. Don't ever have me callin' you in again. Do ye understand?' says he.

'I won't, I promise,' says me.

The Man stands up and goes to Briege's Ma. 'OK, Mrs McAnally, anymore trouble, ye come straight to me,' says he to her and heads out.

'Is that it?' she says after him, ragin'. She stabs her finger at me. 'You tell yer Ma to watch her mouth too or she'll be next.' The door slams behind her.

The door opens again. The room fills up with people, talkin', gettin' out their sweets, all in great form.

'Yes, Mickey Donnelly's in it. He's the Explorer. He wrote it himself. The queue's right round the street. Everybody's dying to see him,' says Sue Ellen from *Dallas*.

'I paid £100 for my ticket,' says Pamela Ewing.

'That's nothing, I paid £200!' says JR.

'I paid £1,000,' says Bette Davis. 'It'll be worth every penny to even be in the same room as such a great talent.'

They're all really famous actors. John Travolta and Olivia Newton-John. Wonder Woman, the Bionic Man, the Bionic Woman, Judy Garland and Toto. I'll have to tell Judy she's not allowed to bring dogs in. Toto changes into Killer. Judy Garland is lookin' after Killer in Heaven. The lights go down. Everyone goes quiet. Spotlight on me.

'Thank you all for comin'. It's so wonderful to look at this audience and see so many of my dear, dear, close friends.' Doris Day blows a kiss. I catch it and slap it on my cheek. 'This story is very special to me. I wrote it last night and I was doin' changes til the wee hours.'

Rustlin' and whispers.

'Thank you.' I bow. A huge round of applause and then silence. You could hear a Black Jack bein' unwrapped.

I – Explorer – walk in the big wind. Hailstones the size of gobstoppers. I fall to the ground, reach out to the audience, like Helmet Head did but much better. Bette Davis reaches out to me. My actin', so amazingly brill, she thinks it's real. I collapse. Death by enormous hail. I juke up. I see a tear roll from Olivia Newton-John's left eye.

The Dolls, clumpin' towards me, wake me up. They grab me, holdin' down my arms and legs. Queen Briege of the Dolls stands over me. Her head Exorcists round and instead of the back of her head, it's her Ma's face. She leans forward to eat me, her head turnin', the audience gasps. Wind blows the curtains lettin' light shine through the windows onto her and the

Dolls. They let go of me and put their funny hands over their eyes. They can't stand the light.

I know what they are. I know what to do. I grab my hatchet from my belt and chop Queen Briege in her chest and her ribs split like sticks. She screams and the Dolls scream too. Smoke comes from the Queen's mouth, and nose, and ears. She sizzles. She melts, like the Wicked Witch of the West. I look round at Judy and wink – she knows what I'm goin' through. The Dolls melt too cuz they can't survive without her. All of them disappear, leavin' just their clothes.

Martine comes runnin' out from behind the counter in a nun's outfit like Julie Andrews in *The Sound of Music*. 'Mickey, oh my God, Mickey. You're alive.' She raises her hands to Heaven. 'Thank you, Jesus.'

Martine rips off her habit. Underneath she's wearin' the dress Sandy wears in *Grease* when she turns into a dirty bitch.

'Mickey, I can't go on as a nun any longer. I love you. And I know God won't mind me leavin' the convent, cuz I know now that God has put me on this Earth for one thing and one thing only. And that's to give all my love to you.'

She little kisses me.

'Enough of these little kid kisses,' I say.' There's somethin' I wanna show you, Martine.'

I grab her and lumber the face right off her. The light fades to black. The audience are on their feet shoutin', cheerin', cryin' and clappin'. 'More!' they shout. 'More!' But we just keep on lumberin'. Even after the lights come back on. I push Martine off me. I have my audience to think of. I stand before them. Martine looks like she's goin' to faint.

'Thank you. Thank you all so much,' I say. I take Martine's hand and pull her in front of me, so she can get some applause. But she doesn't look at the audience. She can't keep her eyes off me.

Briege is at the door. 'There's definitely somethin' wrong with you,' she says. 'Get out and never come back. You'll never get in here again.'

I walk scundered to the door. Outside, I hear her shout behind me, 'And your Da isn't in America. My Ma saw him yesterday at the bookie's.' I feel sick. 'So you're not goin' to America. But I am. I'm gettin' sponsored because my Da's in jail for his country.'

I can't say anythin'. She's won me. Forever. I can never win that back.

# 18

'Is that it?' says Martine, turnin' her nose up, lyin' back on the grass.

'Yes,' I say, lookin' across to the mountains. 'Have you been up to Cave Hill? The view is amazin'. And you can watch the boats. They go all the way to America. I'm goin' to go there one day. Get out of Ardoyne forever.' I want to take her with me.

'Why do you want to do that?' says she.

Can she really mean that? I look at her. The longer I stare at her face the more different she looks. Maybe cuz I've never been with her this long. She's still gorgeous but not her.

'Show me again,' she says.

I roll on top of her, close my eyes and go in, mouth open, tongue out. Her lips are really soft so I'm really gentle. Her tongue, slimy and horrible. It doesn't feel any nicer than lumberin' Teresa McAllister, except in my head.

She breaks off. 'You're not gettin' hard.'

I near swallow my tongue. My Martine isn't like that.

'I mustn't be doin' it right,' she says.

The poor thing. She's just worried about what I think. 'You have to keep doin' it,' I say. 'Once more and I bet you I will.'

I go for it again. I lumber her a bit harder this time. Not even a semi. I open my eyes to see her. That feels better. She opens hers. I close mine, scundered. I lean off her a bit cuz I don't want her to feel nothin's happenin'. I see Girl's World in my brain TV. And me kissin' it. There's a wee throb down there. I think of the Girl's World cool, plastic lips. Tiny hard lips. No slime. No tongues. No weirdness.

A wee twitchin'. 'Look.' I roll off and press my shorts tight over my hardner to show her.

'I did it right,' says she. 'Thanks, Mickey.' She kisses my cheek.

'So, will we go and tell everybody?' I say.

'What?' she says with a scrunchie face.

'Not that we were lumberin',' I laugh. 'I mean, that we're boyfriend and girlfriend.'

'You can't tell anyone we did this. You promised.' She looks scared.

'I won't. God, I wouldn't do that,' says me. 'Are we goin' out in secret?' That could be cool. But I'd rather everybody knew so they'd be dead jealous and stop callin' me names.

'No, Mickey.' She shakes her head and stands up, brushin' the grass from her dress. 'We're not goin' out.'

'But . . .why?'

'You know why. How could we? Nobody likes you, Mickey. And the way you get on like a wee girl. Are you gay, Mickey? I won't tell anyone.'

My heart's bein' hit with a hammer. How could she say that to me?

'I have to go. Remember your promise.' She runs down the hill.

I sit up. I can't think of anything to say. Did she . . .? She's a user. I hate her. 'I didn't even like it,' I shout, as she crawls through the fence. 'And there's more I haven't even told you!' She runs down the Bray. I thought she was different, but she's just like everybody else. I hate her. I hate them all.

I kick the grass. Stub my foot in to bring up the dirt. I look up at those bloody mountains. I'm goin' to run. Run til I get to them. And then run up them. And . . . and run over them and I'm going wherever it is that's on the other side. Out of here and away from them all forever. And I'm never comin' back.

I run. Double speed. Down the hill. Bang into the fence and through.

Triple speed. 400 billion, trillion miles per hour . . . per minute . . . per second.

At the top of the Bray. I look down the gigantic, deep slope.

*Will I do the run of certain death?*

Yes.

*Let's see you try, gay boy!*

I'm not bloody gay. I will run down it. Then you'll see. You wouldn't run down there if you weren't a real boy.

I run down that hill like someone not scared. Like an Ardoyne big man. Yeah.

*Faster, faster! Fly, ye little fairy.*

Shit! I can't keep up with my legs.

'Come in Legs, are you receivin' me? Over.'

'Brain is that you? This is Legs, you're breakin' up . . .'

My legs aren't gettin' the message. I can't control them.

'We've lost him, says Mind Control HQ.

I lose control and slow motion kicks in. I am Steve Austin.

Crash! I hit the ground. I feel nothin'. And again. Still nothin'. I'm the bouncin' bomb, like in that movie. I hit the ground again. This time it connects with my knee and I feel it. I hear somethin' crunch. Tinglin' all over my body.

*Roll, roll, roll the gay, gently down the Bray.*

Dead stop. Stop dead. Dead. How many lives do you get?

Mickey Donnelly – a boy barely alive. But we can rebuild him. We have the technology to make the world's first Bionic Boy.

My T-shirt is ripped. My shorts are piggin' dirty. My

elbows and knees are scratched and bleedin'. I can't feel my lips and my head hurts.

Someone walks down from the Eggy. I don't want them to see me. I try to get up. I can't hold my knees straight. Everythin' hurts. A girl is lookin' at me. I try to run, but my knees won't let me. They keep givin' way so I'm runnin' like Egor.

*You rang, Master?*

'Are you alright, Mickey?' It's Teresa McAllister. On her way from Glue World.

I hobble off through the back entry of Havana Street.

My T-shirt's ripped – my American flag T-shirt! My do-you-for-the-whole-summer-holidays T-shirt. Ma's gonna kill me. She'll murder me, then murder me again. It's the best T-shirt I've ever had in my entire life. The one that makes me look like a big boy. The one that makes people jealous of me.

*Nobody wants to be your friend, Mickey.*

All the boys and girls are playin' in the waste ground as I come out of the entry. They can see me cryin'. Evil Briege and User Martine.

'Mammy!' Even though I know she's at work I call her anyway. I hear laughin'.

'Mammy!' I get to our big door. It's closed. Why's our door closed? It's never closed. Everythin's against me. I bang and bang. It opens. Measles.

'Mammy!' I scream into the livin' room.

'Oh Holy Mother of God!' Ma jumps from the chair.

'Mammy, you're here.' Thank you, God. A miracle.

'Oh Holy Christ, look at him. Paddy!' shouts Ma.

'Whaddye want me to do?' Paddy looks out from the kitchen then goes back in. I fall onto the floor cryin'.

'Mammy, Mammy,' I cry. Ma holds me. All she keeps sayin' is 'What happened? What happened?'

Wee Maggie starts cryin'.

'Look at my good T-Shirt, Mammy, it's all ripped.'

'Who cares about your T-Shirt?'

'I do, Mammy. It's for the summer, Mammy.'

'But sure the summer's over, son. You've school next week.'

'Next week?' Oh God. 'Don't make me go, Mammy, please! Please! I can't go to St. Gabriel's.'

'Look at his hands. What did you fall on? Wood?' says Ma.

'The Bray,' I cry.

'But your hands. Jesus, Mickey, son.' Ma starts to cry.

I hide my hands behind my back.

'Oh Mary,' cries Ma, 'take him into the kitchen quick, I can't . . .'

I hop into the kitchen and see Paddy out in the yard puttin' somethin' in Killer's box. Again! I can't believe it. I'm goin' to tell Ma. *Remember the IRA man warned you, Mickey.* Yeah, but Paddy wouldn't hand me into the IRA. Would he?

'Here, Mickey, sit down here,' says Measles.

'Is it really bad?' I ask.

'You'll be alright,' says she.

Paddy comes in with a look of utter disgust on his face. 'Cryin' like a wee girl.'

I hate him. He's the worst of them all. 'So, what are you?' I shout. *Don't Mickey! Don't!* 'You're just a big murderer.'

Freeze. I'm in the doorway of the kitchen. The only thing movin' is Ma's eyes between me and Paddy.

'What did you say, Mickey?' asks Ma.

I look at Paddy.

'Nothin', Ma,' says he. 'He's probably makin' up stories as usual, playin' with wee girls.'

'I don't play with the wee girls.' It's so not fair cuz I don't. 'And I'm not makin' it up.'

'You'd better shut your fruity wee mouth or I'll fuckin' kill you.'

'Paddy, stop it.' Ma stands. 'Mickey, that's enough.'

'Are you takin' his side?' I can't believe it. 'It's all his fault. Cuz he hates me. Everybody hates me. Now you hate me too.'

'I don't hate you, Mickey,' says Ma.

'What are yous all doin' home anyway? Yous were talkin' about me!' I shout. They all look at each other. 'See! Yous were!'

'Shut up, you. You don't know nathin',' says Paddy.

'Yous aren't tellin' me somethin'. What is it?' I shout.

'Keep it down, Mickey,' Ma says.

'Tell him.' I point. 'You're takin' his side and it wasn't even my fault,' says me.

'Fruity boy,' says he.

'Killer!' I say.

Paddy's face turns to stone. 'What about Killer, Mickey?' Paddy says.

I can't swallow. I've stopped breathin'. He knows. He's going to tell. No. No. He won't win me.

'What about the bomb you put down the street and the . . .'

Paddy dives at me and I turn to run. He grabs me by the back of my T-shirt and it rips down my back.

'Paddy!' Ma screams.

'What the fuck is goin' on in this house?' a voice I half recognise booms from the livin' room.

No. It can't be. It can't be.

I turn back.

Da is standin' at the bottom of the stairs in his pyjamas.

∽

I can't sleep cuz of the shoutin' downstairs. I don't know how Our Paddy sleeps through it. It's hard to read in the dark. I wanted to find out how to be a brilliant actor and get to Hollywood. The book is borin' though.

I look for sex in the index. Montgomery Clift – Mammy loves him. I turn to the page. Holy crap! I don't believe he was gay. I bet you that's just people sayin' that. Like they say about me. He was probably just nice. He went with men and women! I've never heard of that before. Is that what actors do?

Shoutin' again. I can't make out what Da's sayin'. I crawl out from under the bed. Paddy's still asleep. Or pretendin'.

The bedroom door opens. I freeze.

'Mickey, what are you doin' out of bed?' Measles asks. She's all dolled up. Must have just come home.

'Nothin'. I can't sleep.'

'Go you into my bed and sleep. I want to talk to Paddy.'

'He's asleep.'

'Never you mind, go on.' She pushes me out onto the landin' and closes the door.

I listen at the top of the stairs. Behind me there's snifflin' from Maggie and Measles' room.

I go in and lie down next to Wee Maggie. 'It's goin' to be OK.'

'Why's he shoutin'?' says she.

'He's just havin' a laugh. I swear,' I say. 'Like he's singin' to her but pretendin' she's far away,' I say.

'Is he, Mickey? Really?'

'Yes,' I say. 'Do you believe me?'

'You said he was in America,' she squints. 'Was Briege right?'

'No. He was. Now he's here and there's so much to sort out. He has to go back again,' I say.

'I don't like it when he's here. I want him to stay in America and we stay here.'

'Do you want to hear the sea?' I say, eyes wide.

She nods, makin' a crinkly sound on her Cabbage Patch Doll pillowcase.

'Close your eyes,' I say, and put my hand over her unpillowed ear. I'm goin' to protect her. I make wind sounds in her ear. I'm her big brother.

Ma's shoutin' now too. Not like her. He's only back and it's started. If he hits her, I'll kill him. I swear to God I'll go down there.

Ma hasn't even gone to work. Lucky I've got money now. I'll make more sticks tomorrow. Maybe go round the other shops.

Wee Maggie's out like a light. I remember when I used to sleep. 'I promise,' I whisper, 'he's goin' to go away for a very, very long time. I'm goin' to fix it.'

I creep slowly off the bed and out to the landin'. Glass smashes. Everybody knows what happens next. I listen for Maggie. Nothin'.

I open my bedroom door. Our Paddy and Measles jump.

'Get into my bed, Mickey,' says Measles.

'And don't come out again,' says Paddy.

I give him a big dirty look. Some big brave IRA man he is. He's not even goin' to stop Da. I close the door. I could go down, listen at the door, but I want to see too. Keep my eye on him.

Openin' Maggie's bedroom window, lookin' down into the yard, I wonder how bad it would be if I fell onto Killer's box. If I feel myself fallin', I'll jump, then there'll be more control on the land. *Smarter than the average bear.*

Twistin' my bum on the window sill, I stick my feet outside, grab the old, metal drainpipe and pull myself over and cling to it. *Mission Impossible. Dun, dun, dun-dun, dun, dun.* I hope the pipe doesn't self destruct in five seconds.

My bare feet grip the joins holdin' it to the wall and hand

208

by hand, foot by foot, I make my way down like a monkey, but I'd rather be doin' it like a fireman. My hands hurt from the splinters.

I step onto Killer's box. I can't feel sad now, I have to look after Ma. Jukin' in the kitchen window, the livin' room door is open. Da is pacin' back and forward. Ma shoutin' and pointin'. I wish the window was open. It'll be about money. And Paddy, maybe.

Da goes to the livin' room door. Ma pulls him back, shoutin' and angry, not beggin'. He raises his hand. I push the back door. Locked. I'm goin' to kill him. How can I get in? I look in the window. He hits her. I run to the yard door – padlocked. Ma got it to keep Killer in. I'm trapped.

I run and jump up the drainpipe, try to pull myself up, but can't. I look in. He raises his hand again.

'No!' I shout and bang the window. He sees me. He's like *What the fuck?* He's comin'. Shit. He closes the livin' room door so I can't see in. I thump the kitchen window harder.

There's nothin', I can do nothin'. Nothin'.

I climb into Killer's dog box and let the roof close slowly so as not to bang. I lie in a wee ball on the carpet. It stinks, but I like it. I search for Killer's wee blanket and I touch woollen cloth with hard inside.

I take out not-really-Uncle Tommy's Brit-killin' gun and hug the cold metal against me.

I hate him. I want him gone, forever. I promised Wee Maggie. If I could get in there now, I'd shoot him dead. I'll wait. And I'll have to be smart about it.

I hug the gun tight. I will win him.

I'll win them all.

I know what I'm goin' to do.

# 19

THE BOTTOM WAY is blocked now by new barricades they're buildin' to stop the riots. I could go all the way round the back entries, but they'll be full of bins and rubbish. Or all the way round the boarded-up, burnt-out houses they're knockin' down, but it would take forever. Or I could just run straight across the wee bit of waste ground that's left to the back door of the house shop. It would only take a minute.

There's no-one around to see me. Frig it!

I push hard on the handles, gettin' a jerky run goin'. I feel like I'm in one of them strong man competitions on the TV. I give a big growl like they do to get more strength.

The barrow jolts to a stop. The wheel's stuck. I push but can't get it goin'. My hands are throbbin'. Boys noise behind me. Girls noise, too. The whole street together.

'Arggghhh,' I growl, pushin' with everythin' I have, but I'm no strong man.

'Look, it's Molly Malone,' I hear Ma's-a-Whore shout.
'*As she wheels her wheelbarrow,*
*Through streets broad and narrow . . .*' I hear him sing.
The kids are all laughin'.

'Molly Malone, that's a good one,' says Briege.

It is. I can't deny it. It's funny. Why are stupid people so good at being evil?

'What's that in there?' he asks, liftin' a bag of sticks.

Say nothin'. Not a word. No trouble. I look over to my house. Worse than these ones seein' this is our ones seein'. They're always home now, not leavin' Ma alone since the other night.

'Where you goin' with them?' says Briege. They're all crowdin' round me. The two evils have joined forces. Ma's-a-Whore lifts a bag of sticks. If he lifts another bag he'll see my gun. I couldn't risk the IRA comin' to take it, or Paddy, then I can't use it for Da. But if Ma's-a-Whore sees it he'll tell the IRA. For stealin' their gun, I wouldn't just get a beating. I'd get my knees done.

I edge round the side of the barrow and grab my bag of sticks from him. 'Leave them alone,' I say.

'Leave them alone,' he mimics me, soundin' like a wee girl. 'Are you deliverin' sticks?'

Briege squints at me and the hatchet. 'Are you sellin' bags of sticks?' Laughter explodes from her. 'From a wheelbarrow.' Her laugh. If evil had a sound . . .

Don't say anythin', Mickey. You can't let them see the gun. I walk back to the handles while they're busy.

'Where do you think you're goin'?' Ma's-a-Whore, puts his foot on the wheel.

'To the shop, now let me go . . . please,' I say, lookin' past him.

'Listen to gay boy.' He thumps my chest.

I push the handles. The wheel jerks forward. I push through the crowd.

*'In Ardoyne's fair city, where the girl's are so pretty,*

*I first set my eyes on sweet Molly Malone,'* Briege sings. 'That's what we'll call him. Molly.' They all laugh.

*'As she wheels her wheelbarrow, through streets broad and narrow . . .'*

People come out of their houses, starin' and pointin'. I use all my actin' skills to show just how much I don't care.

The singin' stops. The boys and girls all behind me.

'Fruity boy!' Ma's-a-Whore shouts at the top of his voice. 'Sure I saw him buyin' fanny pads. They were probably for him.'

'Did you hear him cryin' for his Mammy all over the street the other day?' Briege shouts, and looks over at our door. 'Mammy's boy!'

If I have to use my gun, I will. If they make me. I don't care anymore.

They all chant, 'Molly! Molly!'

I want to cry but I'm not goin' to. I drop the handles and turn to them. 'I don't care what yous think.' I can be louder than any of them. I scream, 'Do you hear me? All of yous. I'm better than all of yous. Yous are all dirtbirds. And horrible people. And I hate yous all. And I'm goin' to show yous. I know what I am. I'm . . .'

'Gay?' Ma's-a-Whore says and they all laugh.

'I'm not gay,' I shout, 'I am an actor!' Silence. That shut them up.

Sniggers. Laughin'.

'How can you be an actor when ye've never even acted before?' says Briege.

I hadn't thought of that. They don't know I act all the time. I see Our Paddy and Measles followed by Ma come out our door. Laughin'. They think this is a game.

'Is this like your Da bein' in America?' says Briege.

'Shut up, you,' I say. 'I'll get my Mammy for yous all.'

'Mammy's boy,' says Ma's-a-Whore. The others join in chantin' again.

Wee Maggie pushes her way out of the crowd and comes beside me, takin' my hand.

Movement to my right. I turn to see Our Paddy doin' a leapin' Karate kick in the air like he's Bruce Lee. 'I'll fuckin' kill every one of ye's!' he shouts. They scatter in all directions like ants runnin' from under a rock. Only Briege McAnally stands still.

'You'd better not touch me,' she says.

'I'll touch you alright,' Our Measle's beside me.

'Will ye? Then I'll get the IRA to kill you,' says she.

'What did she say?' Ma arrives, her face bruised, one eye swollen. I can't believe she's showin' the street.

Over Briege's shoulder, I see Ma's-a-Whore knockin' Briege's door. Her Ma comes out.

'I can get the IRA. Ask him,' says Briege, pointin' to me. 'He's already been warned.'

Ma and Paddy look at each other and look at me. I watch Briege's Ma comin' across the street towards us. There'll be murder.

'It was nothin', Mammy,' I say.

Ma's face is goin' red. Her chest big, as she gasps in breath like she's drownin'. Or pumpin' herself up like a balloon. It's *The Hulk*.

'Just you stay away from my daughter!' Briege's Ma shouts, as she walks. 'He got what he deserved. I told them. *I* got the IRA for him. Me. What are you goin' to do about it?'

Ma looks down at me. She looks at the sticks, frownin'. 'What have you been doin'?' She takes my two hands gently, and turns them palm up. 'My son,' she says, and her body sort of shudders. She shakes her head. 'Your wee hands are destroyed.' She traces the splinters and welts with her fingers.

'It's OK, Mammy,' I say.

Her face tightens, scrunches up then goes blank. She drops my hands and wipes her eyes. She reaches into the barrow and lifts the hatchet. She holds it over her head like an Indian squaw. 'I'll fuckin' kill you!' she screams and runs at Mrs McAnally.

I launch after Ma. A hand on my chest holds me back. 'Don't,' says Paddy. I look up at him and stop pushin'. I listen to my big brother. All us Donnellys stand together in the waste ground watchin'. Except Da, of course. The gun! I need to get it off side.

I push the wheelbarrow, but it's too stiff.

Paddy snatches the handles off me. 'C'mon, ye wee weaklin', where we goin' with these?'

I point to McQuillan's and we walk there together. I juke over at Ma who's hatchetin' Mrs McAnally's front door. She squeals with each chop.

Paddy drops the barrow outside the house shop.

'Go on, it's OK now,' I say.

'Who was it that warned you?' he says.

'I don't know him, some man,' I say.

'Why didn't you tell Ma? She'd've sorted it.' I don't say anythin'. 'If anyone calls you names again, you come to me,' says he. 'And in St. Gabe's. You just tell them who your brother is. I leave this year. We rule the school. I rule the school,' he says.

'OK,' I say.

He spits on the ground and walks away. 'Just keep your mouth shut so they don't hear your voice. And try not to be such a poof, Mickey,' he says. He spits again and heads off towards our house.

Ma's stopped, holdin' the wall for breath.

'Mrs McQuillan, I've got the sticks,' I say. 'Another shipment, all the way from Woodsville, Tennessee,' I say, in my American accent.

'You're good at that,' says she, lookin' over her shoulder at Ma.

'That's cuz I'm goin' to go to America very soon,' I say.

'I bet you are, Mickey Donnelly, that wouldn't surprise me at all.' She smiles. 'Here you go.'

I smile back, stickin' the money straight in my pocket. She bends down to grab the bags.

'I'll do that, Mrs. I wouldn't have a lady like you bendin'.'

'Mickey Donnelly,' she laughs. 'That's made my day.' She sighs. 'I dare say you will make it to America and be an actor.' She must have been watchin' the whole thing. 'Hollywood, here you come. I'll have to get your autograph now, before you make it and won't want to know me.' She giggles as she walks in.

Ma's takin' on the whole street like some horror-story hatchet murderer. 'Any of yous say one word against my son, or any of my children, IRA or no, I'll kill every fuckin' one of yous!' Ma holds the hatchet over her head.

My Ma is completely nuts.

I root out the gun and stick it down my trousers. Now it's my turn to protect Ma.

∼

'No messin' about for Mary,' says Ma. 'Your Da's not in. But he'll be back tonight at some point.'

I look at her eye. The street seein' is one thing, but everyone comin' in the chippy and the Shamrock Club?

'Don't go to work, Mammy,' says me. 'Don't let them see your face.'

Ma puts a hand on her stomach. 'The money man's dead, son.' And Da back too. Takin' her money for drink. I didn't think I could hate him any more than I already did. Just makes what I'm goin' to do all the easier.

'Say you fell, Mammy,' I say. 'Round the old houses with

all them bricks.' She smiles and tucks the blanket under the mattress. 'Or a rubber bullet hit you in the eye.'

'Look at the state of you. Sure, they'll all be sayin' yer Ma beats ye,' she says.

'You do!' We laugh. 'Sure they all know I'm an eejit!'

'You're no eejit, Mickey Donnelly,' says she. 'You're stronger and braver than any of them out there. I don't know where you get it from.'

'You, Mammy. I get it from you.'

Ma shakes her head. 'Shut up, wee boy and go to sleep.'

At the bedroom door, she does her routine. She looks round the room – I wonder what's she's lookin' for when she does that. She pats her coat pocket for her purse – so Da can't get it. And she twists her ring on her finger – cuz she still loves him after everythin' he's done.

'Be a good boy,' she says.

Not tonight, Mammy. No.

She leaves and I'm scared. 'Mammy,' I say.

She comes back in. 'What is it, Mickey, I'm goin' to be late.'

'Can I ask you something?'

'What is it, Mickey? Hurry up.'

'Do you promise not to laugh?'

'Mickey, I'll dig ye if you don't tell me nigh,' she says.

'It doesn't matter,' I say.

'Fuck me, wee boy, you're mustard,' she says, and leaves again. She reaches the top of the landin'. I'm so scundered to ask, but after what I'm going to do she mightn't ever love me again.

'Mammy, will you hug me?' I shout.

Her footsteps stop. Silence. I hide my head under the blankets. I can't believe I said that. So stupid. I scrunch up into a ball. Nothin' happens. It's OK, but.

Weight on me. Through the blankets. Leanin' heavy. Blankets tuck in all round me. I get a slap on the arse. I laugh. I poke my head out.

'You're in bed early,' says Measles.

I look past her but Ma's not there.

'Just me and you tonight,' says she. Wee Maggie's at Aunt Kathleen's. That's another reason tonight is perfect.

'Look,' she says, opening a plastic bag, 'A party for us.'

'Jesus,' I say.

'You're gettin' spoiled rotten tonight,' says she. 'Ma loves you, licky arse.'

I smile. Mammy loves me. The sweets prove it. Even Measles said it.

'Well, go on then,' she says.

I take out a packet of crisps. Nothin' says *I love you* like a packet of Tayto Cheese and Onion. Measles watches me eat. 'Do you want some?' I say.

'They stink your breath,' she says.

'So,' I say. 'Who cares about that?'

She looks out the window and waves. She doesn't want cheese and onion crisps and she's wavin' outside. It doesn't take Sherlock Holmes.

'Have you got a boy out there?' I say.

'Yes,' says she. 'Mammy says I can't bring him in.' Her eyes go all *Me is woe, I'm Juliet kept from my Romeo.*

'Sure, go on out,' I say. 'I won't tell.'

Her eyes light up like petrol bombs. 'I couldn't, Mickey,' says she.

I burst out laughin'. 'Aye, but you could really.'

She laughs too. 'Are you sure?'

'Yes,' I say. This is even better. If no-one's here. In case it all goes wrong.

'Mickey, I love you,' says she, and gives me a big hug and a kiss on the cheek. Jesus, bein' in love makes her happy. I wish it was like that for Ma.

'Before you go, will you sing me one of your songs?' I say.

'OK,' says she, wavin' out the window with a smile that Doris Day would be jealous of. 'Which one?'

I know exactly which one. 'The one about the mum and her son with the gun,' I says.

'OK, lie back,' says she. She nudges in close to me.

She sings. I close my eyes and play the words in my head like a filim:

There's an IRA man. He's wearin' a black beret, balaclava, dark sunglasses, green jumper and trousers and big black boots. He's got a gun. His Mammy comes out of her house arms raised to the sky, like in silent movies. She doesn't want him to go to war.

He's in a dark alley waitin'. An army patrol passes. He shoots a Brit in the head. Blood flies out everywhere. The patrol runs off, leavin' the Brit to die. I see the Brit that got shot outside Aul Sammy's lyin' all alone.

*'Oh Mother, Oh Mother, comfort me.*
*I know these awful things are meant to be.*
*And when this war of freedom has been won,*
*I'll promise you I'll put away my gun.'*

An orchestra is playin' big filim music. He runs to the Brit, puts a rifle to his head. 'Please,' the Brit sobs, 'have Mercy. Let me live.'

Now I'm the IRA man. I take off my sunglasses. I've seen the Brit's eyes before. Scary and sad. From the *Loose Talk* posters.

My Mammy comes, covered in a black shawl. She lifts the Brit's head up, restin' it on her lap. This isn't in the song. She strokes his hair and hums to him. The Brit turns into Da.

*But to your memory, mother, his life I spared.*

Mammy doesn't know what's good for her. I pull Da off Ma's lap and shoot him in the head.

~

Heavy thuds on the stairs. Moanin'. Da's talkin' to himself. I crawl out from under Paddy's bed, tiptoe to the landin'. I peek round. Da's fallen on the stairs, passed out.

'C'mon, Da,' I whisper. 'It's time to go to bed.'

Moanin'. His head lifts. 'Mickey, is that you, son?' he says.

'Yes, Da,' I say, puttin' his arm over my shoulder. 'Let's get you to bed.'

'Yes,' he says, on his knees. He uses the wall to push himself up and leans on me. We take it one stair at a time.

I put my arm around his waist and drag him up. He's like the Leanin' Tower of Pisa, but manages to keep goin'. At the landin', he falls onto the wall and slides along til his head hits his bedroom door.

'Hey, hey, hold on,' I say, openin' the door. He staggers forward and I guide him to the bed where he collapses on his back. 'There you go,' I say, and start loosenin' his laces.

'Have I been a good Daddy, Mickey? Have I?'

'It's OK,' I say.

'I've tried . . . I have. I know . . .'

'Stop it, Da. You're drunk,' I say.

'No, son. It's important. Have I been a good Daddy? Tell me, have I, son?' He starts cryin'. 'I'm sorry, son. I am. I swear to God, I'm sorry for everythin'.' He grabs me and hugs me on top of him. 'I had to try . . . to get out . . . I'm sorry. I love you.'

Shut up! I hate you! And you stink! You dirty, filthy bastard!

I try to get loose, but he's holdin' me so tight I can't move.

*Dear Jereon,*
*This is Mickey Donnelly here. Remember me? I'm your pen pal from Belfast. I'm really, really sorry that we lost touch.*

*It was my fault. I was in a desperate car crash. It was in my Daddy's BMW. I actually died but there was a miracle and I am living now. But don't worry, I'm not a zombie.*

'Have I been a good Daddy? Have I?'
No, you bloody haven't, you big bastard! Stop askin' that.

*I was in the hospital for months. They were going to cut my legs off but then my Daddy paid for this special Doctor from America who came over and cured me.*
*So I'm writing to ask you if please can I come over to the Philippines? Would you ask your Mummy and Daddy can I come and live with you? I'd get a job and everything. I'd do all the cooking and the cleaning around your house and everything too. And I could be your best friend in the whole wide-world ever! I promise I will never, never snipe off and play with other people. Only you. And I'm not a hard man so you don't have to worry.*

'Please, Mickey.' He's sobbin'. I can feel his tears on my skin.
'Yes. You've been a good Daddy,' I say. Not like it matters any more what I tell him.

*Please write back soon and let me know. It's urgent.*
*Your pen pal,*
*Master Mickey Donnelly Esquire*
*PS. My Mummy and Daddy and brother and sisters all died in the crash. I'm an orphan now. So if I can't come to you I'll have to go into an orphanage.*
*PPS I'll do anything you want.*

He lets me go. Passed out. I walk to my bedroom and get

the gun from my box of secret things. I know no miracles are comin' out of the sky. I know no pen pal is goin' to help me. I have to take care of this myself. I hold the gun tight in my two hands and walk to his bedroom.

## 20

I HAD IT ALL figured out. I thought for sure an army patrol would come past before Ma came back. It all would have been done. I look up and down the street, but it's still empty.

Measles came back first and went to bed. Paddy came in later and is snorin' away. They wouldn't go into his room anyway. Nor Ma. She's been on the sofa since he hit her. She should have been home hours ago.

There's normally Peelers and Brits walkin' around every two minutes and now when I need them . . . shit, there's Ma. I jump back into the house. I look around for somewhere to hide. The coal hole.

'What the frig are you doin', wee boy?' says Ma. She must have seen me and run up here.

'I couldn't sleep,' says me. She looks wrecked. 'Where have you been all this time?' I say.

'They had a lock-in. I thought I'd stay on after and do the cleaning straight away and save me havin' to go back.' She looks upstairs.

'He's in bed,' I say. 'I carried him up. Don't wake him, Ma.'

Ma twists her ring. She puts her purse on the hearth and goes out to the kitchen. I pounce on it but struggle with the metal clasp.

'What are you doin'?' Ma's behind me.

'Nothin',' I feel myself burnin' up, shovin' the purse back on the hearth.

Ma walks over and slaps me hard across the face. 'Why would you steal from your Mammy?' She bites her fist.

'I didn't, Mammy,' I cry.

She slaps me hard again. 'Just like your fuckin' Da.'

'No, Mammy. I was . . .'

Ma slaps me again. 'Don't lie to me. I can't take it.'

'I wasn't, Mammy, I swear to Almighty God!' I grab her elbows. 'I was puttin' in the stick money. I didn't want to scunder you by givin' it to you.'

'Mickey. Mickey,' she cries.

'I'm sorry, Mammy,' I say.

Ma goes for me and I jump back. 'Don't hit me, Mammy, you're hurting me.'

'I'm sorry, son.' She grabs me and holds me to her. 'I'm tired. Your Mammy's tired, son.' Mammy cries. I've never heard her say sorry before.

Ma stops and stares at the floor. She moves to the stairs.

'Our Mary said I've got school today,' I say to distract her.

Ma looks at me, twistin' that bloody ring. I'm goin' to get that ring off her somehow and flush it down the bloody toilet.

She sits on the arm of the sofa and stares out the window. I wait. I move towards her like when you don't want to scare a bird or a butterfly or a bee. I touch her leg. Like Maggie used to do for me when I spaced out, in case I never came back. Ma takes my hand. My Mammy holds my hand. Not since I was a little tiny boy has she done that. It really hurts because of the splinters, but it's so nice I don't want to say anythin'. I can't help flinchin' a wee bit. She looks at my face and then to my hand. She pets it. Blows on it. I'm Mammy's wee boy again.

'Come on, you're comin' with me,' says she.

'Where?' says me.

'That's for me to know and you to find out,' says she.

'Where, Mammy?' says me.

'Shut up, nigh,' says she. 'C'mon.' She marches out and I follow, takin' one last look up the stairs. No-one will go near that room anyway. I'll find a patrol when I'm out.

~

We walk up the Bray, down into the Bone, and cut across into the Cliftonville Road. All the way without sayin' a word. I really need to go to the toilet. It feels like two fists are pushin' into my belly and squeezin' everythin' out. I'm not even jokin'. Ma's bein' weird.

She's in a phone box. My Ma. On the phone. In a phone box. Never in my long-legged life have I ever seen or heard tell of my Ma usin' the phone. One 10p after another as well. For ages. Like she's made of money. She can't know what I've done. She can't be phonin' the police.

Phone the police. That's it!

I watch Ma cry on the phone. Beggin'. She looks out at me, points. 'My son,' I hear her shout. Oh God. I could run. How could she know? They say Ma's know everythin'. But she wouldn't turn me in anyway. And to the Peelers. Would she? For Da. Would she?

Remember, she loves him more than you.

I look up and down the Oldpark Road. I could run into the Proddy estate behind, but they'd probably kill me. The Bone? But then where?

Mammy comes out of the phone box blowin' her nose, her eyes veiny red and eyelids swollen.

'Mammy, can I have 10p? I want to phone Fartin'. Can I?' says me.

She's distracted, all upset. Gives me 10p out of her pocket. I pull the heavy red door with the little windows and it shuts behind me with a thud. I watch Ma, she's too busy gettin' herself right to notice I don't need 10p to make this call.

'Is that the police? I want to report a murder,' I say, in a deep, grown-up man's voice. 'I did it, it was me,' says me. The most important actin' I've ever done. 'Donnelly, 23 Havana Street,' says me. 'Yes, I'm givin' myself up. I'll be there in twenty minutes. I have the gun . . . Under my bed.' I slam down the phone and push the big door with my bum.

Me and Ma walk. Ma twistin' her ring the whole way down the Bray.

'That's where I fell,' says me. Ma doesn't respond. We take a left, round the back of the new estate. 'What are we goin' this way for, Mammy? Is it another message?'

'Yes,' says she and stops at the back of Minnie the Tick Woman's house. 'Wait here.' She must be givin' the money I put in her purse. And wages from last night. Good. I don't want Ma in trouble. Things could get nasty. She's probably worried Da's goin' to nick from her purse. She doesn't have to worry about that anymore.

A boy comes from the entry. I kick the ground and don't look up.

'Alright, Mickey?' he says. I look up and see Helmet Head. But his hair's different, he doesn't look Helmety anymore. And he's tall. What are they feedin' him? I mean, it's only been nine weeks.

'Yeah. You?' I say.

'Yeah,' he stops. Looks around him. 'So, you not at school today?'

'No, my Mammy said I didn't have to,' I say, like I'm Little Lord Fauntleroy.

'Me either,' he says, and laughs. He looks different to me. Like the Milky Bar Kid mixed with a choir boy off the telly. His golden hair shinin' in the sun. Like a boy Martine. 'We're the same.' He taps me on the belly. My belly sinks in. I get tingly all over and my willy jumps.

'Come on,' says Ma. 'Is that your wee friend?'

I look at him and smile. He smiles back.

'Yes, I'm Mark, I was in Mickey's class at school,' says he, stickin' out his hand to shake hers. I don't think I've ever seen that in real life. I'm definitely goin' to do that if I don't get life in prison.

Ma shakes his hand. 'Aren't you lovely, son?' says Ma.

He takes a big redner. Like I do. And that's what people usually say to *me*. We are the same. And I'm not even ragin'. How could I have been so stupid before? Why didn't I see we could have been mates? Maybe we still could.

'See ya at St. Malachy's, Mickey,' says he.

'See ya,' says me, my stomach bein' rung out like clothes in our sink. Ma grabs me and pulls me with her. So Helmet got to go there. I knew it. He still thinks I'm goin'.

As we get to the street, we hear the screech of tyres round from the back of the Eggy into our street. Ma looks over. I keep walkin'. I pull her now.

At the bottom of the path, Ma stops. She smells trouble.

'Go in, Ma,' says me.

'Go you in, wee boy,' says her.

A Saracen and a Jeep pull up and the Peelers and Brits jump out, runnin' to our door. Ma holds both pillars at our gate blockin' the way, but they push through easy.

'What do yous want?' she screams, runnin' after them. People come out of their houses.

'Paddy!' she screams. 'Paddy, Paddy . . .' She breaks down sobbin', holdin' her stomach.

Fuck! I forgot about Paddy. They'll think it was Paddy.

I bend down to tie my lace beside the soldier on his hunkers in the garden. I whisper, 'It wasn't my brother. My Da's in the back bedroom. The gun's under the bed.'

Women come runnin' to our house.

The soldier takes his walkie-talkie and repeats what I told him. I watch.

Thumpin', bangin', shoutin'. 'Got the gun.'

'What are yous doin'?' Ma screams hoarse, fightin' to get by the Brit at the front door. 'Leave my son.'

'It's not Paddy, Mammy.' I grab on to her.

The thumpin' comes nearer and Da is dragged out past us into the street. Trailed with legs behind, he isn't even tryin' to walk. Still passed out. They throw him into the back of the Saracen. Ma's behind, but she's not shoutin'. The women crowd around her. They shout. The bin lids go.

'She's in shock,' Aul Aggie says. 'Somebody get her a chair. Get her a cup of tea.'

The women surround Ma. Our Paddy runs out. 'What the fuck?' he says. He looks like he's still asleep.

'Get her a cup of tea, plenty of sugar,' orders Aggie, and pushes Ma down on a chair that's appeared.

I watch the Jeep drive away. And the Saracen behind. Ma looks up at me. Her face like a ghost.

'Get Mrs Brannagan,' says Aggie.

'No, I'm alright,' says Ma. 'I'll be alright. I've to get their school uniforms in.'

'Don't be stupid now, Josie, you're not thinkin' right,' says Aggie.

'I am, Aggie,' says Ma, shakin' Aggie's hand from her arm and standin' up. 'Paddy, you're comin' with me.'

'Fuck sake,' says Paddy.

'How would I know what size you are, you're like fuckin' Frankenstein. And get some clothes on, paradin' yourself at the door,' says Ma. 'Mickey, you stay and look after the house, keep an eye on Wee Maggie.'

Ma goes inside. The women stand with folded arms, lookin' at each other.

'Shock,' I say.

Aul Aggie nods, pleased with herself and she mouths to the others, 'Shock.' They nod at each other and whisper.

∾

'You tell me how one of your guns ended up in my house,' Ma says.

'Your husband has nothin' to do with us,' says not-really-Uncle Tommy. 'He's nearly had his knees done a couple of times, but out of respect for you, Mrs Donnelly, he's been spared.'

The coal hole is the perfect place for listenin'. Normally I wouldn't risk it but . . .

'My Paddy's sayin' nothin', but I know yous put that gun in here, somehow,' says Ma. 'We had an arrangement. It should've come through me.'

'I know, Mrs Donnelly. What we can't understand is why it was under his bed with his fingerprints on it. Someone suggested he might've found it on the street, picked it up on his way home, you know, not realisin' because of the drink.'

'Or planted on him. To frame him and get yous off the hook,' says Ma.

I near choke.

'Mrs Donnelly, I can assure you that did not happen. We did not frame your husband.'

Silence. A tiny scratchin' in the corner of the coal hole. Too dark to see, but I know it's a mouse. It better not come anywhere near me or I'll scream the friggin' place down.

'Well, my husband may be many things,' says Ma, 'but stupid isn't one of them. He wouldn't find a gun in the street and bring it home.'

'We'll look into it. And rest assured, we'll get to the bottom of this,' says him.

Rustlin' and muffled movement. Luckily it's not winter cuz this is where Ma would've put his coat.

'And of course,' his voice softer, coming from behind the wall at my head, 'you'll have our full support. You don't need to be worryin' about anythin'. It doesn't look good, Josie. But you're not alone.'

Snap! The trap cracks. Dead mouse.

## 21

I HAVEN'T SLEPT ALL NIGHT. Not even one minute. Like there's glue on my eyelids stickin' them open.

I tried to wank. I kept checkin' Paddy was asleep. Not that he bothers when he has a go and his blankets bounce. I did it like the boys do with their hands when they call somebody a wanker. I did it for ages waitin' for somethin' to happen, but all that happened was my willy got sore. Will that be enough for my puberty? Will I get my man's voice today? If it's not here, I'm not goin' to say anythin' again til it comes. And if it doesn't, I'll pretend I'm deaf and dumb til I get to America.

I don't wanna go to St. Gabe's. Our Paddy told me how bad it really is. People think that the monsters in horror filims aren't real. They are. They live in Ardoyne. He said St. Gabe's is the roughest school in Ireland. All the Ardoyne boys want to go and be evil together. Ma's-a-Whore will be King of them. I know he'll tell everyone about me. He's gonna make every-body hate me. They'll all love him. It'll be all of them against me. The school will hate me. I never thought I'd say this, but thank God for Our Paddy.

God, can't I go to sleep and when I wake up it's all been a dream?

*God'll never help you. Not after what you've done.*

'Mickey, come on son, you've got to get up for school,' Ma says, shakin' my foot. I give her the look of my life – *Mummy, I'm shittin' myself, please don't make me go to St. Gabe's!* She doesn't respond.

'Paddy, come on. Get up!' Ma shouts.

I crawl out of bed.

'Here's your new uniform,' she says to Paddy, hookin' a hanger on the wardrobe, a black blazer with a St. Gabriel's tie wrapped around it.

'Mammy, I don't want to go,' I cry.

'I'm tryin' to sleep here,' Our Paddy shouts.

'Shut up you and get up off yer lazy arse and get dressed for school.'

'Shut up, woman,' says he.

'Get up, nigh!' Ma digs him in the leg.

He jumps up. Ma nods for him to follow her out of the room. She must want to have a talk with him about lookin' after me.

Wee Maggie comes in. 'You look all grown up,' I say. She's so nice in her Holy Cross Girls uniform. She's gonna be in P4. She's all excited, waitin' for Ma to walk her up cuz they have to go past the Prods at the top of Alliance Ave.

Paddy comes back in and starts gettin' dressed.

'Did you not get washed?' Ma says.

'I shouldn't be goin' to school, anyway,' says he. 'After Da.'

'What good would it do sittin' round here?' says she. 'And do you think I came up the Lagan in a bubble? I know fine rightly you're only usin' it as an excuse.'

'No, I'm not.' He frowns, but walks out to hide his redner.

'C'mon, Mickey, I have your stuff in my room,' she says, pushin' me out into the landin'. I don't want to go into their bedroom. I grab the handle of their bedroom door and for the first time I think about him. Passed out on the bed and me puttin' his fingerprints all over the Brit-killin' gun.

Ma's hand squashes mine and pushes the handle so we open it together.

A black blazer lies on the bed. The whitest shirt in the world lies beside it. Shiny black shoes on top of a box. All brand spankin'.

'Mammy,' I say, lookin' at her. She's a smile like it's Christmas. Her eyes watery. Wee Maggie squeezes in beside her, Measles on the other. Paddy leans over her shoulder.

That's what she must have seen Minnie for. She shouldn't have. Now she'll owe her loads.

'Pick up your blazer,' Ma says.

'You got the wrong tie, Mammy,' I say, pullin' it out of the breast pocket. I don't want to be the only one with the wrong tie. They'll all pick on me. I look at the badge on the pocket. St. Malachy's Grammar School.

'Mammy,' I say. I look up. They're all beamin' at me, even Paddy. 'Mammy?'

Mammy's cryin'. 'Put them on, son,' she says.

Measles pinches me on one cheek and kisses the other. 'One man in this family with a brain.' She heads out.

'Go down and get your breakfast, Maggie,' says Ma, pushin' her out.

'How Mammy?' I say. Ma twists her ring. When she stops, I see. There is no ring. Ma's twistin' skin where a ring used to be. 'Oh, Mammy,' I cry.

'Do you have to?' Paddy leaves disgusted.

'Oh Mammy, I . . . I did a really bad thing,' I say, huggin' her, hidin' my face in her chest.

She strokes my hair. 'Shush,' she says.

'No, Mammy, I have to tell you.'

'I know,' she says.

I pull away and search her face.

'I know about Killer, son,' she says.

I swallow. 'Killer.'

'It doesn't matter, son, it was the bomb, it wasn't your fault,' she says.

'No, Mammy, that's not . . .'

'Promise me you'll stay away from those bad places, Mickey. Don't have your Mammy worrying. I can't take it.' Her eyes drop to the floor. 'I can't take any more.'

'I . . .' I nip my legs hard and bite my lip. I'm not going to give her anything more to worry about. Not ever. 'I promise, Mammy.'

Ma looks at me and puts her hands on my shoulders. 'You're a big boy now. You can't go around tellin' stories and actin' the way you do.'

'I am a big boy, Mammy,' I nod. 'I'll be good from now on. Wait til you see. I'm gonna make you proud. I'm goin' to be President of Ireland one day.'

Whack!

'Ach, Mammy. What was that for?'

'That's enough of that shite talk, Mickey. What did I tell you?'

'OK,' I say. I'm goin' to try really, really hard not to be me.

'Nigh hurry up and get dressed, you're goin' to be late for the bus,' she says. 'Two bloody buses. Champagne Charlie!' I watch her disappear downstairs.

I pick up my blazer and rub the badge. I'm going to St. Malachy's. Me. I sit on the bed smellin' the newness of the blazer and rub the coarse material on my face.

233

~

'Yes,' I tell the air hostess. 'I'd like a Coca-Cola, please. Thank you. All by myself, yes.'

I check my seat belt. Out the little airplane window I see big white clouds that dissolve, showin' Cave Hill and the famous view of Napoleon's Nose below. Napoleon comes alive and turns his head to me.

'Clever boy, Mickey. You got there in the end.' Napoleon winks at me.

'Winkin' on a Sunday, Napoleon!' I say, smile and wink back.

'I'm used to goin' places by myself,' I say when the hostess returns with my iced Coke with a tiny umbrella stickin' out the top. 'I'm quite the loner,' I laugh. 'Well, to tell the truth, I'm from Belfast, and you Americans very kindly send money for poor children of the Troubles, like me, to come and visit you. Yous are so generous. Not everyone, no, only the children of IRA men if their Da's are in prison. It was a terrible tragedy but . . . we had no idea, you know.'

I look out the window. Napoleon tips his hat. The plane turns towards the sun. The big, golden blindness. I pull down my eye mask and pray for jet lag.

THE END

# THANKS

I'D LIKE TO thank P. P. Hartnett for publishing my first short story that would become this novel. Tania Hershman, John Fox and Vanessa Gebbie for reading and their encouragement. Vanessa also for last minute guidance. Laura Kenwright and Holly Dawson for their attention to detail. Tabitha Pelly for working hard at publicity.

Special thanks to Lou Kuenzler for her advice and support on the many early drafts and to Sarah Butler who gave her time and expertise to the final version of the novel. I owe a great debt to these two writers.

For their generosity I'd like to thank the Lawson family, Sandy Ellis and John Stephenson. To New Writing South and The Literary Consultancy for my critique bursary and Spread the Word writer development agency for their ongoing support.

Most importantly, I'd like to thank my agent Carrie Kania and Jen and Chris Hamilton-Emery from Salt who believed in this novel.

To my family for their unwavering support throughout the years.

# PERMISSIONS

W ITH THANKS TO the following, where extracts of this book first appeared:

Haworth Press, of the Taylor & Francis Group, where 'Mickey Donnelly – The Incredible, Invisible Boy' was published in *Harrington Fiction Quarterly*.

Millivres Prowler Group Ltd who published a short story, 'What I Did on my Summer Holidays' in the *New Century, New Writing* anthology.

# NEW FICTION FROM SALT

RON BUTLIN
*Ghost Moon* (978-1-907773-77-8)

KERRY HADLEY-PRYCE
*The Black Country* (978-1-78463-034-8)

IAN PARKINSON
*The Beginning of the End* (978-1-78463-026-3)

CHRISTOPHER PRENDERGAST
*Septembers* (978-1-907773-78-5)

JONATHAN TAYLOR
*Melissa* (978-1-78463-035-5)

GUY WARE
*The Fat of Fed Beasts* (978-1-78463-024-9)

MEIKE ZIERVOGEL
*Kauther* (978-1-78463-029-4)